At ten o'clock in the morning, Salito received a phone call. "There's been an accident."

He leaned forward, suddenly sweating. "Details?"

"Sketchy. Our plane was pulling up when a Libyan jet accidently fired a heat-seeking missile."

"Any other accidents?"

"None . . . our boys flew back to the carrier."

"The pilot?"

"Never had a chance."

"Whatever the Libyans have out there, they sure are making sure that no one sees it."

"More than by just having accidents. . ."

Salito took a deep breath. "What do you mean by that?"

AGENT OUT OF PLACE

IRVING A. GREENFIELD

CHARTER
NEW YORK

A DIVISION OF CHARTER COMMUNICATIONS INC.
A GROSSET & DUNLAP COMPANY

51 Madison Avenue
New York, New York 10010

AGENT OUT OF PLACE

Copyright © 1982 by Irving A. Greenfield

An Ace Charter Original

First Ace Charter Printing: March, 1982
Published simultaneously in Canada

2 4 6 8 0 9 7 5 3 1
Manufactured in the United States of America

THIS BOOK IS RESPECTFULLY DEDICATED TO

BOB ABEL

AGENT OUT OF PLACE

I

Jack Groggins was a broad-boned man of average height, about five ten. Muscular with a strong jaw and sensual lips. He had light brown eyes and blond hair. His complexion was on the dark side.

He sat scowling at the sheet of paper in the typewriter.

"I went to Angola for money, not for glory. The opportunity had come to make my own killing."

Groggins fought down the desire to pull the paper from the typewriter. Crumple it and throw it to the floor. But that would only mean he'd have to begin the page again. He hoped the two sentences might spark a third. And in turn the three would lead him to a fourth. That way, sentence by sentence, he'd be able to crawl down the page.

"Angola, shit!" he suddenly exclaimed. Turning to the open window on his right, he looked down on Queen Square.

Brown grass. Brown leaves. The great city of London panted for breath in the double stranglehold of the worst drought in two hundred and forty years and a scorching end-of-summer heat wave.

"The damn park is deserted," he commented.

"Too bloody hot," Paula Bennet answered from the bedroom.

A moment later she stood at the door of the living room. Paula was twenty-four. She was a secretary for Mr. James Crimins III, of KBI, a multinational corporation. The flat belonged to her.

She was born and raised in Penzance, Cornwall. At twenty-one she came to London to go to business school. Sometimes she returned to Penzance to visit her parents and see her younger sister and brother, but she never really enjoyed those visits. Since she began living with Groggins, she kept in touch with her family by sending them a brief letter every Sunday.

Groggins faced her. Except for a black gossamer peignoir, she was nude. Her body was svelt. From his experience with it, he knew it was also very supple. Her breasts were small. The nipples on them were light pink and prominent. The hair on her head was black, long and silky. On her pubis it was also black, though kinky, pleasant to touch. Her face was childlike with wide, black eyes. She was smiling at him.

"I don't see why you hang with it, love," Paula told him, "when it isn't coming?" At the end of her statement the inflection of her voice went up, making a question out of a statement.

"Because it's there," he answered in a theatrically intense voice. He didn't really know what else to say.

Her laughter had a pleasant lilt. She thought he was slightly bonkers. But most Yanks were.

Groggins watched the roll of her breasts. He felt a

sudden ignition of heat in his groin, like the quick flare of a match.

When her laughter subsided, Paula said, ''But don't you see, it's not there?'' Again her inflection made it a question.

''It's hiding,'' Groggins replied. He looked down at the paper. ''An African wood carver once told me,'' he explained, ''the spirit of whatever he carved was hidden in the wood to begin with. If he carved an elephant, then the spirit of the elephant was in the wood. The man would sit and stare at a piece of wood for days until the spirit of whatever was hidden in the wood revealed itself to him. The spirit of whatever I'm going to write is likewise hidden in the blank paper.''

''You don't really believe that, do you?''

''Oh, absolutely!''

''Nonsense,'' she laughed.

Groggins cocked his head to one side. He squinted at her. With a slow nod, he said, ''It was a lot easier being a mercenary in Angola than writing about it now.'' With a shrug, he leaned back into the chair and stretched his hands up toward the ceiling. He yawned loudly. Switched off the light above the typewriter. Then he rubbed his hairy chest. ''Gorillas always scratch their chests when they're perplexed,'' he told her. ''See, if I close my eyes like this and scratch my chest, I'm really into a Gorilla type, TM.''

''You're too much, Jack,'' she exclaimed, ''you're really too fucking much!''

Within moments her near-naked body was in his lap. Her arms went around his neck. She pressed herself against him and swirled her tongue in the channels of his right ear.

Groggins moved one hand over her breasts. She smelled good.

Her nipples hardened.

His other hand glided between her thighs. He pushed a forefinger deep into her.

Paula trembled, sucked in her breath and pressed her body down.

"Unless we intend to put on a show for the entire neighborhood," he told her, "I suggest we move into the bedroom."

She glanced out of the window. "No one's there," she said.

Groggins disregarded her response. He eased his finger out of her. Moved her off of his lap. Led her into the bedroom.

Paula slipped out of her peignoir. She dropped onto the bed, splaying her thighs. She moaned softly.

Groggins stripped. He was erect. Fucking was better than beating his head against a blank sheet of paper. At least it was easier.

She caressed his balls.

He looked up at the mirror on the ceiling. The two of them were actors in that big porno flick in the sky. He turned to her. Sucked the nipple of one breast and then the nipple of the other.

"Sixty-nine?" she asked.

"Only if you do all the work."

Avidly she swung herself over him, momentarily pressing her bottom against his face.

He eased her slightly forward. Just as he put his mouth against her her lips formed a deliciously warm ring around him.

They did each other.

Groggins tried to tear himself away from the damn book. But it hung in there. So close that when he turned his head just slightly toward the bedroom door, he could see beyond the slight convexity of Paula's ass, the blank sheet of paper. It lay limply over the back of the typewriter.

To escape from the book, he shifted his attention fully to her. With his tongue, he made her bounce up and down.

"Eat it," Paula exclaimed, "eat it hard!" She reached back and separated the lips of her vagina, and shuddered with pleasure.

Groggins was outside the chrysalis of pleasure surrounding his body. He struggled to drown his thoughts in Paula.

She gyrated her bottom over his mouth. He pushed his cock deep into hers.

Paula backed off. With a laugh, she said, "I can't swallow it all, love." She started again. She moved her tongue with practiced deliberation, working from the underside of his balls to the head of his cock.

Trembling, he uttered low throaty sounds. The inside of his eyelids flooded with red and yellows. He slid his hands down the length of her body. Closed them over her breasts. Slowly rubbed her nipples between his fingers.

They devoured each other.

Her body tensed.

The heat slowly spread upward from Groggins' toes, centering deep inside of him in a place just above his balls.

Paula's body suddenly jumped with orgasmic release. She pressed herself down on his lips. She moved her body from side to side. She spat his cock from her mouth. In a wordless shout of pleasure, she cried out. Her body continued to tremble with spasms of lesser intensity.

Groggins guided her head back to his organ. For a moment, he watched. Her movements were very rapid.

He closed his eyes. Gave himself up to the boiling intensity coursing through his body. Suddenly he arched, and growled with pleasure. With gimlet eyes he watched her swallow. To see a woman do that always added to his satisfaction.

Paula lifted her mouth from his organ, drew the back of her hand across her lips, and then settled down next to him.

They were wet with sweat. For awhile, neither one of them spoke.

Groggins gazed around the room. It was small. One window opened on a narrow courtyard. A dresser stood against one wall. A mirror hung over it. Two chairs, a straight-back near the window, one with armrests in a corner, close to the door. A night table with a cheap green vaseline glass lamp stood on either side of the bed.

"That wasn't bad at all," Paula commented. "Really, it was damn good!"

"I'd recommend you for head anytime," he responded. Her vaginal fluids were beginning to dry on him. Her scent was strong.

After a pause, she asked, "Would you really?" She turned on her side and looked at him. "Would you really recommend me to one of your friends?" she questioned, pushing the black hair away from her face.

Groggins neither liked the question or the tone in which it had been asked. He sensed a scene. He did not want to take part in one.

"I mean," she said, "I don't want you to think I'm your ball and chain."

He pushed himself up and a moment later left the bed. He went into the bathroom. Washed her scent from his face. Rinsed his mouth.

When he returned to the bedroom, Paula was sitting up, smoking a small cigarlike cigarette.

He started to dress.

"Where are you going?" she asked.

"Out."

"Is that all the answer you're going to give me?"

He slipped into a white polo shirt.

"Well is it?" she demanded. She held the cigarette away from her. A slender column of white smoke rose toward the ceiling.

"If I stay," he told her, "we're going to argue. And I don't want to do that."

"Tell me what's wrong."

"Nothing . . . I'm sorry I said what I said. I didn't mean it the way you took it."

"It's not that alone," she responded with a shake of her head. "It's your whole damn attitude!"

Groggins started out of the room.

She called to him.

He stopped and faced her. "Remember, I told you when I moved in I wouldn't be the easiest guy to live with. And you said you'd be willing to chance it. Well, you have. Right now I'm in a funk. The book isn't going. I don't have a helluva lot of money left from my advance."

"I never asked you for money," she said accusingly.

"You never did," he agreed. "But it's not my style to ask a woman for money either. But if something doesn't happen soon, I won't have any damn choice!"

With a shrug that lifted her bare breasts, she told him, "It won't make any difference to me. Sooner or later the book will work out; then you'll be able to pay me back."

Groggins shook his head. She had more faith in him

than he had in himself. But then he knew himself. He moved back to the bed. Sat down at its foot. He looked at Paula.

Her breathing was shallow. Her breasts rose and fell rapidly, and her face and neck were suffused with color. She was a beautiful woman, or perhaps not as beautiful as she was attractive.

She blew a cloud of smoke into the air.

Groggins didn't know what to say to her. He did not think he loved her. Besides enjoying her companionship, she was a good lay. Their bed-sharing arrangement had started three months before. He had come from New York with a five-thousand-dollar advance from his publisher, C.P. Hawkins, to do a book on his experiences in Angola. He'd receive another five grand when the publisher accepted the completed manuscript. When he had started to write, he had been full of fire to burn the Company. But by now that fire had all but gone out.

"Are you just going to sit there staring at me?" she asked, stubbing out the remainder of her cigarette in a white shell that served as an ashtray.

He put his hand on the calf of her leg closest to him.

"Don't," she exclaimed, jerking her leg away from him.

"Give me a day or two," he said, "and I'll be out of here." To continue their relationship made little sense to him. It could only deteriorate further.

"Is there someone else?" she questioned. Her voice was tight. Almost a suppressed scream.

"It's me, the book, and the damn Company!"

"The fucking Company!" she exclaimed, spitting the words out. "You should be damn glad you're done with them."

"They're the ones who finished with me," he answered, dolefully.

"And that's what's bugging you?"

Groggins walked to the window. Looked down into the drab courtyard. Not much to see. Other windows. Two squares of burnt grass framed by cobblestone walkways. Using one arm for support, he leaned against the bottom of the open window.

"I wasn't responsible for what happened in Angola," he explained. "But it came down on me." He looked back at her to see if she really understood. "There were a dozen of us and fifty, maybe sixty, rebels led by a Russian colonel name Aleksander Fedorovich Grachev. There was no way my men could have taken that convoy."

She sighed wearily.

He faced the courtyard again. He said, "Well, I got shafted, and I can't do a damn thing about it."

"You could stop thinking about it and finish your book. You could spend the rest of your life writing as Hank Carter and to hell with the Company."

He bit his lower lip. She was right. But he also knew he was not Hank Carter. Since '72, after he had resigned from the Marine Corps, he had been with the Company. First in 'Nam, because he had fought there. Then later in Chile. Finally in Angola. He had liked the work. He had thrived on the danger. He knew better than anyone else that if Jack Groggins had not been with the Company, there never would have been a Hank Carter.

Paula said, "It's good between us, I mean, I like being with you, even when we're not humping or sucking each other off."

A smile slipped over his face. He turned to her.

"I just don't want to feel as if—as if part of you is not there when we're making it."

He nodded. But didn't say anything.

Paula left the bed and padded over to him. "I've never lived with a man before like this," she said. "Sometimes a weekend. But nothing like this."

He held her and nuzzled her hair. He didn't want to hurt her.

"Come back to bed," she told him. Her black eyes were wide and pleading. She led him across the room.

Groggins undressed. He settled down next to her, wondering if she realized time was running out for them. That no matter what happened, he was somehow going to find a way to square himself with the Company.

"This time just let's screw," she said, "for a long, long time."

"Sure," he answered. "Sure."

She opened her thighs.

He straddled her.

She reached down and, arching toward him, gently guided his cock into her body. When he had entered her completely, she asked, "Doesn't that make you feel better?"

Groggins closed his eyes. Nodded. "Yes," he said. "Yes, it's about the only thing that does."

II

Monday. A pallid sun. By late morning, the air was soggy. Dark clouds were building over the city, creating an unnatural twilight. But in the afternoon the clouds drifted slowly away, giving the sun the opportunity to pour its bright heat down on the gasping metropolis.

Paula was at work. The apartment was silent, except for the sound of Mozart's Symphony No. 39 coming from the radio. . .

Groggins rubbed sweat from his eyes. He looked down at the paper in the typewriter.

"It's just not there," he said, more to hear the sound of his voice than to remind himself of his failure. He wasn't able to move beyond what he wrote the previous day. He glanced down at the square.

A few young mothers and nannies were out with their prams.

His attention returned to the paper. So far, no hidden

spirit had manifested itself to him. "And it never will," he said, continuing aloud. "Not on this book. Maybe not on any book."

He walked into the bathroom. Urinated, washed his hands and face. Then used a towel to dry the sweat from his chest.

As he entered the bedroom, he wondered how long he'd be able to stall his publisher. "Probably for a few months," he said aloud.

He opened the closet and took a short-sleeved, light-tan sport shirt and put it on, leaving the top buttons open.

He thought about writing a note for Paula but discarded the idea. He did not want her to have any illusions about their relationship. It was strictly short term.

He left the flat. The street was bathed in hot sunshine.

Groggins had no need to move quickly. He wasn't going anywhere in particular until later, when he'd go to a pub and drink with some of his friends. But he wouldn't do that until the sun was well down in the west. Now he just wanted to get the cobwebs out of his head.

He strolled all the way to the Victoria Embankment. The dull gray water of the Thames was very low. Not far from him some old men were fishing. He wondered if they ever caught anything. He wondered why so many old men all over the world spent their time trying to catch fish. He wondered if he would do the same thing when he was an old man. That prospect was vaguely disquieting and he moved away.

Big Ben tolled five.

Groggins left the embankment. He wasn't going to

wait to start drinking. He hailed a cab and told the driver
to take him to Dolly's Pub, Antigua Street.

"An' where's 'at?" the cabby asked.

"In the West Indian Dock Section. It's one of those
streets that end up on the river."

"You sure?"

"Yes, I'm sure I want to go there," Groggins said,
settling back for the ride.

Traffic, was heavy, and they moved slowly.

The cabby complained about the weather.

Groggins left the man's comments unanswered. The
weather had to be tolerated, like it or not. For a brief
interval he closed his eyes. He tried to think his way
past the two sentences on the sheet of paper in the
typewriter. Nothing! He was unable to move.

The cab eased over to the curb. The driver said,
" 'at's Antigua Street 'ere. But I don't see no sign of
Dolly's Pub."

"It's alright," Groggins answered, "I can find it."

"You sure you want to be 'ere after dark?" the cabby
questioned. "I can tell you're a Yank." The cabby's
face was round. His hair was gray and his eyes a watery
blue. He looked very disturbed. "T'isn't a safe place
after dark."

"I'll be with friends," Groggins assured him. He
handed the fare. And for his solicitude gave the driver a
good-sized tip.

The cab pulled away.

Antigua Street was really an alleyway lined with old
dark brick warehouses. The far end opened on the river.
Dolly's Pub was built into the street level of one of the
warehouses.

Several large trucks were still at the loading docks.
The men Groggins passed were covered with dirt,

and sweaty. Some looked at him with unabashed curiosity. Others did nothing to hide their hostility.

Groggins ignored them. He entered the dimly lit pub crowded with dockworkers, truckers and sailors. A sour smell hung heavy in the air. There were booths on either side, all of them occupied, some by men, others by prostitutes and their johns.

Tim, the barkeep, spotted Groggins and gestured him toward the bar. "You're a bit early this evening," he commented, in a sandpaper voice. He was a tall, thin man with deep-set brown eyes and a balding head. Because of a shattered left knee, he walked with a limp. Without waiting to be asked, Tim drew a half-and-half for the American. "By sixish it'll empty out a bit," he said. "Most of the blokes'll go home to their nagging old ladies and squawling kiddies, or they'll take off with one of them birds for a couple of hours of fun an' games."

Groggins drew on the mug of brew. Though tepid, it quenched his thirst. He set the mug down on the darkwood bar.

"You look like you needed that drink," Tim said, coming back after waiting on another customer.

"Like a hound needs a bitch."

"The weather makes everyone more thirsty than usual," Tim commented. "I hear it's something in the air. Get into the throat an' lung—"

Groggins threw up his hands. "Don't tell me about it," he said. "I have enough to think about without thinking about the air." He picked up the mug. Took a long draught from it.

The barkeep moved off.

Groggins turned from the bar. He looked toward the door. More men came in. His eyes went to the tables. They were still occupied. He started to turn back to the bar when a man called out to the barkeep, "Ay, Tim, 'ow come you lets queers in 'ere. I 'tought this place was only fer men an' real pussy.'' He was a hulking man, with bull neck, a red face and big hands.

The hubbub stopped, almost as though it was turned off by the twist of a spigot. The men near him edged away. Embarrassed, several of them averted their eyes, while some plainly showed their fear. But all too many faces reflected their inner lust for blood.

Groggins set his mug down on the bar.

Tim glanced anxiously at him.

Groggins rested his elbows on the top of the bar. He put his right foot on the brass railing. He waited for something to happen.

"You ain't givin' me no answer," the man said, looking over at Groggins.

"Why don't you drink Ed, if that's your pleasure," Tim answered, "or better still why don't you leave an' give me some pleasure."

Nervous laughter flitted around the dim room.

Ed scowled. He pushed his way toward Groggins and stood behind him. He bellowed, "We don't like no bloody fags 'ere. We don't like guys that show the 'air on their chests. So why don't ya take a walk."

Groggins didn't move.

"I'm talkin' ta ya, fag!" Ed bellowed.

"Ah señor," another man said, "you make so much noise you wake up all the little fish in the river. I tell you to go away quietly or maybe you don't go away on your feet."

A hint of a smile touched Groggins' lips. The Hispanic accent belonged to José Ortega. Who like himself from time to time had worked for the Company. He had first come to know him in Chile. In Angola they had become friends.

"Mind yer own fuckin' business," Ed said to Ortega. "I'm 'aving a private talk 'ere wit' this fag."

Groggins could see their reflections in the dirty mirror behind the bar. Oretega was a small man, with a neat black moustache. He was almost boyish looking.

"But señor," Ortega persisted, "you will be my business if you are dead."

"Wot the 'ell are ya talkin' about?"

"*Señor*, permit me to introduce myself," Ortega said, whipping out a white business card. "Hosé Ortega, funeral director."

A puzzled expression came over Ed's florid face. He looked at the small man and then at Groggins.

"*Señor*," Ortega told him, "that man you insult is a killer of many."

" 'Im?"

"Si, señor," Ortega answered gravely. "I bury some he put down himself."

"A fag—"

"*Señor*,-- Ortega told him, "*il esta muy malo hombre,* he is a very bad man."

" 'E don't look so tough to me," Ed said. But there was a definite note of uncertainty in his voice.

Ortega nodded.

"Come on, Ed," Tim cajoled, "why risk more than you can handle. Come have a drink on the house."

"Wot about it, Tim, is that bloke as tough as this spic says?"

"Worse. Much, much worse."

Ed hesitated. He couldn't seem to make up his mind whether to fight or back off and take Tim up on the drink.

Groggins made the decision for him. He whirled around. Snapped his knee into Ed's groin.

The man groaned, blanched and sagged, grabbing himself.

Clasping his hands together, Groggins used them as a hammer. He struck again, delivering a smashing blow to the side of the man's head.

Ed dropped to the floor before most of the pub's customers realized what had happened. When they did, it was only the women who made any sort of a noise.

Groggins turned back to the bar and picked up his mug. He motioned Ortega to join him.

Tim called for some of Ed's friends to help the poor man to his feet and give him some fresh night air. Even as Ed was being carried outside, the volume of noise rose to its previous level. Business continued at the bar as though nothing had happened. Nothing really had.

"I tried to talk him out of it," Ortega said with a shrug, "but some men are like that one, mule-headed."

Groggins nodded. He asked his friend what he wanted to drink.

"Anything that's wet," Ortega answered.

Near six o'clock many of the pub's patrons began to leave. One of the booths became available. Groggins and Ortega settled in, opposite each other.

Tim came over and said, "Ed's goin' to have a big head for a day or two."

"It will not be big enough to match his mouth," Ortega said.

"Some of his friends are angry. They said you set him," he explained, looking at Ortega, "for you to work him over." His brown eyes went to Groggins.

"*Madre mia*," Ortega answered, "I know what my friend can do. I did not want to see him get hurt."

"Thanks for the tip," Groggins said, "but you tell Ed's friends if we had set him up, he'd be in the hospital. Or in the morgue.''

"I told him that," Tim responded.

"Tell them again," Groggins said softly, lifting his mug. He drained off what was left of his half-and-half, handed the empty mug to Tim and asked him to fill it.

"What about you?" Tim asked Ortega.

"Not yet," he answered. After the barkeep left the table, Ortega faced Groggins. "How are things going for you?"

"They go," Groggins said. "What about you?"

Before Ortega was able to answer, Tim returned with the half-and-half. "You really a funeral director?" he asked Ortega.

"Si," Ortega said, holding out a white business card. "But I only do funerals for Cubans. I specialize in those Cubans who are for Castro. But lately I have not had much work."

To keep himself from laughing, Groggins drank, choking on the half-and-half.

"You know it is true," Ortega said, looking reproachfully at Groggins.

Still coughing, Groggins nodded vigorously. "Absolutely true," he managed to sputter. "I swear it!" He raised his right hand to accentuate the integrity of his oath and Ortega's statement.

"Never could figure you guys," Tim said, shaking his head. "Never!" And he went back to the bar.

"Think he's playing with us?" Ortega questioned, watching the man limp away.

"Who the hell knows," Groggins answered. He looked toward the bar. "Maybe he just keeps an eye on things for MI5. I sure as hell don't know."

Ortega drank. Then he said, "Tony Salito is still watching over Company business here in London . . .

But everyone knows he's in charge of European operations.''

"Interesting," Groggins commented, leaning over the table. "When did he come up?"

"About ten days ago."

Groggins knew Salito from Angola. He was the only man who stood up for him when the shit hit the fan over there. Salito knew two dozen mercenaries couldn't have stopped the convoy. He told that to Bob Machlin, the Company's Chief in Angola.

Ortega bent closer to Groggins. "I think the Company is recruiting men again."

"Tell me about it."

"A friend told me there is a man around who says he has people who are willing to pay good money for men with experience in small arms and explosives."

Groggins pulled away from the table. He rested against the back of the booth. "I'm not in the game anymore. I'm a writer now."

"I forgot to ask, how is the book coming?" Ortega asked.

"It's not!"

Ortega clicked his tongue in commiseration. Then he asked, "How's Paula?"

Groggins managed to mumble, "She's okay."

"If a man has a woman who pleases him, he already has the best part of his worldly possessions."

"Sounds like it's more Chinese, or Arabic, than Hispanic," Groggins said.

"I must have heard it somewhere," Ortega laughed.

"I don't think it'll last much longer between us," Groggins commented.

To signify the ease by which a man loses or gains a woman, Ortega made an open gesture with his hands.

Then he said, "Why don't you contact Salito? Maybe he will be able to do something for you. He has a lot more, how you say it—?"

"Clout."

"Si, more clout with the Company than before."

"Why don't you go to him?" Groggins asked.

"I am always with the Company," Ortega said.

Groggins nodded. He had thought as much, but had never asked. Men like Ortega would seldom say as much as he already had. Their lives frequently depended upon them holding their own counsel.

"Besides," Ortega said with a smile, "I have a woman that pleases me very much."

"Did Salito ask—"

"No, no amigo," Ortega interrupted. "But if you went to him—"

"Crawl you mean."

"It does not matter what name it goes by, as long as you do it," Ortega said with a shrug. "If the Company needs men with your experience then maybe you have a chance to get back in."

They finished their mugs without further conversation about the Company. Groggins suggested they leave together, "Just in case any of Ed's friends might want to even things out for their friend."

Ortega agreed and asked, "Are you armed?"

"A gravity knife," Groggins answered.

Ortega smiled. "The same."

Groggins went to the bar and paid the score.

"Careful," Tim cautioned, "Ed has some mean friends."

Groggins threw him a quick salute and joined Ortega at the door. "See anything?" he asked.

"Too damn foggy to see much," Ortega answered.

The two men walked down the middle of Antigua Street. But no one came after them. When they were outside of the West Indian Dock Area they shook hands and separated.

III

Groggins's book began to move ahead. He stayed with it. Taking time only to sleep and eat.

After two days and nights, he completed the entire sequence leading up to the attack on the convoy. The words poured out of him.

When he took time to reread all he had written, Groggins was stunned by the similarity between himself and the hero in the book. Like him, he wanted the gold more than he wanted to stop the convoy.

Groggins switched the light off above the typewriter. He leaned back in the chair, his hands on the back of his head.

Paula was asleep in the bedroom.

A slight breeze washed over him. He was tired. He rubbed his eyes with the back of his hands. He was having trouble separating what he was writing from what had happened. His discovery was a downer. He had been with men who had gone in for looting in a big

23

way. But he had never developed a taste for it. He had always been well paid by the Company. He never really had been moved enough by anything he had seen to want to carry it around with him. He had preferred to be as mobile as possible.

Groggins found himself wondering if Salito had guessed the real reason why the attack on the convoy had failed.

Sure, his men had been outnumbered. But they had the advantage of surprise. They might have carried it off successfully, if he had not tried to separate the last four trucks from the rest of the convoy. He had figured the ingots of gold and silver would have been equally divided between the fifteen vehicles.

Had his plan worked, he and every man with him would have had the opportunity to lift a few bars of gold and silver. The men would have kept their mouths shut and no one else in the Company would have stopped to count the ingots. Within hours the bulk of their booty would have been flown out of the country.

The rebels under Colonel Grachev had fought hard to keep the four trucks from being taken. But their fighting had been a ruse. Grachev had diverted attention from the rest of the convoy, and when they had finally broken off the fire fight, the four trucks had been blown apart, leaving nothing but burning rubber, gutted chassises, and the sand they had carried so that they would appear fully loaded.

If Salito had any suspicions about the action, he had kept them to himself. Or had he?

There was the possibility that Salito's defense had been the Company's way of letting Groggins know they were on to him.

For the first time since Groggins had left Angola, the enormity of that possibility made him break out in a cold sweat. If that was the way the Company handled the matter, then he would never be able to get off their shit list.

He rested his elbows on the top of the typewriter carriage and covered his eyes with his hands. There wasn't any way for him to find out if he had finally come to an understanding of the Company's actions. There wasn't anything he could test. He had to find some scheme that would give him the real reason for the Company's attitude toward him.

It also occurred to him that Ortega could have lied, that Salito had used Ortega to play the game of cat and mouse. Through Ortega, Salito might have put out feelers to him. If he responded positively he would speak to Salito in an attempt to return to the Company. Salito might use such a visit for a fishing expedition, hoping to get more information than he already had; or he might pretend he knew nothing about what Ortega had said. On the other hand, if he responded negatively and did not go to him, Salito might interpret that as a confirmation of his own suspicions, provided of course he had them to begin with.

Groggins dropped his hands and clasped them together. He'd been with the Company long enough to know it was unforgiving. There might even be a contract out on him, and he wouldn't know it until it would be too late to run. Not that running would do any good. Sooner or later he'd be found and blown away.

"Alright, Mr. Salito," Groggins said in a low voice, "let's see if I can be a smarter mouse than you're a cat." He placed the pages he had written in a neat pile. One by one, he tore them to pieces. Making sure there wasn't a regular pattern to the way he did it.

"That's for openers," he whispered. "Now there's nothing about the mission except what I know and what you think you know. That still leaves us about even.''

Groggins gathered the bits of paper together. He tossed three handfuls out of the open window. He flushed the rest down the toilet. Then he stripped, showered, and went to bed. Knowing he would have to begin writing the whole sequence all over again the next morning. In the past hour or so the book had become the least of his concerns. If Salito was playing with him, his chief concern would soon be how he would remain alive.

Sleep did not come quickly to Groggins. When it finally did, it was filled with nightmares. He tossed and turned throughout the night.

In the early hours of the morning, Groggins accidently brushed against Paula's naked body. Aroused, he eased his penis into her while she was still asleep.

Reflexively, she pushed her buttocks against him.

He reached over her with one hand and fondled her, slipping the other under her and caressing her breasts.

She made a soft purring sound. Quickened her movements.

The soft mound of her buttocks felt good against him.

"I thought I was dreaming the whole thing," she whispered, reaching back to trace her fingers over his scrotum.

"Is the real thing as good as the dream?" Groggins questioned.

"Oh yes," she exclaimed. "Yes!"

Groggins quickened his thrusts.

"Roll me over," Paula gasped.

Within moments Groggins was on her back.

She thrust her rump up at him.

He slammed into her.

"Faster!" she cried out. "Faster . . . Fuck me . . . Fuck me!"

Her body tensed, and she uttered a wordless wail. She clutched at the pillow.

Their sweaty bodies made loud smacking noises as they came together and separated.

"More," Paula shouted. "Give me more!" Her body quaked with orgasmic fury.

Groggins' fluid gushed from him. For a few brief moments, his vision dimmed. He was hurled into an exquisite oblivion. When it was over, he rolled off her and lay on his back.

She nestled close to him, her head on his chest, one thigh crossing his body.

Groggins glanced at the digital clock. "You'll have to get up soon," he said.

"More is the pity for that," she answered lazily.

He splayed his fingers over her breast. "I'm going away for awhile," he said. The words came without any premeditation. As soon as he said them, he realized his timing was off. Yet there they were. The words that preceded the act!

Paula didn't move or speak.

Under his hand, Groggins felt the sudden quickening of her heart. Silently she was waiting for him to give some sort of an explanation. He said, "I have something to take care of. Something personal."

She pulled away from him. . . . "God," she exclaimed, "but you're a bastard!"

"I guess from your point of view I am."

"A final fuck," she said, leaving the bed, "and it's goodbye to Paula!"

Groggins pushed himself into a sitting position. He rested against the headboard. "I won't be here when you come back this evening," he said. He wasn't going to become involved in an argument with her.

Paula went into the bathroom. She slammed the door after her.

He could hear her sob but made no attempt to go in and comfort her.

After awhile, Paula came out and dressed. Without a word, she left for work.

Groggins packed his clothes, typewriter, and papers. He was out of the flat by nine o'clock. After four cab changes, he was ensconced in a small, airless room on the fifth floor of a rundown hotel on Frith Street in the Soho section of the city. It was one-thirty.

His purpose now was to make it as difficult as possible for any of the Company's men to find him. Tomorrow he would tail Paula. When he was sure no one was following her, he would make arrangements to fly back to the States, or perhaps he'd go to Italy. He would leave his options open; there was no need for him to decide anything just yet, other than how to occupy his time.

He opened his suitcase and took out his clothing. He separated a dummy panel from a side section and removed a .22 automatic. He pushed the weapon into his belt. Despite the heat, he would now have to wear a jacket if he wanted to have more protection than just the gravity knife.

Groggins left the room. He locked the door and went into the street. He was hungry and stopped at a stand for some fish and chips and a cold can of Seven-Up.

He began to walk. Sooner or later he would have ended his relationship with her. But he knew damn well he had hurt Paula. It came much sooner than he had expected in a way he couldn't have foreseen. But he hadn't wanted to risk her life for whatever time remained for them. If the Company had put out a contract on him and Paula had somehow gotten in the way, the hit man would not hesitate to waste her too.

Groggins spent the afternoon getting to know the neighborhood. He discovered the hotel had one rear and one side entrance. Each of them opened onto a different alleyway. The one in the rear led to the next street. In one direction it went as far as the Square; the other all the way to Shaftsbury Avenue.

There were a great number of pubs in the area. And many, many antique shops. A few streets down from the hotel was London's Chinatown.

By four o'clock Groggins was hot and tired. He returned to the hotel. Showered in the bathroom down the hall from his room. Napped briefly. By six, he was on his way to the Dolly again. This time he intended to press Ortega for more answers.

"I haven't seen your friend," Tim said, "since the other night when he was here with you."

"That was the beginning of the week," Groggins said, lifting his mug and drinking slowly.

The barkeep nodded. "I wondered if the two of you made it out of the dock area alright."

"No trouble," Groggins told him. "What about Ed, have you seen him around?"

"Last evening. Just about this time."

"Have anything to say?"

"No more than usual. He's a noisy bloke."

"That's one way of describing him." Groggins pushed his empty mug toward the barkeep for a refill.

After a few minutes, Groggins settled down in the first booth on the left. He faced the door, hoping to spot Ortega the moment he walked into the place. Behind him were a group of four men. He'd seen them in the pub several times before. None of them were steadies.

They were speaking to one another in low voices.

Seven o'clock came and went. Ortega still hadn't showed.

Groggins was beginning to become more and more edgy. Fear about Ortega's connection to whatever seemed to be coming down between himself and Salito increased, putting knots in his stomach.

In the next booth a man with a thick German accent said, "It's goot money. . . . I vus der ven he put hiss offer on da table."

Another added, "He wants guys who have experience with small arms and explosives. I mean he's looking for guys like us. A couple of hundred from what I could gather." He was obviously an American.

"I will have to think about it," the third man said in an English accent.

"Count me in," the fourth told the other two. "I am getting tired of dear old England. Or is it merry old England."

The four men laughed. The Americans called for another round of drinks.

Groggins strained to hear more. Their conversation turned toward women. After a half hour they left. But not in a group. Not even in twos. They went singly.

Groggins pulled himself back into the corner of the booth. He considered the possibility that Salito had sent them to whet his interest. But they were in the pub before him, and he had chosen the empty booth. There was also the possibility that if he hadn't landed near them, they would have found a way to sit close enough to him so he could not fail to overhear their conversation.

He shook his head. Though something like that was possible, it would be improbable for it to happen.

Groggins decided Ortega wasn't the go-between for Salito. Most probably Ortega had told him the truth. He had picked up word about the recruitment drive and thought the Company was behind it.

Groggins left the booth. Went to the phone. He dialed a number, then hung up.

Several moments passed.

The phone rang. Groggins answered it.

The disembodied voice of a recording machine at the other end said, "Give your ID number, the code color, and the individual to whom you wish to speak."

Groggins gave his old ID number. He said, "The color yellow. I want to speak with Tony Salito."

More time passed. Groggins heard the whirring of wheels. The rapid chatter of print-out typewriter.

"Salito here," a man with a pleasant voice announced.

Groggins swallowed and said, "Jack Groggins here. I want to meet with you."

"No dice."

"It's important to me," Groggins said.

"I know where to find you if I need you," Salito said crisply. "I'll call you. But don't call me."

"I'm not there any more," Groggins said. The Company knew he'd been living with Paula.

"If I need you, Groggins, I'll find you."

"Listen, Salito, you may need me more than you realize. I want to meet with you tonight."

"Impossible."

"Tonight."

"What's it about?" Salito asked.

"I'll tell you when I see you. But it could mean your ass, Tony. I owe you," Groggins said. "Now I'm just trying to pay my debt."

"Alright," Salito answered, after a momentary pause. "I'll meet you. Do you know where the Chesire Cheese is?"

"Yeah."

"Be at the bar about eight-thirty," Salito told him.

"I'll be there."

The line went dead. Groggins hung up.

IV

Groggins arrived at the Cheshire Cheese before Salito. The bar was crowded with reporter types from the nearby Fleet Street newspaper offices. There was a forty-five-minute wait for a table. Because the Cheshire Cheese was once the haunt of such former literary lights as James Boswell, Dr. Samuel Johnson, Charles Dickens, and scores of others, it was constantly frequented by culture-hungry tourists from the States and other countries.

Groggins eased his way to the bar. He ordered a Pimm's Cup. He was aloof from the hubbub around him. His chief concern was whether or not he was about to put himself in an extremely dubious position. The answer might cost him his life. *If* the Company saw fit to take it. But if he ran now, the only way he'd ever stop running would be—

"Drink up," Salito said from behind Groggins. "And let's walk."

He turned.

Salito was dressed in a light tan suit, white shirt, and brown tie. He smoked a large bowl, curved-stem pipe. He was a tall dark-haired man with a boyish face and black eyes. Since Angola he had put on a few pounds.

Groggins finished his drink, paid for it, and started out of the restaurant with Salito behind him. Side by side they walked through the arch onto Fleet Street.

"Which way?" Groggins asked.

"Toward St. Paul's," Salito answered. "There's a garden there where we will be able to sit down."

Groggins said nothing. His heart was beating very fast.

"Suppose you tell me what's going on?" Salito questioned.

"That's what I wanted to ask you."

Salito stopped. "You mean you got me here just to put that to me?" he asked angrily. "I thought you had something important."

"Listen," Groggins said, "I know how the Company feels about me, but I want in again."

Salito shook his head.

"Why? You yourself said my men couldn't take the convoy."

"You know why the Company doesn't want you as well as I do," Salito said. "I don't think I have to spell it out."

"Then you knew—"

"Yes," Salito answered. "My orders were to provide you with a cover story."

"Machlin know too?" Groggins asked.

"Just that you fouled up."

Groggins uttered a deep sigh. Some of what he had guessed was true. "Why did the Company let me off the hook?"

"Hard to say," Salito answered, emptying his pipe against a lamp post. "But my guess is they wouldn't have if you had managed to get your hands on any part of the gold shipment."

"So there's no way you want me for your new operation?" Groggins questioned.

"If I had a new operation, no," Salito said. "But I don't have any, and I sure as hell don't know what you're talking about."

Groggins moved his hand across his jaw. "There's word going around," he said, keeping Ortega's name out of the conversation, "that the Company needs men who have experience with small arms and explosives."

"Not through me," Salito responded. "I'm looking for men with fluency in one or more African languages."

"Listen, I heard it from two different sources."

"Somebody is playing with you," Salito told him.

For several minutes neither of them spoke. Groggins didn't know whether to believe Salito or not. But neither could he come up with a good reason for thinking Salito wasn't telling the truth. Especially since he leveled with him about what had happened in Angola.

"We're not into anything requiring men with your experience," Salito said, blowing smoke into the warm humid air.

"Okay," Groggins replied, "maybe you're not. But somebody sure as hell is."

Salito pointed up at the illuminated dome of St. Paul's. "If I hadn't become involved with the Company, I might have become an architect."

"Do you know who's on the buy for mercenaries?" Groggins asked.

"No," Salito answered. "But for the past few days

some of my field men have been asking the same thing.
I questioned headquarters about it. They don't know
either.''

''Suppose I offer to find out?'' Groggins said, suddenly stopping.

''Let's walk,'' Salito told him.

''Well, are you going to answer me?''

''Do I have to? You know where you are with the
Company. My advice to you is to stay with your writing.''

''Call Virginia,'' Groggins urged. ''Find out what
they have to say?''

Salito shook his head.

''I told you on the phone I owe you,'' Groggins said.
''Give me a chance to pay my debt.''

''You should have thought about what you owed the
Company when you hit that convoy,'' Salito answered.

They reached St. Paul's and walked around to the
side where the garden was. The big wrought-iron gate
was closed and locked.

''Too bad,'' Salito commented. 'It's a good place to
sit and talk.''

They turned around and started back in the direction
from which they had come.

Salito emptied and refilled his pipe before he said,
''Maybe if I were in your place, I'd have tried the same
thing. I don't know. I'm not throwing stones at you,
Groggins. You pulled your shot. It failed. Now you
have to bite the bullet no matter how damn much it
hurts.''

''It hurts,'' Groggins commented softly. 'If it didn't
hurt, I wouldn't be begging you for another chance. I
want to clear myself with the Company.''

''It's over and done with. Keep on with your writing.
I read your first two books and liked them.''

"Look, don't you understand, I'm beginning to have trouble living with myself. The damn book I'm writing isn't working, and I walked out on a woman."

Salito threw up his hands. "Your troubles are your own. I don't want or need them."

Groggins fell silent. He was ashamed for opening up the way he just had. He would have apologized. But he felt that would only embarrass Salito more. "I don't have anything more to say," he said, "except, thanks for meeting with me."

They stopped and shook hands.

"And thanks for the compliment on my books," Groggins said with a weak smile. He felt small, very small. Now all he wanted to do was leave Salito as fast as possible. He was disgusted with himself.

"I could use a drink," Salito said. "What about you?"

Groggins hesitated.

"Have one with me for old time's sake," Salito offered.

Groggins nodded.

In a few minutes they were standing at the bar in the Cheshire Cheese. It was less crowded, less noisy.

Salito did all of the talking. Telling Groggins how much he was enjoying London. How some of the other men they knew left the Company when it began to take so much flak from the media during the congressional hearings.

Salito insisted on a second round. "What is your new book about?"

"Angola," Groggins answered. "I mean it's a novel about a mercenary."

"Nothing like writing from your own experience," Salito responded, picking up his half-and-half. "To the success of your book."

They touched mugs and drank.

"You know," Salito said, "most people have no idea what we're like. Company men, I mean. We do our job, just the way they do theirs. Damn few of us ever really understand what we really do."

Groggins agreed with a nod.

"Tell me, what would you have done, if you had gotten away with it?"

Groggins used the tip of his forefinger to draw three intersecting circles on the top of the bar.

"I really hadn't thought about it," he said.

"You must have had some idea."

Groggins shrugged. "I guess bring it to Switzerland," he answered.

"You know if you had really knocked over the convoy," Salito told him, "you might have gotten some of the gold and no one would have been the wiser. As far as I know, there wasn't one Company man in Angola who knew how many bars were in those trucks."

"I should have spoken to you before the mission," Groggins commented in a low voice.

"Maybe you should have," Salito answered.

Groggins looked at him questioningly.

Salito stared him down. "Two days later the Portugese hit the convoy."

"I didn't know that," Groggins admitted.

"Not too many people do."

"Would you have thrown in with me, if I had come to you before the mission?" Groggins asked.

"I don't know," Salito answered. "Let's say that I'm as weak as the next guy when it comes to a woman; and I imagine that the smell of gold would make me even weaker. As I told you, I'm not the one to throw stones at you."

"Thanks for being honest with me," Groggins said.

"I just wanted you to know where it was at."

"It helps."

Salito bought a third round of drinks.

"You know I'd be willing to go it alone," Groggins said before he drank. "But if I find out anything interesting then the Company picks up on the expenses."

"I can't tell you to do it," Salito told him.

"Then ask the people in Virginia. Someone there could give you the authorization."

Salito started to shake his head, stopped and said, "Maybe, with some luck, I might be able to do something on a limited basis."

"Try it. The worst they could say is no."

"I'll be going way out on a limb," Salito commented. "Way out."

"I understand."

"Alright," Salito told him. "Contact me the same way. About seven tomorrow night. But don't count on anything."

"Some luck is the best I could hope for," Groggins answered.

Salito lifted his mug and toasted, "To luck."

"To luck," Groggins responded, touching Salito's mug with the tip of his own.

They drank looking at each other over the rims of their mugs. . . .

V

Five minutes to seven, Groggins walked jauntily up to a telephone kiosk. Within sight was Foys, the largest bookstore on Charing Cross Road. He had gone in there earlier to see if they still stocked his first two books. They did. He was immensely pleased. He interpreted it as a good omen.

He deposited the coin. Dialed Salito's number. Answered the computer. Anxiously waited to hear Salito's voice.

Salito came on.

Groggins cleared his throat. "How did it go?"

"It didn't go anywhere," Salito answered. "Your name isn't worth shit."

Groggins was silent.

"Are you still on the line?" Salito questioned.

"Yeah, I'm still here."

"I told you not to count on anything," Salito said.

"Can't those fuckers in headquarters understand what—"

"Don't come down on me," Salito cut him short. "I tried. I caught more damn attitudes because of you than I want to remember."

Groggins took a deep breath. He apologized. "I know you did and I'm grateful."

"It's alright," Salito responded.

For several moments neither of them spoke. Then Groggins said, "I have one more favor to ask."

"If I can, I'll do it."

"You probably know I've been meeting with José Ortega."

"Yes."

"I haven't seen him for a couple of days. I'd like to rap with him. But I don't know where he lives."

"It's against Company policy."

"I know what the policy is," Groggins shouted. "But damn it, I'm not someone from the other side. Remember I just tried to get back into the Company." He couldn't keep the anger out of his voice, even if he tried. He didn't try.

"I'll give you Ortega's address. You get off my case. And that means no more calls. Nothing. I don't want to hear from you."

Groggins nodded. Salito was giving it to him straight. The Company wanted nothing more to do with him.

"Do we have a deal, Groggins?"

"We have a deal."

"Ortega rents a flat at Fifty-six White Lion Street. . . . That's in the Pentonville Section. His phone number is 01-730-8147."

Groggins repeated the telephone number.

"You know there's nothing personal in my actions,"

Salito told him. "I'm really sorry you're not going to be back with us."

"Thanks again." Groggins hung up without giving Salito the opportunity to continue the conversation. Anything more would have been a waste of words.

He deposited several more coins into the slot. Dialed Ortega's number. After five rings he gave up and left the kiosk.

Groggins considered going to Paula. He could tell her why he thought he had to leave. Now that he was irrevocably finished with the Company, maybe they might be able to make it work between them again.

He decided against contacting her. At least when he was down. He didn't want her to pity him.

Groggins quickened his pace. A wind had suddenly sprung up, whirling pieces of newspaper in the air. Somewhere in the distance thunder boomed. He looked up. The night sky was heavy with clouds.

He stopped at St. Giles Circus and hailed a cab. "Fifty-six White Lion Street," he told the driver.

A violent thunderstorm struck the city. Streaks of lightening came so fast the thunder was almost continuous. The wind-driven rain made it difficult to see out of the cab's windows.

It was still raining when Groggins reached his destination. The lightening and the thunder had moved off to the south. He paid the driver and hurried into the vestibule of the three-story building.

There were four apartments on each floor. Ortega's name appeared next to 1-D. Groggins pushed the bell button with his forefinger.

No one answered.

He stabbed at the bell again.

Silence.

He shook his head. Could the bell be out of order?

There was no way to tell. Unless someone on the inside buzzed back, the front door could not be opened.

He could wait for one of the other tenants to open the door, or he could ring anyone of the bells and pretend he was delivering something. The first might lead to an awkward situation. The second might not work at all.

He decided not to try either before he visited the local pub. He had seen it at the end of the street when the cab had slowed down to make the turn onto White Lion Street. There was a chance Ortega might be there.

Groggins left the vestibule. The rain had stopped. The wind was still blowing though not nearly as hard as it previously had. The air was cool, almost chilly. The long summer heat wave had been broken. Autumn was ready to make its appearance.

Halfway to the pub, Groggins stopped. He looked around him. The houses on either side of the street were recently renovated turn-of-the-century structures, some six floors high. All of them possessed a certain dignity, especially those with high stoops and Gothic-type windows. He guessed most of the residents were professional people: lawyers, engineers, a few doctors, and probably a great many writers and artists. He had not figured Ortega for such a quiet, respectable neighborhood.

The pub was busy. Unlike the noisy clientele at the Dolly, its customers were subdued. Even those at the dart board played the game with a minimum of raillery.

Groggins stepped up to the bar. Ordered a scotch neat. He took it down with one swallow. Asked for a second. He drank that one as rapidly as the first. Neither drink had any effect on him. He was still depressed.

When the barkeep brought him his third, Groggins asked, ''Do you know a man by the name of Ortega?''

The barkeep shook his head.

Groggins said, "He's rather short. Dresses very well and has a small black moustache."

"He must be the spic who comes in here," the man said. Seeing the look of disgust on the customer's face, he heatedly apologized. "I didn't mean any offense. He's a quiet fellow. Comes in. Has two or three and usually sits over in that booth with his lady friend. She's a looker. Small like him. But built. Blonde too."

"Has he been here today?"

"Not for a few days," the barkeep answered. "I think it was Monday the last time I saw him. He ain't in any trouble is he?"

"No," Groggins told him. "I'm an old friend. I just got in from the States. He doesn't answer his bell."

"Might be with his lady friend," the man said with a broad wink.

"Might be," Groggins agreed. He finished his third scotch. Paid what he owed and walked back to where Ortega lived. That neither Tim at the Dolly, nor the barkeep in the local pub had seen him in the past few days was not in keeping with Ortega's habits. He was a drinker, though not a lush.

It occurred to him that Ortega might be on Company business. But that didn't seem too probable, since Salito hadn't mentioned it. If Ortega was away on a Company assignment, Salito would have suggested he wait a few days before paying him a visit.

Groggins went straight to the panel of bells and randomly pushed one belonging to an apartment on the top floor.

The door was buzzed.

Groggins quickly opened it.

A woman called down from the top floor, asking who it was.

Groggins did not answer. He went straight to Ortega's apartment. He turned the knob. It moved.

Groggins' heart began to thump. He pushed against the door. It swung open.

The all too familiar stink of death leaped out at him. He entered the apartment and stepped into the living room. Flicked on the light.

The window was open. Everything nearby was soaked from the storm. Nothing else seemed to have been disturbed.

Groggins turned. Crossed a narrow foyer. Stepped into the open doorway of the bedroom. His three drinks tried to leap out of his stomach. He forced them down again.

Ortega and his lady friend were dead. Half of Ortega's head was splattered over the pillow. The woman had three holes in her. They lay soaked in each other's blood.

Rats swarmed over the two bodies. From time to time the rats looked up at him but didn't scamper away.

Groggins ran his hand over his face. He was sweating profusely. He moved back into the foyer. He paused to wipe his fingerprints off the door knob with a handkerchief, and left the apartment.

Once he was in the street, he took several deep breaths. He found a telephone kiosk. He asked the operator to connect him with Scotland Yard. He told the officer on the other end, "A man and a woman were shot to death in apartment 1-D at Fifty-six White Lion Street." He hung up and hurried away from the telephone.

Groggins was having trouble thinking. His brain seemed to be a soft thing in his skull.

"The goddamn rats," he muttered to himself several times.

He walked as far as King's Cross Station. Hailed a

cab and told the driver to take him to Queen Square. He got out of the cab and looked up at Paula's window. It was dark.

Groggins checked his watch. It was nine-thirty. Too early for Paula to be in bed. Unless she had someone there with her. He didn't think she did.

Using his own key, Groggins opened the front door. The furniture was all in place. But even from the doorway, he could see everything else had been taken away. He rushed into the bedroom. None of Paula's clothes were in the closets.

Groggins went back into the living room. He stood at the window, feeling as though he had been struck on the head a few dozen times. He glanced back at the bedroom for a moment. Then turned to the window again.

"Ah Mr. Groggins," a man said, from the doorway, "I thought I saw lights up here."

Groggins turned. It was Mr. Jeffrey, the building's caretaker.

"I didn't expect to see you again, sir," Jeffery told him. "Miss Bennet said you'd not be coming back."

"That shows how wrong a woman can be," Groggins replied. "When did she leave?"

"Yesterday evening. Gave me a full month's rent, she did."

"She didn't say where she was going, did she?"
Jeffery shook his head.

"Did she leave a forwarding address?"

"She asked that all her mail to sent to KBI Industries. I believe that's the company she works for."

"I have no use for these any more." Groggins handed him the keys to the building and the apartment.

"I'm going to miss the clickety-clack of your type-writer," the caretaker told him.

Groggins almost responded, *I'm going to miss it too.*

But instead he said, "I'd appreciate it if you would hold my mail. I'll stop by in a few days to pick it up and leave a forwarding address."

"I'll hold it."

"Thanks." Groggins shook his hand. Out on the street he felt a dull throbbing at the top of his skull. He was unable to think of anything.

Groggins walked the streets to clear his head. The night became chillier. He turned up his jacket collar. Dug his hands deep into his pockets. The Company was gone. Ortega was gone and Paula too was gone.

He passed the great dark mass of the British Museum. At the intersection of Great Russell and Bloomsbury Streets, he stopped a cab.

Groggins needed to feel the security of familiar surroundings. Be with people. Maybe even talk to a few about anything. Anything at all. As long as the conversation would keep him from thinking about Salito, Ortega, and Paula. He was on one of the worst trips he had ever experienced.

When Groggins came up to the bar in the Dolly, Tim looked at him for a moment and said, "Whatever you want is on the house."

"A double scotch."

"You'll need more than that tonight," Tim commented.

Groggins nodded.

VI

It was near closing time. The Dolly was practically empty.

Groggins sat in a booth, elbows resting on the table, head in his hands. Next to him was a woman. Her name was either Tinna or Lina. He couldn't remember which one. Now and then she pressed herself against him. He felt the softness of her breast on his arm, smelled the cloying sweetness of her perfume.

"Why don't we go to my digs?" she asked in an eastern European accent.

But he couldn't place it with any accuracy.

She asked the same question again.

"Soon," he answered, lifting his face from his hands. "Soon."

"I'm going to the ladies room," the woman said.

He gestured her away from the table. When she was gone, he picked up his mug and drained it. He moved over to the end of the bench. Slued his head around and

49

watched Lina (or Tinna) walk to the rear of the establishment. Good ass! Cheeks nicely separated. He nodded approvingly and moved back to his former position, trying to decide whether or not to go with the woman. In his condition, he wouldn't even be able to get it up, let alone get his money's worth from her. If he went, he'd have to tell her he'd sleep first. Then screw.

Groggins was looking toward the door. Two men entered. He had never seen them in the Dolly before. They weren't locals. Each wore a loose-fitting topcoat. One was dark, a Latin type. The other was fair and tall. Neither of them wore a hat.

Groggins followed them with his eyes.

They went to the bar. The dark one spoke to Tim.

Tim looked at Groggins, and the two men came toward the booth.

"Groggins?" the dark man asked.

"Yeah, I'm Groggins."

"Someone wants to see you," he said.

"If he sent you," Groggins answered, "he knows where I—"

The fair-complexioned man thrust his hand into his coat pocket.

A moment later Groggins found himself looking at a snub-nose .38.

"It wouldn't bother me if I pulled the trigger," the man said. His blue eyes, like his voice, were expressionless.

"Tim," Groggins called out, "tell the lady I had to leave in a hurry. Give her a tenner for her trouble."

"Sure," Tim said.

Groggins slid out of the booth.

The man with the .38 waved him toward the door. The other said, "We'll be right behind you."

"I have no doubt about that," Groggins told them.

Once outside, he was directed to the rear of a van. He lay face down, with his hands over his head. He smelled gasoline and oil.

The man with the gun came in after him. The other went around to the front of the vehicle.

As soon as they began to move, he was frisked. Without a word his automatic was taken away from him.

They drove for a half hour or so, making many turns. Neither of the men spoke to him or to each other.

Groggins didn't even try to figure out where he was being taken, or who the heavies were working for. One or both could have wasted Ortega and his woman. But he was sure they weren't from the Yard.

The van slowed, turned to the left and came to a stop. Metal moved against metal. A gate was opened.

The van started again. Moved in second gear for a short distance. Then jerked to a stop.

"Sit up," the man with the gun ordered. "Put this on," the man said, handing him a blindfold. "Make sure it doesn't slip."

Groggins put the blindfold on.

The guard tested it. Then called out to his companion to open the back of the van.

They led Groggins across a small courtyard through a door and into a narrow passageway, then through another door and to a chair.

The blindfold was removed.

Groggins found himself facing Salito. He was sitting behind a large dark wood desk. "Aren't you going to ask why I had you brought to me?" Salito questioned.

"The Yard probably phoned you about Ortega, or you found out some other way he had been wasted. He and his woman."

"Did you?"

"I was the one who phoned the Yard," Groggins said, flicking his eyes around the room.

The walls were covered with bookshelves, except for one area where there appeared to be a window overlooking a garden. But it was an illusion, what the French called a *trompe l' oeil*. There wasn't any rug on the hardwood floor. The only light in the room came from an ornate brass lamp on the desk.

Salito motioned to his men to leave. When they were gone, he said, "You had a good reason to blow him away."

Groggins looked at him questioningly. "Tell me," he said. "I can't think of one."

Salito leaned far back in his swivel chair. "I want you to tell me," he said.

Groggins' brow wrinkled. It had never before occurred to him that he had been Ortega's only assignment.

"From the look on your face," Salito said, "I'm sure you've come up with a reason."

Groggins started to speak.

"No," Salito told him. "I want you to look at it from my point of view. You find out what Ortega was doing. You tail him and when the opportunity comes, you blow him and his woman away. Then to cover yourself you pretend not to know where he lives and ask for his address."

"How long was he tailing me?" Groggins asked.

"Since you came to London," Salito answered. "The Company wasn't sure if those four trucks were really empty."

"You mean it wasn't sure whether I had some deal worked out with the rebels."

"You said it, I didn't," Salito commented with a shrug.

A trace of a smile flickered across Groggins' lips. Ortega had completely suckered him in.

"You had cause to blow him away," Salito said.

"So did a lot of other guys," Groggins answered. "Any of Castro's goons would have been happy to do it, to say nothing about those from Chile and Angola."

"It could have happened that way," Salito agreed.

"Then the rap about the guy who has a friend. . . ."

"That's true," Salito said. "Ortega heard about it, and as I have already told you, word has come from other quarters on the same subject."

Groggins rubbed his chin. It was scratchy. He was tired, angry, and confused. "All right, Salito," he said, "I didn't kill Ortega. Now where the hell do we go from there?"

"A great many people in and out of the Company are going to be upset about Ortega."

Groggins remained silent.

"You understand he was just doing his job," Salito said. "I want you to understand that. The Company had to know if you were clean."

Suddenly Groggins started out of his chair. "Paula—"

"Sit down!" Salito ordered.

Groggins dropped back into the chair.

"You've been damn slow tonight," Salito told him.

"You bastards," Groggins exclaimed in a low harsh voice. "You fucking bastards!"

"We do what we must in any way we can," Salito said.

"Then her job at KBI. . . ."

"Absolutely straight. Let's just say our Company and hers have some business dealings."

Groggins took a deep breath. His stomach knotted.

His head felt heavy.

"Now you tell me," Salito questioned, "where do we go from here?"

"I found Ortega dead."

"But you did have a motive."

"Listen," Groggins said, "I didn't know I was his pigeon. I didn't even guess. I didn't know I was fucking one of your agents. If you believe it, fine. If you don't—well, I don't have to tell you what you'll do, do I?"

Salito rested his elbows on the desk. "They both reported you were clean," he said, looking down at the papers on the top of the desk. "I have their statements here."

"Okay I'm clean. I could have saved you a lot of work, all you had to do was ask me."

"Some people high up in the Company are going to point their fingers at you. They're going to demand you be taken out."

"At this point," Groggins said, "I don't give a flying fuck. I'll take my chances. Unless, of course, you intend to have your heavies blow me away." He slumped back in the chair.

"Do you want to deal?" Salito asked.

"You hold all the cards."

"Then let's say I want to deal," Salito told him. "As things stand now, you're out of one trouble and in another. I'm not saying you did or did not waste Ortega and his woman. But I'm telling you, you had a damn good reason to. And that's exactly what the people in Virginia are going to think."

"Are you going to put another tail on me and give me another woman to fuck so you can prove my innocence?" Groggins asked angrily. "If you do, how do you know I won't waste them?"

"You're going to prove your innocence," Salito answered. He came around to the front of the desk and rested against it. "You're going to find out who killed Ortega. Then you're going to take him out."

"You're out of your mind!"

Salito shook his head. "If you want to live, you better do what I ask. I'll stall my people from putting a contract out on you. But I can't do it for more than a few days. After that I'll have to tell them to go ahead with their plans, or that you have some inside info and I've given you time. Say two months to come up with something."

"What happens if I draw a blank at the end of that time?"

"I'm counting on you not to," Salito said, returning to his chair. "If you didn't waste him, I want you to find the man who did."

"I don't see where I have much of a choice."

"You don't."

Groggins nodded.

"If you have to, contact me at the second phone number," Salito said. "Tomorrow I'll send you a new passport and other papers. I suggest you start with the Yard. Find out what they know."

Groggins remained silent. He was trying to put it all together. Trying to make that gray mass in his skull function. He could understand, even condone, Ortega's role. Had the situation been reversed, he would have done exactly what the Company asked. But his feelings about Paula were completely different. He was angry and he was hurt. Angry, because she had used him. More accurately, she had misused him the way no woman had before. Hurt, because he could have easily fallen in love with her.

"You'll be paid two thou a month and another K for

your expenses in the next two months," Salito told him.

"Generous," Groggins commented.

Salito ignored the sarcasm. "If you take off," he warned, "you won't be giving us any choice. We'll put out a contract on you. And you know that sooner or later one of our men will get you."

"At least I know where you stand," Groggins said.

"I didn't want you to leave here with any doubts." Salito buzzed for his two heavies. The tall, fair one handed him Groggins' automatic. He looked at it, smiled, and suggested Groggins get himself something with more killing power.

"I'll think about it," Groggins answered.

Salito handed the automatic back to him. He stuck it in his belt. He was blindfolded again and taken back to the van. This time he was allowed to sit up in the rear.

A half hour after they had passed through the gate, Groggins was left standing in front of the Dolly. It was closed.

With a shrug, Groggins began to walk.

VII

By noon the following day, a bellboy brought Groggins two packages from Salito. In one, a new American passport, driver's license, voter's registration card, and social security card. All identified him as Robert Harris, journalist from New York. There was a letter of introduction to an Inspector Harris W. Southby at the Yard and a note from Salito, telling Groggins he was already receiving flak from the Company over Ortega's death. Salito wanted him to move quickly.

Groggins put all of his old identification papers into a large envelope and addressed it to himself, care of the American Express Office in London.

The second package was a box. From the weight of it Groggins knew it was a gun. He opened the box. Salito had sent a snub-nose .38, complete with clip-on holster and two boxes of cartridges. With one chamber empty for the hammer, Groggins loaded the remaining five and put the safety on. Then he left the room.

Groggins paused at the desk for stamps, and again at the corner of the street to mail his credentials to himself. The sun was out. The sky was bright and clear. By evening it would be cool enough for a topcoat.

He stopped for a breakfast of sausage, eggs, and coffee. He phoned Inspector Southby. Told him he was on his way over.

A short while later Groggins looked across a green metal desk at a tall, broad man with a florid face and steady gray eyes.

"According to the coroner, Mr. Ortega and Miss Cooper were killed approximately seventy-two hours before they were discovered by an unknown caller," the inspector said very precisely. "No doubt a silencer was employed. The bullets were fired from a .357. No one heard anything unusual. And that's the sum of it."

"I suppose that's what you've already told my employer?" Groggins asked.

"Yes," Southby said. "Which leads me to ask why you came here?"

"My employer likes everything verified in triplicate. I guess I'm the triplicate."

"There are no clues," Southby told him. "It was a completely professional job."

"I never had any doubt it was anything but professional."

"We do have one thing, though," Southby said. "The pub keeper gave us a very accurate description of you."

"I was the one who called the Yard."

"I thought as much," Southby commented.

"What about the newspapers?"

"Can't stop them from getting hold of a nice juicy piece like this. They will treat it as some sort of love murder. Irate husband follows wife. . . ."

"Was the woman married?"

Southby nodded. "She used her maiden name Cooper. She was some sort of model-actress type. The city is full of them. We have no knowledge of where her husband is. The best we can make out is that he is a seaman."

"Then it could have been a love murder type thing?"

"Too professional for that," the inspector said. "Unless the husband hired what you fellows call a hit man. But that does not seem too likely."

"And nothing more about Ortega?"

"He ran a small import-export business," Southby said. "I have the address here, Caribbean Associates, 148 Fournier Street."

The phone on the inspector's desk rang. He identified himself and then listened.

Groggins' eyes roamed over the room. A picture of Queen Elizabeth and Prince Philip hung on the wall behind the inspector. A lone snake plant with brown edges was on the windowsill. There were three green metal files.

The inspector put down the phone, excusing the interruption. "I can't tell you any more than I already have."

Groggins thanked him, stood up and shook his hand.

"If I can be of any more help," Southby said, "please do not hesitate to call."

Groggins smiled, and left the office to the obvious relief of the inspector. If the visit served any purpose, it allowed Salito to show him his vulnerability. He was identified by the pub keeper and could be given a very difficult time by the Yard, should his behavior warrant it. Nothing else came out of the meeting with Southby. He doubted the inspector would have given him more information even if he had any, without first checking for Salito's okay. Groggins stepped out into the street. The sun was gone and the sky was filled with clouds.

Fournier Street was in the slums. Old, ugly buildings coated with grime. Many had boards nailed across the windows. Garbage was everywhere.

Groggins went to number 148, a small, basement-type store. White-washed windows. Caribbean Associates in black lettering on the door.

It was probably used as a mail drop. Possibly a meeting place for other Cubans.

The building superintendent was a grizzled old man. Groggins asked, "Did Caribbean Associates do much business?"

"Didn't seem like 'e did any," the man answered. He was standing in the half-opened doorway of a flat directly above the store. "Came 'ere a couple of times a week. Now and then 'e'd come with some men at night. But 'e paid 'is rent on time. You a copper?"

"Mr. Ortega was a friend of mine," Groggins said with a shake of his head.

"Coppers been 'ere early," the man told him. "Said 'e was done in. Said 'e 'ad a woman with 'im."

"Did you ever see a woman with him?"

"A real looker."

"Blonde?"

The man waved a scrawny finger at him. "A dark 'aired one. She was with anot'er man. I 'eard 'er call 'im Tony."

Groggins' blood began to race. He thanked the man, and left. For several moments he paused and looked at the white-washed windows. Then he walked away. Knowing he must not let anything from the past get to him if he wanted to stay alive.

Late afternoon drifted over the city. Rain was in the

air. Groggins returned to his hotel room for a raincoat and hat and left immediately. Went to KBI Industries to wait for Paula. She was as suspect as Salito.

Groggins stood in the green travertine lobby. KBI occupied four floors in a new building just off Edgeware Road on Oxford Street.

At five o'clock the elevators began to spill out people. Men in conservative business suits. Women in dresses and skirts.

Groggins spotted Paula.

She wore a simple long-sleeved blue dress with a mandarin collar. She carried a light gray raincoat. She was with a man. An office type, complete with black leather attache case.

He waited until they reached the automatic door. Then called Paula's name.

She recognized the voice and stopped.

Groggins came up to her. He caught the momentary dulling of her eyes. Fear? He wasn't sure.

"I don't think we have anything to say to one another," she said.

The man with Paula drew himself up about to speak.

Groggins flicked his eyes over to him. "Don't do, or say, anything stupid," he told him. And pushing his forefinger against the inside of his coat pocket, he said, "I'd just as soon pull the trigger as not."

The man saw the bulge in the pocket. His lower jaw became unhinged. Beads of sweat popped out on his forehead.

To Paula, Groggins said, "Walk out of the building in front of me. I'll be directly behind you."

She nodded.

Then to the man he said, "This is a family matter. If you're very smart you won't call the police."

A few moments later Groggins fell in alongside of

Paula. A misty rain was falling. Lights came on. They walked without speaking. Crossed to Hyde Park.

"So you know," Paula finally said.

"Know what?" He wanted her to squirm.

She stopped suddenly. Faced him and said, "There was no way I could get out once I was in it."

"There never is," Groggins answered. He began to walk again.

She came after him. Grabbed hold of his arm. "I was falling in love with you!" she exclaimed.

He stopped. Wheeled around and said, "Ortega was taken out."

She blanched. Her lips quivered.

"I know you visited him at Fournier Street. You were with Salito."

She nodded. "But I never knew where he lived," she told him in a low voice. "Never."

They continued to walk.

Groggins pointed to a bench. He said, "Let's sit down."

"In the rain?"

He didn't bother answering. Took hold of her arm and steered her to the bench.

"Salito told me about Oretega and about you," Groggins said. "Now I want you to tell me about Salito."

"I don't know anything," she answered. "I mean, I know who he is but. . . ."

"He recruited you from KBI?"

She nodded.

"Your Mr. James Crimins. . . ."

"He was with me in the lobby."

"Is he a Company man?" Groggins asked.

She shook her head. "No."

"And did he try you out before he suggested you to Salito?" Groggins asked.

"We sometime—"

Groggins threw up his hand. "Who you fuck is your business. I want to know more about Salito and Ortega."

"I was to report anything you said about Angola, gold, and the Company."

"Which of the three was the most important?" Groggins asked.

"The gold."

Groggins rubbed his chin. He smiled. "When Salito asked you about our conversation, you tell him I said things are adding up. Now tell me did either of them ever mention someone was on the buy for mercenaries?"

"Ortega thought it might be the Company," she said. "But he didn't really know."

"When did he tell you that?"

"Just before he went to meet you at the Dolly. He phoned and said he was going to suggest you contact Salito. He said you were clean. I told him I thought you were clean too."

"And when you asked Salito if he was putting the word out for men, what did he say?"

"That he wasn't."

Groggins stood up. "The Company wants me to find the man or men who killed Ortega," he said.

"So you are back in the fold," she commented, walking alongside of him. "Happy now?"

He gave her a quick look.

"It's what you want," she told him, "even if it means getting yourself killed?"

"I'm not especially looking for that to happen."

"But it could," she said.

"It could," he responded after a long pause.

They were out of the park.

"I'd offer to give you a lift," Groggins said, "but I don't know where you live."

"It's all right. I'll find my way."

He nodded.

"I don't want to see you again," she said in a choked voice.

Groggins was torn between wanting to take her in his arms, and leaving. He didn't know what to say. The misty rain made her hair look silky. He nodded. "Wrong time, wrong place, Paula."

"Wrong man. Wrong woman," she responded.

Groggins turned and walked away.

A few moments later a cab passed slowly.

He saw her looking at him through the rain-stained window.

The cab accelerated, then swung into the stream of traffic.

Groggins turned up his collar. Dug his hands deep into his coat pockets and walked quickly toward Marble Arch. From there he would go to the Dolly.

The Dolly wasn't crowded when Groggins arrived. He took a booth for himself. He couldn't get Paula out of his mind. Remembering what she had been like in bed made him ache for her. Several times he told himself he was off the wall for letting her get to him. But that line didn't stop him from thinking about her. From wanting her!

Tim limped over to the booth. He held out a late edition of the *Express* to Groggins. "Your friend," he said, "caught it. Paper says he was mucking around with someone else's wife."

"Can't believe all you read."

" 'Love Murder' it says here."

Groggins shrugged. He wanted to be left alone.

"You want to read about it?" Tim asked.

"No. But thanks anyway."

"I guess it's better your way," Tim commented.

"What way is that?" Groggins questioned. Looking up at the man.

"Out of sight. Out of mind."

Groggins' eyes hardened. "Yeah," he said in a low hard voice, "that's the way it is. Now how about bringing me a double scotch."

"What I meant—"

"It's okay," Groggins interrupted, "I know what you mean."

Tim nodded and left the booth.

Groggins went to the free lunch counter. He put several pieces of ham on a plate and two hard-boiled eggs. He hadn't eaten since noon. His stomach was growling.

The double scotch was on the table when Groggins returned to the booth. He downed half of it in one swallow. He ate with no interest in the taste of what he was eating.

Ed came in and went to the bar.

Groggins stiffened. If the job on Ortega hadn't been so professional, he would have gone after Ed. He glanced back at the bar.

Tim was showing Ed the story in the *Express*. Ed nodded and started for the booth.

Groggins faced around. He swallowed the rest of his drink and waited.

Ed hulked over him.

Groggins looked up. Pushed back his jacket to show the .38.

Ed's eyes went wide. He licked his lips and said,

"I'd 'ave gone after you, not yer mate."

Groggins nodded slowly.

"I wanted ya to know," Ed said.

"I know," Groggins answered.

Ed backed off. Turned and went straight to the bar.

Groggins signaled Tim he wanted a refill. Something about Ed reminded him of the four men he had overheard the night he met Salito. Since then he had not seen them.

Tim set the drink down on the table. He looked back at the bar where Ed was. "He was worried you might think he killed your friend," Tim said.

"Tell him not to worry," Groggins answered. "He's a brawler not a killer."

Tim's eyes were on the .38.

"That's the difference between us," Groggins said.

Tim didn't answer. He limped back to the bar and took to washing and drying the dirty mugs.

Groggins didn't pick up the double shot of scotch. He turned and called Tim to the booth.

"Be there in a sec," Tim responded.

Groggins suddenly realized Salito might have had nothing to do with Ortega's murder. That he could have been blown away by someone with totally different connections. Say the man who was fronting for the people buying the mercenaries? Ortega could have stumbled onto the real buyer.

Tim came to the booth.

"Couple of nights back when I was in here, there were four men sitting in a booth behind me. One was a Kraut. There was an American and there were a couple of Englishmen in the group. Have they been around?"

"One was."

"One Englishman?"

"How did you know?"

Groggins waved the question aside. "And the other three?" he asked.

"They're a mean bunch," Tim said. "Did some fightin' in Angola, so they say."

"That doesn't answer my question."

"Gone to Rome," Tim said. "That's if you can believe Bucky. He's one of the Englishmen. That's his nickname."

"Do you think he'll drop by tonight?"

"Who knows?"

Groggins thanked him. He finally drank his second drink. He stayed in the Dolly until closing time.

Bucky didn't show. On the way out, Groggins said to Tim, "Tell Bucky, someone wants to talk to him. Tell him to be here around nine for the next couple of nights. Tell him it's about Rome."

"Sure."

Groggins handed him a ten-spot to be sure Bucky would get his message.

The misty rain had turned to a steady downpour. The street was deserted.

Groggins reached the end of Antigua Street. He was about to turn the corner when suddenly he was blinded by the glare of several searchlights.

Two black sedans sped toward him and screeched to a stop.

A voice on the bull horn ordered him to freeze and lift his hands about his head. "Groggins, this is Inspector Southby of Scotland Yard. Do what you're told."

Groggins raised his hands above his head.

Six men rushed at him. One quickly took his .38 while the others hustled him toward one of the cars. They forced him onto the rear seat of the car, pushing his head down.

Inspector Southby came in through the other door.

"What the hell is this all about?" Groggins asked.

"Did you know a Miss Paula Bennet?" Southby responded.

Instantly aware of the inspector's use of the past tense, Groggins heart began to thump. "I know her," he said.

"She is dead. Her body was found in Hyde Park by a man walking his dog."

Groggins uttered a deep sigh. He sank back into the corner.

"You were last seen with her," Southby said. "Her employer, Mr. A. J. Crimins—"

"Skip the horse shit, Inspector," Groggins cut him off in a flat voice. "When we get to the Yard, get on the fucking phone to Salito. Tell him I want him there, or I'll blow all of you away."

"Just who do you think you are speaking to?"

"Just do it. Do it, Inspector, before I'm brought before the examining magistrate. You have me under arrest, but I got you by the balls."

Southby took a deep breath and turned away.

The room was small and windowless. The lighting was indirect. Groggins sat on one side of a green metal table. Salito on the other.

Groggins finished giving Salito a full account of his activities from the time he had met Paula until he had been arrested by Southby.

"Mr. Crimins said you had a gun on him," Salito told Groggins.

He shook his head. He explained what he had done.

"Crimins is the nervous kind," Salito said with a smile.

Groggins stood up. Palms down, he leaned on the

table. "When do I get out of here?" he asked.

"You had a motive for killing Paula," Salito said in a nonchalant manner.

Groggins eased away from the table. "I also had a motive for wasting Ortega but I didn't."

"I'm not saying you killed her," Salito told him. "But looking at it from the inspector's point of view. . . ."

"Are you trying to tell me something?" Groggins questioned.

"Just presenting an alternate viewpoint."

Groggins sat down. He wondered if Salito was into fun and games at his expense.

"Once you knew about Paula's relationship to the Company, you should have left her alone," Salito said. He filled his pipe and lit it. "You should have been on your assignment, not chasing cunt."

"I was on my assignment," Groggins answered. He did not explain any further.

Salito puffed on his pipe. "Going to Paula was one kind of mistake but threatening Southby was really stupid," Salito said. "You're becoming a pain in the ass, Groggins."

"Yeah, I suppose, from your point of view."

"Mr. Crimins and the inspector share my point of view."

"What the hell am I supposed to say to that?" Groggins asked. He stood up again. Walked a tight circle behind the chair. Stopped. For a long time, he looked at Salito, trying to understand his position. Then he said, "I didn't kill Paula, and I know you know that I didn't."

Salito shrugged. He took the pipe from his mouth and, pointing the stem at Groggins, he said, "It can be arranged—but I don't have to tell you what you already know."

"No. . . . But you could tell me what you want."

"I want you to find out who blew Ortega away. . . . I don't want anything else from you."

"That's what I have been trying to do," Groggins answered. He was about to tell him about Bucky and the other three men who went to Rome but changed his mind. This wasn't the right time for that.

"Paula was raped before she was killed," Salito said.

Groggins ground his teeth together. His brain was filled with the image of her behind the rain-washed cab window.

"Southby has several men on it," Salito said.

"You can tell him that the last time I saw her she was in a cab," Groggins told him.

"I'll tell him," Salito responded. He stood up and went to the door. He knocked on it.

An officer opened it.

"Would you ask Inspector Southby to step in here, please."

The officer nodded and closed the door.

A few moments later Southby entered the room. His eyes flicked from Salito to Groggins and back to Salito.

"Mr. Groggins understands his position," Salito said. "And I am sure Mr. Crimins will explain that he gave you the description of the wrong man."

Southby nodded. Looking at Groggins, but speaking to Salito, he said, "I do not want him ever to come to the Yard again."

"Don't worry, Southby, I won't," Groggins told him.

Southby looked at Salito.

"I think he understands," Salito said, "that it would be the kind of mistake he would not survive."

A short time later, Groggins and Salito left the Yard. Dawn was just coming over the city. To the east, the clouds were pink and yellow.

"Do you want a lift?" Salito asked, pointing to his chauffeur-driven black limo.

"No thanks," Groggins said. "I think I'll walk for awhile. Oh by the way, I'm going out of town for a few days."

"Where?"

"Rome. I haven't been there for awhile."

"Remember," Salito cautioned, "the Company is paying for your time."

"I can hardly forget," Groggins answered.

They shook hands and went their separate ways.

Groggins walked. The city was awakening; heavy trucks were already rolling, factory workers were on their way to their jobs.

Paula's death saddened him. He didn't know how to deal with his own feelings about it. Grief had long since been denied him by his profession. And he honestly couldn't have claimed to have loved her. They had enjoyed each other. She had told him she was beginning to fall in love with him. He had mentioned something about his feelings for her, although he had never said he loved her. But maybe he had and didn't know it.

Groggins stopped at a newsstand. He bought the morning edition of the *Daily Telegraph* and tucked it under his arm. He continued to walk.

He entered the Lyons Tea Shop and found an empty table. He drank two cups of coffee and stared into space.

After awhile, Groggins opened the paper. News about the pound and other national matters occupied the first page.

He wasn't interested. He moved through the paper page by page.

Then he spotted a small item. A man was struck by a hit-and-run driver at the intersection of Westro Street and Lancaster Terrace. The man was later identified as Arthur Buckingham, known in his neighborhood as Bucky.

Groggins nodded. If he had thought about it, he'd have predicted something like that happening to Bucky.

The story said that Bucky was a soldier of fortune and was known to have worked for several foreign governments. The story did not say whether there were any next of kin or if the authorities were investigating the incident.

Groggins went to the telephone booth in the rear of the establishment. He deposited coins in the box, waited for the operator and asked for Scotland Yard.

When the duty officer answered, Groggins said, "Tell Inspector Southby that Arthur Buckingham, known as Bucky, was not killed accidently."

"Who are you?" the officer questioned.

Groggins hung up. He went back to the table. Scanned the rest of the newspaper. Nothing about Paula's death in it. He closed the newspaper.

There were links between the dead people. Ortega and Bucky knew about the mercenaries. And Paula knew about them from Ortega. Or perhaps from some other source. Her death, like that of Ortega's and Bucky's, seemed to be connected to the people on the buy for mercenaries.

Groggins paid the cashier, then walked way back to the hotel. On his way to his room, he glanced out of the hall window. A man leaned against the wall of the building across the street.

Groggins figured he was from the Company. Courtesy of Salito. He nodded and went into his room. Placed his .38 on the night table. Removed his coat and jacket. Loosened his tie, kicked off his shoes, and dropped onto the bed. He closed his eyes and slept.

VIII

Because of the severe thunderstorms over Da Vinci Airport, the ninety-minute flight from London to Rome had already passed the two-hour mark. Turbulence rocked the plane.

Groggins occupied a window seat, his eyes closed. He was finding it difficult not to think about Ortega or Paula. Regardless of the fact that Ortega had been his tail, he still liked him. As for Paula, well, he might have fallen in love with her.

The plane suddenly dropped.

"No matter how many times it happens," said the man next to him, "I just can't get used to the bumps." The accent was unmistakably New York.

Groggins opened his eyes. The man was pale. Short. Middle-aged with a receding hairline and horn-rimmed glasses.

"I didn't mean to disturb you," the man said. "But

the last drop really got to me.'' He touched his heart.
''Probably got to my pacemaker too.''

Groggins nodded. ''We'll be going in soon.''

''How can you tell?''

''From the way we're flying.''

A moment later the stewardess confirmed what
Groggins said. They were beginning their approach to
the Da Vinci Airport.

Groggins turned toward the window. Except for the
red glow at the tip of the wing, he could see nothing.
Suddenly the clouds became ragged, and in the distance
lightning streaked across the sky.

The plane dropped below the clouds. The ground
became visible. The landing gear snapped into place.
The plane lost more altitude, banked to the right, then
straightened out. The dome of St. Peter's came into
view. Then most of Rome, gray in the rain.

The plane made another, very steep turn to the left,
then flew over farm land, some ruins of a Rome long
passed, a highway and a line of high tension lines. Then
lower over a hurricane fence.

Moments later the plane came down hard on the
runway, bounced and came down again. A curtain of
water exploded in front of the window as the plane
rushed forward. With a loud roar the engines reversed.
The plane slowed and taxied to the terminal.

''This is my first trip here,'' the man said. ''I figured
I'd like to see the old country before my chips are
cashed.''

Groggins faced him. His color was better. He was
smiling.

''Name is Arthur Fioredelliso,'' he said, offering his
hand.

Groggins was about to answer, when he remembered

the name on his passport. "Robert Harris," he responded, shaking Fioredelliso's hand.

"My folks came from Garda. A small town on Lake Garda. That's up north. But I figured since I'm coming here I might as well see Rome too."

"It's a beautiful city."

"Then you've been here before?"

Groggins nodded. "Several times."

"I envy anyone who has traveled," Fioredelliso said. "Only time I did any traveling was during the war. To look at me now, you wouldn't believe I was a Marine. Fought with the First Division from Guadalcanal to the end of the war, with some time out for a bout with malaria and a Jap bullet."

The plane turned into a bay at the terminal and came to a stop.

"I'm staying at the Hotel d'Inghilterra. Near a place called the Spanish Steps. Do you know it?"

"Yes."

"Why don't you give me a call? Maybe we can have dinner together, or at least a drink?"

"I have a very busy schedule," Groggins said.

Fioredelliso threw up his hands. "Hey, if you can, fine. If you can't, that's the way the ball bounces."

"I'll try," Groggins said, though he had no intentions of doing it.

"After all, we're fellow countrymen," Fioredelliso commented smiling broadly.

The passengers started to deplane.

Thirty minutes later Groggins had his single suitcase and cleared customs. He shook hands with Fioredelliso. He was anxious to get away.

"Listen, we could share a cab to the city," Fioredelliso suggested.

"I'm supposed to meet someone in the cocktail lounge," Groggins lied. His new friend was swiftly becoming a pain in the ass. Ordinarily, it wasn't his style to become involved with a fellow passenger. He'd even eschew the casual friendship of a woman when it might have led to an interesting sexual experience later.

Strangers had a tendency to unburden themselves to other strangers. Groggins didn't want any share of their problems. He carried around a sackful of his own.

"I hope we can get together," Fioredelliso said.

Groggins shook his hand again. He picked up his suitcase, and turned toward the main cocktail lounge. He found a place at the bar. Ordered a Campari on the rocks.

He spoke fluent Italian, as well as French, German, Vietnamese, and several African dialects. He even understood some Arabic. He had an ear for languages.

Groggins sipped his drink and looked at the clock. He'd wait twenty minutes before leaving the cocktail lounge for the Eliso Hotel. He had called earlier in the day from London to reserve a room.

He drank slowly. Twenty minutes passed.

Groggins paid for his drink and hurried to the taxi stand. The rain had stopped. There were patches of sunlight and blue sky. A short time later he was deposited in front of the hotel on the Via Pinciana, across from the Villa Borghese.

Groggins checked in, left his passport at the desk, and went up to his room on the fourth floor. His window overlooked the street and the Villa Borghese. The room was small. A large bed occupied most of it.

He had never stayed at the Eliso before. He had passed it the last time he visited Rome, liked its location, and decided he'd try it if he returned.

There wasn't much he could do until the cafes in the Trastevere section would be open for business. That wouldn't be until seven P.M. the earliest. Like himself, many of their customers were unemployed mercenaries. If anyone was in the market for men, word of who was doing the buying most certainly would be circulated.

Groggins unpacked and decided to spend the rest of the afternoon enjoying the sights of Rome like any other tourist. A few hours could be his before he began to earn his pay. Besides, Rome was too much like a beautiful woman, whose past made her a challenge and whose present joy of life made her a seductress few men could resist.

The afternoon passed quickly. Groggins visited the church of Saint Peter in Vincoli to look at Michelangelo's Moses. Every time he had visited Rome he had seen it. For him the statue personified the leader of the Israelites. Michelangelo created the image of a man who had been touched by God—if there was a God.

Groggins had seen too much of life and death to believe in anything other than himself. But he understood why most people had to believe in something. It gave them a hold on the future and guidelines to live by. He didn't need either, he learned to live in the present. He made his own guidelines. In his world, the Ten Commandments just didn't exist.

Groggins finished the afternoon of sightseeing in the Piazza Navona. He sat at a small table at the Cafe Tres Scalini, enjoying the gelati he ordered and the constant swirl of activity in the piazza. There were mimes, jugglers, shouting children, artists peddling everything from their paintings to their bodies. And as the light began to grow softer, the shading of color in the piazza changed, too. The yellows and pinks gradually faded into the gray of dusk. When the lights came on, illuminating the central fountain of the Four Rivers, Groggins summoned the waiter and asked for his check.

He went back to the Eliso. At the desk, he asked for his passport. The clerk, a young man with slicked-down black hair, smiled. ''There is someone here to see you, signor.'' He rolled his eyes up to indicate the person was behind Groggins in a small sitting room.

Groggins' heart raced. As he turned, a man of medium height and build wearing a gray silk suit, was just getting to his feet.

In English the man said, ''My name is Mario Rinaldi. I am with Italian Intelligence, something like your CIA.'' He flashed his ID card. ''I would like to have a few words with you.''

Groggins nodded. He guessed him to be in his late forties or early fifties.

''I think it would be better if we were outside,'' Rinaldi said.

''Yes, I think so too,'' Groggins answered.

They walked to the corner without speaking, crossed the street and entered the Villa Borghese. There were couples on the benches. Most were teenagers but a few were older, in their twenties. They passed two couples who were making love.

''Hot Roman nights make one want to be young again,'' Rinaldi commented.

Groggins shrugged. He had no such yearnings.

''Well,'' Rinaldi said, ''do I address you as Signor Robert Harris, or do I use your real name, Signor Jack Groggins?'' Then he explained. ''One of our spotters recognized you in the airport. You were talking to another man; then you went into the cocktail lounge alone. Waited about twenty minutes and took a cab to the hotel.''

"Use whichever one makes you feel more at ease," Groggins answered.

Rinaldi laughed. "I want you to be at ease, Signor. I am almost always at ease.''

"Did you also pay a visit to the man I was seen with?''

"Signor Fioredelliso is as clean as the newly fallen snow,'' Rinaldi answered. "By the way. Your room has been searched. It too is clean.''

"I'm glad to hear my traveling companion wasn't a setup,'' Groggins said sourly.

"I think we can sit down now," Rinaldi suggested, pointing to an empty bench.

"What do you want to say to me?'' Groggins asked, dropping down on the bench.

"Well, Mr. Groggins—''

Groggins chuckled. "So you made the choice after all.''

"I much prefer to deal in reality," Rinaldi said. "Since we know who you are, we'd very much like to know why you're here.''

"Italy is my favorite country,'' Groggins answered. "Someday, I hope to come here and live.''

Rinaldi took out a pack of cigarettes and offered one to Groggins. "Your former employer—''

"Is still my former employer," Groggins said, blowing smoke into the air. "I told you. I'm here on a visit.''

"With a fake passport?''

"Old habits are hard to break,'' Groggins responded.

"An Inspector Southby at Scotland Yard gave some

vague hints that you might have had something to do
with two murders. A man by the name of Ortega and
your former mistress, Paula. . .''

Groggins was on his feet. "Listen, I didn't kill either
of them!"

"I was only telling you what Inspector Southby
hinted at," Rinaldi said. "But we're not interested in
what you did in London or, for that matter, anywhere
else. We want to know why you're here."

"I already told you."

"To look at Michelangelo's Moses and eat gelati in
the Piazza Navona."

"Tomorrow I'll find something else to do. Tell your
man to be up early. I'm going to the Sistine Chapel, and
if you don't get there when it opens, it just becomes too
crowded to see anything."

Rinaldi stubbed out his cigarette. "Try to understand
our position. We have terrorists from the left and from
the right. We don't need men with your background
giving either group the benefit of your experience."

"Neither group interests me."

"For money a man could suddenly find himself
interested in something that he might otherwise even
laugh at."

"I'm not here to become involved in your politics,"
Groggins said.

"Then why are you here?"

"A visit," Groggins said.

"We could deport you. Even hold you for having a
fake passport. Our detention prisons aren't exactly
what you might expect."

"I don't like threats, Signor Rinaldi," Groggins
said, grinding the remainder of the cigarette under his
heel.

"I was only stating what could happen," Rinaldi

answered. He took another cigarette and offered Groggins one.

Groggins waved it aside. "What are you going to do?"

"For the time being, nothing," Rinaldi answered, lighting up. "We'll wait and see what you do. If you do nothing, then nothing will be done to you. But if you do something that involves you in our political situation, be assured we'll act and, if necessary, kill you."

"But in the meantime, I'm free to move around."

"Not completely."

"Of course I know I'll be followed and that's what'll make it so interesting. I'll not only have the pleasure of enjoying the sights, but I'll also have the sport of evading my shadow."

"I have nothing else to say," Rinaldi said.

Both men stood up and walked back the way they came. When they reached the entrance, Rinaldi offered his hand. "You know there's nothing personal in this."

"I know," Groggins said as he shook Rinaldi's hand.

Groggins returned to the hotel.

The desk clerk handed him his passport. "I'm sorry for having held it so long," the man said.

"Not your fault," Groggins replied with a smile. He walked to the end of the hallway and rode the small elevator up to the fourth floor.

Though his clothes had been searched, everything was as he had left it. The only thing Rinaldi's men might have found was his gun. But he had hidden that and the extra bullets for it in the water tank behind the commode. He checked. It was still there, safely wrapped in oilskins. He took it out and put it on the dresser. Then he switched on the air conditioner, took off his jacket and loosened his tie. Groggins stretched out on the bed and closed his eyes. Having an Italian Intelligence agent on his tail would only keep him more alert. The more alert he was, the better chance he'd have of staying alive.

Groggins slept for an hour, then showered. Before he left the room, he took the .38 and slipped it into a belt holster.

He walked downstairs. No one was in the lobby or sitting room. He asked the concierge to call a cab for him.

"Where shall I tell the dispatcher you're going?"

"Just for a drive," Groggins answered. "For a drive around the city."

Later in the cab, he caught sight of the car tailing him. He couldn't see the driver, or his companion, clearly. "There's a car following us," Groggins told the driver. "I'll give you ten thousand lire extra if you can lose him."

"No problem," the driver answered. "Just sit back and hold on." He made a series of fast turns into narrow streets.

"They're still with us," Groggins said.

The driver sped across a bridge spanning the Tiber. Then picked up a street that ran behind some warehouses. "Where are they now?"

"Just turning."

The car tailing them rushed by.

"Stay here for a few minutes," Groggins said. He handed the driver a ten thousand lire note and a cigarette.

To play it safe, Groggins had the cabby take him to the Piazza de Popolo, where he switched to another cab and went to the railroad station. There he changed cabs again and told the driver to take him to the Via Ugo

Bassi, off the Viale Traste Vere.

The driver glanced back at him and said, "That's a rough place, even for a Roman."

"Yes, I know," Groggins answered. "But I have friends there. A couple of crazies who like living in the slums."

"They must be crazy if they live in the Traste Vere, when they could live somewhere else."

Groggins let the conversation lapse. He had other things to think about. This time he managed to shake off Rinaldi's men. But the longer it took to find the men he sought, the better Rinaldi's chances to follow him. Groggins had to even-up the score for Paula and Ortega.

The cab crossed the Tiber on the Palatine Bridge. A few minutes later it stopped at Via Ugo Bassi.

"Walk in the middle of the street," the driver cautioned. "Stay away from the alleyways."

"Thanks. I'll be careful," Groggins said, handing the driver the fare and a generous tip.

The Via Ugo Bassi led directly into the heart of the Traste Vere, one of the worst sections in Rome. The small, narrow twisting streets were crowded with society's outcasts and poor. It was a thieves lair and a haven for murderers. Each year a certain number of unsuspecting tourists wandered through it's streets in search of some new pleasure and never lived to come out.

Groggins turned into one of the narrow streets opening on the Via Ugo Bassi. The multistoried buildings on each side were ugly and left only a ribbon of sky between them. Here and there a figure lurked in the dark entrances.

Once a woman called, "Give you a good fuck for five thousand lire."

Groggins kept walking. Made another turn and entered the brilliantly lit, crowded Piazza Rosolino Pilo. The sidewalk cafes were doing a brisk business. Hawkers were everywhere. Dozens of multicolored balloons filled the piazza. Children ran after them.

Groggins crossed the piazza.

"My bag," a woman shouted. "Someone stole my bag!"

"There he is! That boy there!" another woman cried.

In the next instant Groggins faced a teenaged boy holding a woman's bag. Neither he nor the boy moved.

The boy was breathing hard and then tried to sidestep Groggins.

"Drop it and run," Groggins said.

"Son of a whore, out of my way!" the boy exploded.

Groggins shook his head.

Suddenly the boy had a knife in his hand.

"You just made a mistake," Groggins told him in a flat voice.

The boy slashed at Groggins. But before the boy could recover, Groggins grabbed his hand, forced him to drop the knife and tossed him aside.

The boy scrambled to his feet. "Fucking bastard!" he shouted and ran.

Groggins picked up the bag and handed it to the woman.

"It happened so fast," she said in English. "He grabbed it and the next moment I saw you fighting with him."

Groggins pretended not to understand.

A man interpreted what the woman said.

"Tell him," she said. "I want to give him something for his trouble."

Groggins declined.

"Then at least let me buy you a drink," she said.

"It's not necessary," Groggins said through the interpreter. "Now if you'll excuse me, I must be on my way." He shook hands with the woman and continued across the piazza.

The encounter with the purse snatcher hardly raised a sweat. Had he wanted to he could have maimed the boy for life or killed him. As it was, the boy would be black and blue for a few days from the fall he had taken.

If he hadn't come face to face with the boy, Groggins would have done nothing. He didn't have a complex about law and order. He had no illusions about the law. And as for order—if it meant living in a neat, tidy world where everyone and everything had its place, he was against it. Both the laws and the concepts of order were made by the few to keep their hold on the many. Ordinarily he would have let the boy run. But the punk pulled a knife on him. And that was a mistake.

Groggins turned onto the Via Porta Settimiana and entered Romolo, a restaurant at number 8. It's history was linked with the mistress of the painter Raphael. But Groggins wasn't interested in that or anxious to see some of the celebrities that might be there. His only reason for going to Romolo was to speak with Bruno, one of the waiters.

Groggins didn't know if Bruno was his given or surname. He supposed it was his surname. The family probably came from northern Italy, where that name was common. Bruno was a short thin man with light brown hair, almost blond. A small, well-trimmed moustache hid a harelip. A dapper dresser, Bruno had a penchant for beautiful women and they for him. His mistress always occupied a table overlooking the garden. It was known as Bruno's table.

When he entered the restaurant, Groggins looked toward the table. A woman sat there; a dark-haired beauty, somewhere about twenty-five. She wore a tight black dress that showed every curve of her voluptuous body.

Bruno was one of those rare men knowledgeable about a great deal more than was required by his job. He came by information the way some individuals come by money. People told him things, and he always repeated them to the right people. If someone wanted to buy some smack, Bruno knew who was selling. If a man needed a few thousand in cash, Bruno could arrange the loan. And if someone was on the buy for men with small arms and explosive experience, Bruno might know who the buyer was or where or when to contact interested parties. Bruno was trusted by everyone, or so it seemed.

The maitre'd came up to Groggins. "There'll be a twenty-minute wait," he said.

"Bruno's table," Groggins answered.

The man nodded. "I'll tell him," he said.

Groggins went to the table.

The woman looked up questioningly. She had lovely green eyes, childishly pouting lips. For a moment Groggins imagined how those lips would look circled around his penis. "I'm a friend of Bruno's," Groggins said.

She nodded.

He sat down. He wondered if she knew anything more about Bruno than what he was like in bed.

Bruno came out of the garden and looked toward the table. For a moment he didn't recognize Groggins. But when he did, he smiled broadly and called to the barkeeper, "Give my friend at the table the best scotch in the house."

"My name is Rinata," the woman said.

"Harris, Robert Harris," Groggins told her.

"But you speak Italian like a Roman."

"I also speak French like a Parisian and German like a Berliner."

A waiter put a drink down in front of Groggins. He lifted it, gestured toward Rinata and said, "To luck!"

She smiled broadly.

Groggins swallowed most of his drink. He was finding it hard not to stare at Rinata. She was either wearing flimsies under her dress, or nothing. Her nipples pressed out against the black material of her dress.

Bruno stepped up and shook Groggins' hand.

"Can you spare me a few minutes?" Groggins asked.

"After I serve one of the tables their main course," Bruno said. He glanced toward Rinata. "Keep my friend here happy until I come back."

"I think your friend would only be happy if he had me in bed," she answered.

Groggins colored. She was sharper than he thought. At least more perceptive.

"I didn't say kill him with happiness," Bruno laughed and went back into the garden.

Groggins sipped his drink. He enjoyed looking at Rinata. His imagination went wild.

"Are you going to stay in Rome long?" she asked.

"Probably not."

"Then you're here on business?"

"Yes, on business," Groggins answered.

Bruno returned. "Why don't you take a walk for awhile," he said to Rinata.

She nodded. Shook hands with Groggins and left.

He watched her walk toward the door. "She's not wearing any panties," he commented.

"Doesn't," Bruno replied sitting down. He ordered a glass of wine for himself and another scotch for

Groggins. "I own a piece of this place now," he explained. "A twenty-five-percent piece."

"Glad to see you come up in the world," Groggins said. "To your success as an entrepreneur."

They touched glasses and drank.

"Now tell me what brings you to Bruno's table?" Bruno asked.

Groggins glanced around the room. No one was paying any attention to them. He leaned forward. "Someone is looking for men with special experience.

"I haven't heard," Bruno answered.

Groggins leaned back. "That's like telling me the Pope isn't Catholic."

Bruno smiled. "He's only a Polish Catholic. To be a real Pope he'd have to be Italian."

"Tell me about it," Groggins said.

"Word is you were excommunicated," Bruno said.

Groggins nodded. "I'm freelancing now."

"I heard you were writing books. Is there money in it?"

"Would I be here if there was? I'm looking for work. It's as simple as that."

"I don't know anything myself. But I might be able to put you on to someone who might know."

"I'd appreciate it," Groggins said, slipping a hundred dollar bill across the table. "Where can I find him?"

"Here. I'll phone him," Bruno said. He left the table and walked to the end of the bar where the phone was.

Groggins lit a cigarette. He glanced around again. Several people were waiting for tables. Most of them were Americans.

After two or three minutes, Bruno came back. "Have something to eat. I recommend the seafood pie.

By the time you finish he'll be here. Now I have to go back to work.''

"Thanks," Groggins said.

"He's a German," Bruno told him. "Name is Kurt Wagner. I didn't tell him your name. I figured you weren't really using the same one anyway."

Groggins shrugged. "It could be worse; he could be a Russian."

Bruno laughed and said, "Rinata is probably standing outside waiting for me to leave the table."

"How serious is it between the two of you?" Groggins asked.

"You want to try her?"

"The thought crossed my mind."

"We had our first argument this afternoon. We'll have out second tomorrow. After our third, she'll be gone."

"So you planned it all out?"

"Oh absolutely," Bruno answered with a smile. "I even planned the argument we had this afternoon." He disappeared through the door leading to the garden.

Almost immediately, Rinata returned to the table and sat down.

"What would you recommend to eat?" Groggins asked.

"That depends," she replied, taking a cigarette from a gold case.

Groggins struck a match and held it for her.

She leaned forward. The top of her dress dropped away from her breasts. They were firm. Enough for a good handful. With large pink nipples.

"Food, I mean. At least for now," Groggins said. "Later we can talk about my other tastes."

"Everything here is prepared to order," she

answered, blowing smoke from her nose.

Groggins summoned a waiter. "The seafood pie and a liter of the house white wine," he said.

Groggins was enjoying a second cup of espresso and a cannoli. Rinata wasn't much of a conversationalist. But she was good to look at, and he fantasized about what might happen with her later.

"A man is looking at us," Rinata said, from behind her hand.

Groggins slowly turned toward the bar.

The man nodded. "I'll be back in a little while," Groggins said, facing Rinata.

"I'll tell Bruno," she answered.

"Will you wait?"

"Yes."

Groggins stood up. He walked to where Wagner was standing. In German he said, "Thank you for coming," he said.

"It's best if we walk," Wagner wheezed.

Groggins agreed and followed him outside. Wagner was a heavyset, broad-shouldered man with pale blue eyes and thinning blond hair. He was somewhere in his late fifties, or early sixties. His face was round and florid. The first three buttons of his shirt were open. His chest was covered with a mat of gray hair.

"Bruno thought you might help me find work," Groggins said, going as close to the reason for their meeting as he thought prudent.

"You're a writer, aren't you?" Wagner wheezed.

"I've been other things."

Wagner glanced at him.

"I'm a demolition expert," Groggins said matter-of-factly.

"Where did you gain that kind of expertise?"

"In Vietnam to begin with. Various other places after that, including Angola."

They turned into a dark, narrow street. Wagner hesitated.

"I don't blame you," Groggins said. "The two of us wouldn't be much of a match for a few determined muggers."

"Then we'll walk back to the restaurant," Wagner responded.

"Do you know of any openings for men with my experience?"

"What kind of books do you write?" Wagner asked.

"Novels. . . . Lots of action in exotic places."

"Sex?" he wheezed.

Before Groggins could answer, Wagner said, "I don't read books with sex in them. They're nothing but filth. What kind of people read that stuff? I'll tell you. Only the sick ones read it. Nothing that happens between a man and woman is worth writing about." Wagner stopped. He was breathing very hard. "The only kind of relationship worth anything is the comradeship between men, isn't that so, mister—"

"Harris . . . Robert Harris," Groggins said. "And your name is?" he asked, pretending not to know it.

"Kurt Wagner."

They began to walk again.

"Sex should be a matter of procreation only," Wagner declared.

Groggins remained silent. He wasn't going to attempt to change Wagner's ideas about sex. Obviously the man had his tastes.

When they reached the restaurant, Wagner said, "There are some people who might be interested in a man with your experience."

"How do I meet them?"

"You come to my shop at fifteen Largo Febo. It's a bookstore. Be there around four o'clock."

"I've seen that store. It's across the street from a garden, isn't it?"

"Yes, and it's diagonally across from the Hotel Raphael."

Groggins offered his hand. "I'll be there."

"I don't shake hands," Wagner said.

Groggins withdrew his, certain now he was dealing with a nut job.

"Tomorrow then," Wagner said. He turned and walked away.

Groggins breathed deeply. To take a man like Wagner philosophically was difficult. His comradeship for men was probably limited to boys, or very young men. Groggins had met his type before. A great number of them flourished in the out-of-the-way places of the world, where they could buy the necessary bodies to satisfy their needs.

Groggins reentered the restaurant, walking straight back to Bruno's table. Rinata was still sitting there.

"I told Bruno," she said, looking up at Groggins.

Groggins dropped down into the chair. He signaled the waiter. "Bring me a double scotch," he told him.

"That difficult?" Rinata questioned.

Groggins shrugged. "Not in the usual way," he said, finishing off his scotch in two long swallows.

"I also told Bruno I'd be spending the night with you."

"And what did he say?"

" 'Enjoy yourselves!' "

"Have you a place?" Groggins asked.

"No. But there are places to stay within walking distance."

"As soon as I pay my bill, we'll go."

"Bruno said it was on the house."

"Then let's go find a place to enjoy ourselves,"
Groggins said.

IX

Groggins awoke slowly, conscious of the shouting in the street. Then of a cool breeze against his bare skin. Finally of the soft press of a woman's breasts against his chest.

He opened his eyes. He was facing Rinata. The top of her head touched the bottom of his chin. Like him, she was completely naked. His right knee rested between her legs. She was as good a lay as he ever had.

The shouting from the street drew his attention to the window. A wide swath of sunlight splashed across it, yellowing the wall near a dilapidated dresser. He glanced around the room. Shabby was the only way to describe it. The paint was peeling off the walls. There wasn't even a door between the bathroom and the bedroom.

Groggins raised his left hand to look at his watch. It was only 7:15. Still too early to get out of bed, so he thought about Wagner. But there really wasn't much

for him to think about. The man was obviously a go-
between for the buyer. Probably one of many of such
go-betweens, either in Rome or other European cities.
The men must be needed quickly, or Wagner would
have put the meeting with the buyer off for a couple of
days.

Groggins suddenly realized he had an opportunity to
do more than just meet the buyer. But to do it he'd need
someone he could trust, someone who also knew how
to use a camera. Anyone he knew in Rome would be
suspicious of what he'd want them to do. He needed a
stranger. Groggins glanced down at Rinata. Someone
like her. But Wagner had seen her with him. And
probably knew she was Bruno's woman. Because of
Wagner's sexual preference, he might not have been
aware of her. After a moment's thought, Groggins
decided it would be too risky to get her to do, solo, what
he wanted done. But if she were with someone, say a
man, then photographing whoever entered and left
Wagner's bookstore would be an easy matter. But
who'd be the man?

Groggins couldn't think of anyone. He sure as hell
couldn't go to the Company man at the embassy and ask
him for help. He not only wouldn't get it, but by the
time he was out on the Via Veneto again, Salito would
be told about the request. And probably be pressed as
hell. Maybe enough to stop him. The less Salito knew
about what he was doing, the better off he'd be.

He needed a stranger. Someone who would believe
whatever story he chose to tell.

"That feels good," Rinata purred.

Groggins was surprised. He wasn't aware of doing
anything. He thought she was asleep.

She touched his leg. "Don't stop moving your
knee," she told him.

"I didn't know you were awake."

"I wasn't until you started with your knee," she answered.

He was going to explain he hadn't intended to arouse her, but changed his mind. Instead his movements became more vigorous.

Rinata stroked him but Groggins was still trying to come up with someone he could use.

"Come inside of me," she said in a husky voice.

Groggins eased her over his left leg.

She began to move.

He did too. She was more excited than he realized.

"Faster," she demanded. "Go faster. . . . Yes. . . . Yes!"

Her body tensed. Her pulsing sent exquisite sensations along his penis. He plunged into her.

She began to moan. With a long quavering wail, she huddled herself against him. The next instant she was shaken by spasms of ecstacy.

His own passion rose swiftly. Before she finished climaxing, he uttered a deep growl of satisfaction. Then he remembered Fioredelliso, the little man on the plane.

"I didn't think I'd be so quick," Rinata laughed. "But it was good."

"That's all that matters," Groggins answered. "How would you like to spend the day with me?" he asked.

"Very much." She kissed his right nipple.

"Good. We'll have breakfast together. Then you'll go back to Bruno's place to change and I'll go to my hotel. I'll tell you where to meet me. I'll have a friend with me. He's going to want to photograph you."

She drew away from him. "You want me to—"

"No, no. Nothing like that," Groggins said. "After

he'll take some pictures of you, the three of us will go out to dinner. Then you and I will spend the rest of the night together. But not in this place."

"There won't be the three of us in bed?" Rinata asked, not moving back to Groggins.

"No."

"I don't like it with two men," she said. "Sometimes it's okay with two women and a man. But not the other way around."

"I promise you, there will only be the two of us."

She moved back into his embrace. "Can we sleep a little while longer?" she asked.

"Yes, I'm tired too." He put his hand over her breasts. In a short time they fell asleep.

Groggins phoned Fioredelliso before he returned to his own hotel. He arranged to meet him at the top of the Spanish Steps at two o'clock. Then he bought a single lens reflex camera, a telephoto lens, and two rolls of high-speed black-and-white film.

Before he separated from Rinata, he told her to wear less sexy clothing and a wide-brim hat.

"It's too hot to wear a bra and panties," she complained.

"Just for the photographs," he said. "After that you can take them off."

"Where shall I meet you?"

"At three-thirty at the "Statue of the Four Rivers" in the Piazza Navone. Be there on time."

"I will," she answered and kissed him.

When Groggins returned to the Eliso, one of Rinaldi's men was outside in a car. Another was in the lobby. Groggins was almost tempted to introduce himself. But on second thought realized the overture might not be appreciated.

Groggins took time to shower, shave and dress. He loaded the camera with film and placed it and the telephoto lens in a shoulder bag. He clipped his revolver to his belt, then left the hotel. He was immediately followed by the man in the lobby.

Groggins walked down the Via Veneto to the Piazza Barberini, to the Via Vittoria, and then to where he boarded a bus for the Colosseum. He attached himself to one of the many tourist groups there. When he was sure he was no longer being followed, he left the group and walked toward the Spanish Steps, which were some distance away.

His plan was to meet with Fioredelliso. Explain he was in Italy on a special mission for the Company. And that he must have his help. Of course Groggins intended to swear him to absolute secrecy before telling him anything.

Groggins entered the Piazza di Spagna from the Via de Croce. Looked up to the top of the steps and saw Fioredelliso. He was wearing a yellow polo shirt and green slacks. The area around the Spanish Steps was mobbed with tourists, most of them Japanese. They were seldom armed with less than two cameras and many carried four.

Groggins threaded his way through the crowds. He went up the steps and greeted Fioredelliso warmly.

"I never expected you to call," Fioredelliso said. "I mean you were so intent on getting away from me."

Groggins laughed. "I'll tell you about it." He started to walk.

"Where are we going?" Fioredelliso asked.

"To meet a friend," he smiled. "A beautiful young woman."

They went down to the Piazza and across to the Via Condotti.

"More Japs here than there were on the islands," Fioredelliso commented. "But don't get me wrong, I'm not prejudiced against them or anyone else. But sometimes I look at a woman or a man and I find myself thinking, did I kill your brother? Or your son? Or maybe your husband? You know so many years after the war, I still can remember things as if they happened yesterday."

Surprised by the man's sensitivity, he answered, "I know exactly what you mean. That happens to most men who have been in combat. But let's change the subject. How do you like Rome?"

"It's more than I ever dreamed it was," Fioredelliso said. "I'm like a big kid. I don't know where to look first."

Groggins laughed. "It does that to me every time I come here."

"Now would you tell me why you called me?"

"I need your help," Groggins said.

"If it's money, you can have fifty or a hundred—"

"Thank you. . . . But it's not money," Groggins said. "I need someone I can trust. Someone who'll never tell anyone what I'm going to tell you."

Fioredelliso slowed his pace and stopped altogether. He looked very uncomfortable. "Look, if this woman we're going to meet is another guy's wife and you want me to, well, I can't imagine what you'd want me to do. But fooling around with another man's wife is—"

"Nothing like that," Groggins said with a wave of his hand. "I'm a Company agent."

"A what?"

Realizing Fioredelliso didn't know what he meant, he said, "CIA."

"You?"

Groggins nodded. "Me." He fished out his wallet. Flashed a government press card with his photograph on it.

"Man, that's really something!" Fioredelliso responded.

Groggins started to walk again. "I'm here on Company business."

"Then the woman is working with you?"

"She doesn't know it. I didn't want her to know too much. Women talk about things. She's just a woman I met and spent the night with. But she's part of a plan."

"And you want me to be the other part?" Fioredelliso asked.

"Yes," Groggins said with a vigorous nod.

Fioredelliso frowned. "I don't know," he said. "I just don't know."

Groggins counted on the man's sense of adventure. That was, of course, providing he still had it. Groggins was gambling that whatever drove him to join the Marines during World War II might still be there—or what was left of it—might be enough to make him agree to help.

"If there's any rough stuff, I'd be dead before I could snap my fingers. As it is, my heart is going like a damn triphammer."

Groggins had completely forgotten about Fioredelliso's pacemaker. Maybe it was a mistake to involve him. "There won't be any rough stuff. All you'll do is photograph the girl," he explained.

"Are you putting me on?"

"Whenever someone enters or leaves a particular store," Groggins said. "I need to know who goes in and who comes out for at least an hour or so before I go in and an hour after I come out. It's a second-hand bookstore, so there won't be too many people to photograph.''

"Will I be able to do it without attracting attention?''

"Absolutely,'' Groggins answered.

"I must be nuts for even walking with you,'' Fioredelliso said.

"You could turn around and go back the way we came. I won't be angry, or think any the less of you. After all, this is my game, not yours.''

"Yeah, I know. But this'll probably be the only chance I'll have to do something different. Even if I can't tell anyone about it, at least I'll know it. See, I'm in construction. I have my own company on Staten Island in New York. I build houses. I've made some money. But this is different. This is, as they say, for God and country.''

Groggins slapped him on the back. "You must have been one hell of a Marine!''

"Yeah, I was gung-ho all right.''

"We'll go the rest of the way by cab,'' Groggins said. "And after it's over my lady friend and I will show you Rome at night.''

Fioredelliso grinned broadly.

Rinata was waiting at the fountain of the Four Rivers. She greeted Groggins with a kiss.

He introduced her to Fioredelliso.

"It's a pleasure to meet you,'' she said demurely, offering him her hand.

"Likewise,'' he said, wide-eyed.

"Do you like the way I'm dressed?'' she asked, turning to Groggins.

"You look beautiful,'' he answered. She did. She was wearing a lovely rose-pink suit. High heels. A wide-brimmed straw hat. Even a bra and panties. She looked like a high-class model. "Now I want the two of you to go to the restaurant on Lago Febo, which is just around the back from here. It's located in a small triangular-shaped park. Find a table overlooking a bookstore. Rinata, you sit with your back to the street. Arthur, you sit facing her. Whenever you see someone entering or leaving the store, including me, you photograph them." He peeled off the shoulder bag and handed it to Fioredelliso. "Everything you need is in there. The camera is loaded." Then he gave him two ten-thousand-lire notes. "Order enough for a two-hour session. You don't have to eat much of it. But you don't want to make the waiter suspicious."

"Anything else?"

"If I don't come out after an hour, say, you take the camera and film to the American Embassy and ask for their resident Company man. Give him the camera and tell him everything."

"Does she come with me to the embassy?"

"No. Send her on her way," Groggins said. "But I expect to come out. I wanted you to know what to do if I didn't."

"Where do we meet afterwards?"

"You wait about fifteen minutes. Then come back here. At the far end there, on the right, you'll be able to get a cab. Take it to Romolo. That's a restaurant."

He switched to Italian and gave Rinata the same instructions. Then he said to Fioredelliso, "She knows the place. She'll get you there. Okay, you head for the restaurant. And Arthur make it look good between the two of you. Make people think she's yours."

Groggins switched again to Italian and explained to Rinata, "Make it seem he's your boyfriend. Hold on to him when you walk. At the table, take hold of his hand now and then."

She laughed. "If his eyes were hands, he'd be all over me."

"So much the better. It's got to look real. Now get going."

Rinata linked arms with Fioredelliso.

"See you in a couple of hours," Groggins said. He watched them cross the piazza. When they were out of sight, he went to the Tres Scalini, sat down at an outdoor table and ordered a dish of peach gelati. It was only three-thirty. He could dally for the better part of an hour before meeting with Wagner and his friend.

Groggins entered the Largo Febo from the right. The park was across the street. He glanced toward it. Fioredelliso and Rinata were at a table near the railing. Fioredelliso had a clear view of the bookstore.

The restaurant occupied the base of the triangle. The rest of it was actually a park, with pines, a few oaks, and many stately Lombardy poplars. Children were playing in it. Some mothers watched from nearby benches.

Groggins wondered what would happen if he had to shoot his way out of the bookstore? He shuddered. People would start to run in every direction. He shook his head. If he wanted to survive, he couldn't afford the luxury of that kind of thinking.

He stopped in front of the bookstore. The windows needed a washing. The books displayed dealt mainly with ancient and more recent military history.

Groggins entered the shop. Chimes sounded in the rear. The place smelled musty. Books were piled on shelves, on tables, and on the floor. A battered roll-top desk was directly to the left of the door.

Wagner came out from behind a threadbare blue curtain. "Did you have any difficulty finding the store?'' he asked.

"None," Groggins answered.

"If you will follow me," Wagner said.

"Lead the way."

There was a door behind the curtain. "I told my friend that you were ready to go to work immediately," Wagner said.

"Yes," Groggins answered. He entered a room that was very wide and well furnished with a sofa, several chairs, and a few scatter-rugs on the floor. Each piece of furniture was very modern and carefully placed. There were two windows and a french door opening out on a small garden filled with rose bushes of various colors. A man was framed by the window to Groggins' right. He was examining a blue rose.

Groggins started for the garden.

"No," Wagner said. "He'll come in when he's ready."

Groggins shrugged. "Do you live here?"

"In a flat above. I use this room for entertaining."

"And roses are your hobby?" Groggins asked.

"Yes. I grow and collect books about them." Wagner answered enthusiastically. "You wouldn't be a rose aficionado, would you?"

Before Groggins could reply, the man in the garden started toward the door. He was tall, slender, and very dignified looking with salt-and-pepper hair and a well-trimmed moustache. He wore a blue suit, a white shirt, and a blue and red necktie.

"Well, Mr. Harris," the man said, "Kurt tells me that you're looking for employment? Ah, but before you answer, permit me to introduce myself. I am Hans Dissel." His English was accented.

Groggins shook his head. "Yes, I'm looking for work."

"Kurt, I'd like Campari on the rocks with a twist of lime. What about you, Mr. Harris?"

"Vodka on the rocks."

Dissel gestured to one of the chairs. "Please make yourself comfortable." He sat on the sofa facing Groggins. "Is there anything you wish to add about your experience that you didn't already tell Kurt?"

"Nothing I can think of."

Wagner handed them their drinks.

"To a successful enterprise," Dissel toasted. "You understand, I can't tell you where you'll be going or what you'll be doing."

Groggins nodded.

"The pay is very good. Five thousand dollars for the length of the mission and a five-thousand-dollar bonus at the end of the mission."

Groggins set his drink down on an end table. "Nothing paid to next of kin in the event of death or capture?"

"I'm afraid not."

"The terms are acceptable," Groggins said, taking out a pack of cigarettes. "When do I start?"

"Three or four days. Most certainly within the week."

Groggins lit a cigarette.

Wagner swooped down from the other side of the room. He placed an ashtray next to Groggins.

"Where can you be reached?" Dissel asked.

"Better still where can I reach you?" Groggins asked.

"That wouldn't be better for me," Dissel said with a smile. "Since you're reluctant to reveal where you're staying, I'll tell you where you can go for the information you'll need."

"Fine!"

"Carlo's, It's on the Via Giovagnoli, a few steps in from the Piazza Pilo, in the Traste Vere section. You might meet some of your friends there."

"Who do I ask for?"

"The owner. Carlo. Ask him if he knows a second-hand book dealer. He will ask what kind of books interest you. And you will say anything about the Afrika Korps. Then he will give you the information he has. Check with him every night."

Groggins repeated the instructions.

"If you happen to know of any other men looking for work, tell Carlo. He'll set something up with Kurt."

"How many men are you hiring?"

"Two hundred all told. With you I have one-hundred and eighty."

"If I run into anyone I know, I'll pass the word along. To require two hundred men, it must be something big."

"Take my word, it is big." He looked toward Wagner, who was standing near one of the windows. "You made a good choice."

"Thank you," Wagner responded. "It's always a pleasure to receive a compliment from you."

Dissel nodded. His attention went back to Groggins. "Do you need any money now?"

"I'm not exactly flush."

Dissel took out his wallet and removed five ten-thousand-lire notes. "If you need more, ask Carlo. But don't overdo it."

"This should hold me for awhile," Groggins said.

Dissel stood up. "I'll be going now."

"We'll go together," Groggins said.

"If you don't mind, I'd rather go alone."

"Suit yourself," Groggins replied. "I'll stay here

and look at the roses. I don't ever remember seeing a blue one." He stood up and shook hands with Dissel. He didn't expect to see him again.

"I wish you the best of luck," Dissel said. "Don't bother to come with me, Kurt. I know my way out. Show Mr. Harris your roses."

Soon after Dissel, Groggins left the bookstore. He crossed the street to the Hotel Raphael, found an empty telephone booth and placed a collect call to Salito. It took five minutes for the Rome operator to get through to London and another two minutes before he was cleared through to speak to Salito.

"I was just hired by a man named Hans Dissel," Groggins said. "He has one-hundred and eighty men and still needs twenty more."

"For what?"

"It's blind. Nothing about what or where," Groggins answered.

"You weren't sent there to—"

Groggins cut him off. "Listen Salito, it's all tied together. I'm going to send you a roll of film. See if there's anyone on it you know."

"I don't want you going off on your own. Stick to your assignment."

"Yeah, yeah! But take a good look at the film. Run a tracer on a Hans Dissel and on a Kurt Wagner."

"Don't you have something more than their names?"

"Not for now," Groggins answered. "I'll get back to you in a day or so."

"Remember, stick with the assignment!"

"Sure," Groggins answered and hung up. From the hotel, he walked back to the Piazza Navona. It was the shank of the afternoon, the best part. The crowds in the

Piazza were thoroughly enjoying it. Groggins walked to where there was a line of cabs. He got into the first one.

"The Via Hugo Bassi," he told the driver. He settled back and lit a cigarette. He thought about the way Dissel and Wagner worked. Wagner was a scout and Dissel the buyer. Maybe for himself? Or for someone else? Two hundred men were a lot of men to buy for one operation. Though Dissel didn't say it was one operation. It could be several spaced out over the three-month duration.

Groggins flicked the cigarette out of the window and closed his eyes. He remembered he hadn't eaten any lunch. He was looking forward to having a good dinner and a pleasant evening.

Fioredelliso and Rinata were sitting at a table at the Romolo. Bruno was with them. Various members of the staff were busy getting ready for business.

"I tell you," Fioredelliso said, "I haven't felt so good in years." He laughed and drank the red house wine Bruno had provided.

Groggins reached across the table for the camera. "You can have it, Arthur. All I want is the film."

"I took the film out in the cab on the way here," Fioredelliso said. He dug into his pocket and brought out the film. "You know, I forgot how exciting life could be."

Groggins took the film.

"Give the camera and other stuff to that young lady," Fioredelliso said. "She's just wonderful."

Bruno laughed and translated for Rinata. "By the Holy Mother of God," he exclaimed in English, "she's blushing!"

"Now tell me did anything unusual happen?" Groggins asked, pouring wine for himself.

"The man who left before you came out was picked up in a chauffeur-driven car," Fioredelliso said. "A pale blue Mercedes. Thanks to Rinata we even have the license plate number."

Groggins raised his eyebrows.

"After I photographed the man, she spotted the car. I couldn't photograph it, so she left the table and ran after it. Luckily it was moving slow enough for her to get the number."

Groggins frowned, then glanced at Bruno.

"Don't you want the plate number?" Fioredelliso asked.

"Yes."

"It was a Swiss plate. G-six-seven-eight."

"Easy to remember," Groggins commented. "You don't think anyone realized what you were doing?"

"No way," Fioredelliso said.

"What about when Rinata went after the car?"

"She pretended she was going after a girl friend. She even called her name."

Groggins nodded and lit a cigarette. Nothing would undo what had been done. And he had another scrap of information to give Salito the next time he called him.

"Well, now what do we do?" Fioredelliso asked. "I feel full of piss and vinegar."

Bruno laughed and excused himself. "I have to go to work or my partner will start giving me dirty looks."

"Okay," Groggins said, "it's time for us to go." He shepherded Fioredelliso and Rinata out of the Romolo and into a cab. They went to a cocktail lounge on the Via Veneto; then to a small romantic restaurant on the Via del Portico d' Ottavia in the ghetto section of the city. Groggins had dined there during his previous visits to Rome.

Several times he saw Fioredelliso reach out and touch Rinata's hand. Once he even put his arm around her shoulder. But hastily withdrew it when he realized Groggins was looking at him.

"Let's walk," Rinata suggested, after they left the restaurant. She linked her arm with Fioredelliso's.

"Don't look so worried," Groggins told him.

"But I thought you and her—"

"We're friends. She likes you. Make the most of it."

"I'm old enough to be her father. I have a son her age," Fioredelliso said.

"What are the two of you talking about?" Rinata asked.

"Arturo has a son your age," Groggins said. "He's feeling ashamed of wanting to go to bed with you."

"Ask him if he has a wife?"

"Rinata wants to know if you have a wife?" Groggins asked.

He shook his head. "She died two years ago."

"Tough," Groggins said and translated the answer for Rinata.

"Would you mind if I went back to his hotel with him?"

"No . . . I think that would be a nice thing to do," Groggins said.

"You tell him," she said.

"You do it," he told her. Then to Fioredelliso he said, "You'll be okay with her."

"What? Where are you going?"

"Never mind me," Groggins said. "Just enjoy what Rinata has to give. I'll call you late in the morning." He turned and walked rapidly away. Knowing that

Fioredelliso would never forget his visit to Rome. Never!

Groggins awoke. Someone was banging on the door. "Who the hell is it?"

"Rinaldi, open the door!"

Groggins switched on a light. Got out of bed, unlocked the door and opened it.

"Get dressed," Rinaldi said.

Groggins didn't ask any questions. In less than five minutes he was dressed. He preceded Rinaldi into the elevator, though the lobby, and into the rear of a black Fiat.

A few minutes later they stopped in front of the Hotel d'Inghilterra.

"Fioredelliso?" Groggins asked. His heart beat very fast, his lips were dry.

Rinaldi said nothing.

The elevator climbed slowly to the sixth floor.

"On the right," Rinaldi said. "Room six-ten."

The door was closed. But Groggins could hear the sounds of people inside the room.

Rinaldi moved forward. He opened the door. "Go in."

Groggins stepped into the room. Three men were inside. One was a photographer. His strobe light momentarily illuminated the two nude bodies in the bed.

They had been shot while making love. Fioredelliso was still on top of Rinata. The side of Rinata's head was a bloody plup. There were three large holes in his back.

"We got the tip less than an hour ago," Rinaldi said. "The person who called spoke with a heavy German accent. Usually such tips go to the police. This one came directly to Intelligence. The caller seemed to think Fioredelliso worked for us. He said something about taking the wrong kind of photographs.''

''Is this supposed to mean something to me?'' Groggins asked. He guessed someone in the restaurant had tipped off Wagner.

''That's what I was wondering,'' Rinaldi answered. ''You knew Fioredelliso.''

''You checked him and found he was clean.''

''That's what I found. But obviously I was wrong.''

''Obviously,'' Groggins answered.

''The killer used a .357 and lead-nose bullets,'' Rinaldi said.

''From the look of the wounds, I'd say you were right.''

''Is that all you're going to say?''

''That's all,'' Groggins answered. ''Now could I go back to my hotel and get a few more hours sleep.'' He couldn't allow himself any show of emotion.

Rinaldi nodded.

The two of them left the room and walked down to the elevator together.

''You've managed to give my men the slip each time you walk out,'' Rinaldi said.

''So?''

''We don't have to work against each other,'' Rinaldi said. ''A little cooperation from you would gain a great deal from me.''

''I'm here as a tourist,'' Groggins said. ''You must know I'm on the Company shit list.''

''I know that. But I don't believe it.''

''Believe what you want,'' Groggins said as they stepped into the elevator.

''The killing of a foreign national is an ugly business.''

''Yes, I guess it is,'' Groggins acknowledged, as

they stepped into the lobby.

"Especially if that foreign national happens to be an intelligence agent, or as you would say, a Company man."

Groggins stopped. He hadn't expected that.

"Does that surprise you?" Rinaldi asked.

"Nothing in this world surprises me," Groggins replied. "Absolutely nothing. Next you'll be telling me that the woman was Company too?"

"No," Rinaldi answered. "But she has a record. She was arrested for prostitution on three different occasions."

"It should be legalized," Groggins answered angrily. He was furious with Salito for sending Fioredelliso to shadow him. Suddenly he realized Rinaldi was looking at him and smiling.

"It's difficult to work for men you don't trust," Rinaldi said. "No, Fioredelliso was not a Company man. But you thought he was."

"If it pleases you to believe I'm a Company man, then by all means believe it."

"It neither pleases or displeases me," Rinaldi answered. "But knowing it gives me more than I had before. You're here for something. I want to know what that *something* is."

"I'd like to go back to my hotel," Groggins said, as they left the hotel.

"Use my car," Rinaldi offered.

"No thanks. I'll walk," Groggins said, angry with himself for letting Rinaldi trap him into admitting he was with the Company again.

"Take care, Groggins," Rinaldi said. "Whoever shot Fioredelliso and the girl wouldn't hesitate to pull the trigger on you."

Groggins nodded. Turned and fished out a pack of cigarettes. It was empty, just like most other things in his life.

X

Groggins didn't sleep. After he returned to the hotel, he smoked a great many cigarettes. Paced the length of the room. And tried to tell himself that he wasn't to blame for what happened to Fioredelliso and Rinata.

But it wouldn't wash. He couldn't make himself believe it. He should have guessed that Wagner or Dissel would have a spotter in the restaurant. He would if he were in their position.

He had hoped Fioredelliso would have had something beautiful, something spectacular, with Rinata. A sexual encounter the man would not have experienced unless he'd have the luck to meet someone like Rinata. And that would have been unlikely.

Groggins paused by the window. The pines of the Villa Borghese were becoming clearly defined by the coming of dawn. As for Rinata, he knew she'd have been well treated by Fioredelliso. He might have had her travel north with him to Garda.

Groggins turned and walked to the bed and dropped down on it. His head felt full of wool. He put his right arm across his eyes. If he could have wept, he would have. But years before in the jungles of Vietnam he had lost his tears. Now he could only feel an aching sadness.

Groggins slept. Fitfully, but he did sleep. When he awoke, the woolly feeling in his head was gone. There was a bad taste in his mouth from smoking too much.

He got out of bed, stripped, shaved, and showered. When he went down to the lobby the desk clerk handed him a note. It was from Rinaldi. It said: "Shadows removed." Groggins tore the piece of paper into small pieces. He let the wind take a few at a time when he went outside.

Groggins mailed the film to Salito, care of the S&B Art Gallery, London, the front for the Company's European headquarters.

Groggins breakfasted in a cafe close to the Central Post Office on the Piazza San Silvestro. He ate slowly. When a newsboy passed, he bought a morning paper. There wasn't anything in it about Fioredelliso's and Rinata's murder. The Italian press was censored, and whenever it suited the government's purpose, it determined the news fit to print. He drank a second cup of coffee and milk. Smoked a cigarette. Then paid his bill and left. It was a short distance from the Piazza di Trevi and the famous fountain. He started to walk.

It occurred to him that it was Salito who called off Rinaldi's shadows. But more than likely it was Rinaldi's own idea. He probably decided it wasn't worth the effort and the money it cost to keep tabs on him.

By the time Groggins reached the fountain, the tour buses were already there. The place was nobbed. On the corner of one of the streets opening on to the piazza, Groggins found a telephone kiosk. He dialed Bruno's private number. The phone rang eight times before a woman answered.

"I want to speak with Bruno," Groggins said, thinking that Bruno didn't waste time.

After a few seconds, the woman answered, "He's busy."

"Tell him it's his American friend," Groggins said.

"Bruno here."

"Can you meet me?"

"The police were here. So was some guy from Intelligence named Rinaldi," Bruno said. "He asked a lot of questions about you."

"Can you meet me?"

"I'm probably being watched."

"That's why I can't come to you."

"Okay," Bruno said. "I'll make the trip. Where and when?"

Groggins looked at his watch. "It's eleven o'clock now. Suppose you meet me at the Pantheon at noon."

"I'll be there," Bruno said.

"Make sure you're not being followed," Groggins said. He hung up and walked across the street to look at the fountain and listen to the comments of the tourists. Few understood that they were looking at the most theatrical fountain in Rome, perhaps in the entire world.

Knowing Bruno would probably be late, he waited until 11:45 before he hailed a cab and told the driver to take him to the Pantheon. He arrived there five minutes late. Bruno still hadn't arrived and didn't until twenty after twelve. They greeted each other with a nod and began to walk. Bruno said, "The cops came about

one-thirty. The last time Rinata was arrested for prostitution I put up the money to get her out. I guess I'm
under suspicion."

"I don't think so," Groggins said. "Rinaldi knows
the killing is connected to pictures they took. Only he
doesn't know what the connection is. He suspects it has
something to do with me."

Bruno nodded, and took a cigarette from a gold case
and offered one to Groggins. "They're Egyptian."

"Can you get me a mechanic, a good hit man?"
Groggins asked. He took one of Bruno's cigarettes.
Sniffed at it and said, "It smells like pussy."

"Yeah, I know," Bruno answered. He held his
lighter out to Groggins. "Who do you want taken out
and how much are you willing to pay? And why don't
you do it yourself? You're as good as anyone I could
hire."

Groggins took a deep drag and let the smoke out of
his nose and mouth. "I'll answer the last question first.
I can't become involved in it that way. I'm chasing
something else."

"The buyer?"

Groggins nodded. "I'll pay five thousand American
dollars for it."

"Tell me who?"

"Wagner," Groggins said. "He's the guy who
called Rinaldi. He's the man who bought the gun."

Bruno stopped.

"Keep walking," Groggins told him. "There was a
spotter at the restaurant."

"But how the hell did he find out where Fioredelliso
was staying?"

Groggins shrugged. "Probably overheard him tell
Rinata. I hadn't figured there'd be a spotter. I want
Wagner offed. Can you get the man to do it?"

"Yes."

"Take him out sometime late next week," Groggins said. "I'll get the money to you by tomorrow night."

"In cash."

"Naturally," Groggins said, flicking the cigarette into the gutter. "I like my brand better."

Bruno shrugged.

"Who's taking care of the funeral arrangements for Rinata?" Groggins asked.

"No one. She comes from the south, somewhere around Taranto. I don't think her family has a pot to piss in, let alone money to send for the body. She'll either go into a pauper's grave or be given to the University medical school."

"I'll give you an extra thousand to bury her properly," Groggins said.

"If she meant anything to you, why did you let her go with Arturo?"

"She didn't mean anything special. But she was okay. It was her idea to go with him. It would have been good for him and for her."

"Okay, I'll take care of her. What about Arturo?"

"I guess he'll be shipped back to the States," Groggins said. "He was a nice guy. This was his first trip here. He was going to see family in Garda."

"At least he was in the saddle when he died," Bruno commented. "That's something. That's a good way to die."

"Rinata was his first lay in two years," Groggins said. "He should have had more time to enjoy her. And I know she would have let him enjoy her."

"Anything else?" Bruno asked. They reached the Corso Vittorio Emanuele.

"Do you have someone I could use as an "envelope" for you?"

Bruno thought for a moment. "I have a sister," he said. "I'll send her to you."

"Not at the hotel. I'll be at Harry's Bar on the upper end of the Via Veneto. Say about six. Most likely at an outside table. Send her with one of those large shoulder bags. Make sure you give her a good description of me."

"She'll find you. And remember, Groggins, she's family, so hands off."

"Hands off," Groggins agreed.

They nodded and went in opposite directions.

Groggins had the remainder of the afternoon to himself. He decided to spend it in the ruins of the Roman Forum. Then, if he wasn't too hot and tired, he'd climb up to the top of the Palantine Hill, one of the famous Seven Hills of Rome, where legend has it that the first settlers of the city built their huts under the direction of Romulus.

The early summer evening was still full of sunshine. The heat of the day was lessened by what the Romans call the *Ponentino*—a cool seabreeze. It made outdoor dining a delight. Groggins was at a table for two in Harry's Bar. He had taken several sheets of stationary from the hotel. Oblivious to the crowds of people on the Via Veneto, he spent the better part of a half-hour writing to his brother and sister in New York. They were chatty letters, telling them of his visit to the Roman Forum. No one in his family knew anything more about his work other than that he was a writer. They accepted his erratic life style because it was in keeping with their idea about the way a writer lives.

The third letter was to his father, a man very much like Fioredelliso. Probably as old. He too had fought in World War II. In Europe from D-Day on. But unlike

Fioredelliso, his father seldom spoke about the war. It was something he had experienced and wanted to forget.

The elder Groggins was a widower for the last five years. Though he was still an attractive man, he had no wish to marry again, and he spent a great deal of time reading. When the weather permitted, he worked in his garden. The two shoe stores he owned provided him with a very comfortable income.

Groggins began the letter to his father by calling attention to the fact that he was again in Rome, though he didn't intend to stay there very long. He went on to explain that he was having trouble with the book he was working on and came to Italy for a change of scene.

He wrote, "I'm caught between two loves: England and Italy. That they are so very different doesn't seem to bother me in the least. I am planning to divide most of my time between the two and the remainder in the States.

"I was thinking about having you come over here to spend some time with me. I know London and Rome as well as I know our neighborhood in Brooklyn. Think about it. We could have a good time together. I know your feelings about returning to England or Europe. But think about coming over.

"You won't be hearing from me for awhile. But don't worry. I'll be moving around a great deal. Take care of yourself."

"Your Loving Son, Jack"

Groggins reread the letter. Satisfied, he folded the sheet of paper and inserted it into an envelope, which he addressed to his father. Then he sat back and reached for his vodka.

He looked out on the Via Veneto. Traffic was hardly

moving. Many of the cars were expensive hand-tooled jobs. The kind for which Italian auto designers are famous.

Groggins was never into cars the way some men were. He was satisfied with whatever he had as long as it ran trouble-free. The social or sexual status derived from owning a particular car was, in his opinion, as meaningful as the old adage, *"clothes make the man."* A man had to be substantially more than what he wore. He had known natives in 'Nam and Africa wearing no more than a loincloth who were men in every sense of the word.

His father was a man. From what little he knew about Fioredelliso, Groggins was now sure he was one too.

He picked up the glass of vodka again and realized a young woman was looking at him. She wore jeans, with fancy stitching on the back pocket, a candy-striped blouse, open three buttons down, no bra, and she carried a large shoulder bag. She resembled Bruno somewhat. But her features were more delicate. Her hair was the color of wheat. And when she moved the pink nipple of her right breast was visible.

Groggins nodded.

She came straight to the table and sat down. "I'm Blanch. Have you been waiting long?"

"I came early and wrote some letters," he answered.

The waiter came to the table.

"Have something to drink, Blanch, or whatever else you want."

"White wine on the rocks would be fine," she said.

Groggins nodded to the waiter. When he was gone, he told Blanch to place her bag on the floor, close to his chair. He waited a few moments, then removed an envelope from his breast pocket and quickly slipped it into the shoulder bag.

The waiter came with her drink.

She smiled at Groggins and lifted her glass.

"What amuses you?" he asked.

"My brother said that you were a dangerous man."

Groggins neither smiled nor spoke. He judged her to be eighteen. No more than twenty.

"Are you dangerous?" Blanch asked.

Groggins nodded. She was flirting with him.

"You don't look any more dangerous than any other man here," she commented.

"It's time for you to leave," Groggins said.

"What?" she asked.

"Leave, or I call the waiter and tell him you're soliciting."

She colored. "I don't believe you."

"Waiter," Groggins called. "Waiter, would you please come here!"

Blanch stood up. Took hold of her shoulder bag and with a haughty bob of her head, she left the table.

The waiter came to the table.

"Check, please," Groggins said.

The waiter gave him a peculiar look.

"My check please," Groggins repeated. He left a larger tip for the waiter than he ordinarily would have. And he walked down the Via Veneto.

Remembering there was a bookstore on the street, he decided to visit it. Most writers, Groggins knew, visited bookstores to see if their books were stocked. Sometimes he was moved to do the same thing. But not often. Once the book was written, he felt very little attachment to it. He'd pick up the published book and wonder how the hell he wrote all those words. It was only when he was actually working on a book, or thinking about one, that he had anything like a proprietary interest in it.

The bookstore wasn't crowded. Groggins went to the paperback section devoted to suspense novels. His previous two books weren't there, even though they had been translated into Italian.

He spent the better part of an hour browsing but left the shop without buying anything. Outside he paused to look at his watch. It was seven-fifteen. Much too early to go to Carlo's.

Groggins wasn't hungry enough to find a place to eat. Besides, he preferred to eat in the Traste Vere section, where the prices were cheaper and the food better. He decided to go back to the hotel and relax for a couple of hours.

There was only one man behind the zinc-topped bar. Groggins guessed it was Carlo. He was a tall, broad-shouldered man with a bull neck, blond hair and blue eyes. Around fifty years old, give or take a year or two.

The place was small and dimly lit. Candles were stuck into wine bottles. The walls were begrimed. There was sawdust on the floor. The ceiling beams were blackened from a previous fire. The air smelled of sweat, cigarette smoke, and sour wine. It was crowded and noisy. A juke box pounded out the latest American disco hit. A dozen couples were gyrating in a space too small for half that number.

Groggins went through the ritual exchange of sign and countersign with Carlo.

"Nothing," Carlo told him, then moved down the bar to serve another customer.

Groggins looked around hoping to spot one of the men he had seen at the Dolly in London. He didn't see anyone who looked familiar. Many of the men spoke Spanish. He heard some German and English spoken with an American accent.

Carlo came back. "Do you know anyone here?"
"No."
"Have a drink on the house," Carlo offered.
Groggins nodded. "Thanks."
"What's your pleasure?"
"Wine, Red. An Inferno, if you have it?"
Carlo grinned. "If it's an Italian wine, I have it." He walked halfway down the bar, reached down and picked up a bottle of wine. He came back with the wine and a glass. "If you haven't eaten, eat here. I made some delicious tortellini and baked veal."

"I haven't eaten," Groggins said. He didn't feel like baked veal or tortellini. But his intuition told him he should.

"Take the table over on the side." Carlo pointed toward a table where two men were just getting up. "Sit there. My wife will bring your food. You carry the wine."

Groggins went to the table. He poured himself a glass of wine and drank it slowly. He was placed there for a reason. Possibly two. Either to be photographed or to let the other mercenaries see him. He pretended not to know what was happening. He lit a cigarette. Leaned back. Watched the dancers and tried to see if anyone was looking at him.

If anyone was, he didn't see them. He poured another glass of wine and smoked another cigarette before Carlo's wife came to the table with a large platter of tortellini and baked veal covered with a tomato and mushroom sauce.

Mrs. Carlo was in her forties. A big-breasted, wide-hipped woman. She wore a soiled white apron. Her black hair was pulled back and held by something that resembled a thick shoelace.

She gave him a big smile as she set both plates down.

"If you want more tell me," she said.

Groggins looked down at the food. There was enough for two, perhaps three, people.

"More wine?" she asked, picking up the half empty bottle.

"No, thank you."

"Enjoy!" she said and walked away.

The baked veal and the tortellini were surprisingly good, and Groggins left his plate clean. He drank another glass of wine and decided to leave.

He went to the bar and asked Carlo for his check.

"Nothing tonight," he said. "But next time you pay just like everyone else."

"I'll be here tomorrow night, same time."

"So will I," Carlo answered.

Groggins went into the street and walked toward the Piazza Pilo. Someone was following him. He wasn't the least bit surprised. He figured Dissel had given Carlo the word to find out more about him. There was no longer any doubt. A snapshot would make it easier for Dissel to run a tracer on him. Groggins hoped Salito would hold to the story that he was still on the Company shit list.

Groggins crossed the piazza. He headed for one of the streets leading away from it. He slowed his pace. Then, whirling around, he ran straight into the man following him.

Wordlessly, the man went down.

The charge carried Groggins several yards beyond the man. He turned.

The man scrambled to his feet. Crouching low, he came toward Groggins.

"It'd be a lot easier to tell Carlo you lost me," Groggins said, speaking in Italian.

"I'll cut your fuckin' heart out," the man answered in English.

"Maybe yes. But maybe no," Groggins said in English. The man was very close to him. No more than a large stride. The man was in his late twenties. Thin, muscular, about six feet tall, dark hair. He was good looking, almost a pretty-boy. He wore faded jeans, a white polo shirt, and a blue denim jacket. Groggins didn't have to look at his feet to know he was wearing western-style boots. Lacking was the wide Stetson. Then he spotted it. Some distance up the length of the street, the hat lay where it had fallen when the man fell.

"Don't matter none if you speak English," the man said. "You have a lesson comin'." His right hand reached into the back of his belt. The next instant a switchblade sprung open.

"You sure that's the route you want to go?" Groggins asked. Despite his outward show of calmness, his heart was racing. Any man who pulled a knife was a potential killer. "Carlo might not like it if you cut one of his men."

"Shit man, all you're goin' to do is bleed a little," the man said. "Hell, I'm an artist with a knife." He spoke with a slow Western drawl.

Groggins shook his head. There were too many crazies like the one in front of him. Men who walked a narrow line between sanity and insanity. The small wars around the world gave them a chance to kill for the pleasure of it and at the same time be highly paid for doing it. For every professional like himself, there were ten psychopaths playing soldier.

"Listen," Groggins said, "I'm going to give you the chance to walk away from here."

"Are you some kind of a nut? I got the blade."

Even as the man was speaking, Groggins leaped forward. He grabbed the hand holding the knife and twisted it back, forcing the man to drop it.

He twisted the man's arm, bringing him to his knees. Then he kicked the blade down the street.

"Holy shit!" the man exclaimed in pain.

Groggins twisted the man's arm higher on his back. "You ever pull a knife on me again, I'll tear your arm out of its socket and beat you over the head with it." The man could only gasp.

"What's your name?" Groggins asked.

"None of your fuckin' business."

Groggins twisted his arm a bit more. "I asked your name, wise ass."

"Nelson Boyce."

"Okay, Nelson," Groggins said, loosening his hold. "I'm going to let you up. You move slowly. If you try anything, I'll break your back." He let go of Boyce's arm and stepped away.

Boyce got to his feet, vigorously rubbing his arm.

"It'll hurt for a couple of days," Groggins said. "Now turn around and face me."

"I'm facing you," Boyce said. Tears of pain streamed down his cheeks. "You did a number on my arm."

"And your ego," Groggins answered. "You go back to Carlo and tell him you had trouble with a street gang or whatever story suits you. I won't tell him what happened here. But let me give you a few words of advice."

"I don't need you to tell me anythin'."

"I'll tell you anyway. Don't make the mistake again of thinking you can take someone if you have a knife. He may be better armed than you are just as I am."

Groggins pulled out his snub-nose .38 and showed Boyce. "Aren't you going to ask me why I didn't blow you away? Even if you're not, I'll tell you. Two reasons: a shot would make a loud noise in this narrow street. I don't like loud noises because they attract people; the police. Secondly, Boyce, you told me you were an artist with a knife. As soon as I heard that, I knew you were an amateur. A punk playing at being a soldier. Now go pick up your hat and get the hell out of here. I'll wait until you're gone."

Boyce got his hat and walked back to where Groggins was standing. "I won't forget this," he said.

"If you really remember it," Groggins answered, "you might come back alive from wherever we're going."

Groggins was half awake, when the phone rang, pulling him out of sleep altogether. He glanced at his watch. It was ten-thirty. He knew it was morning because the sun shone through the cracks of the window shade.

The phone rang again. He picked it up but remained silent.

"Groggins," the man said on the other end, "this is Salito."

"I figured I'd be hearing from you as soon as you developed the film."

"Do you know whose picture you have?"

"Mine. The very fat guy is Wagner. The other one is Dissel."

"And the fourth?"

Groggins pushed himself up. He leaned against the back of the bed. "I didn't know there was a fourth person. Couple of friends took the shots for me."

"Crimins is the fourth man," Salito said.

"Crimins. . . . Paula's former boss?"

"Same. Now get this. Dissel is an important stock-holder in KBI."

"I hope you're going to get hold of Crimins and—"

"We'll take care of him in our own way," Salito said. His voice was harder than it had been a moment ago. "The Company still has dealings with KBI."

"Then you're not going to move against him?"

"No. When the right time comes."

"His people killed two more of my friends," Grog-gins said tightly. "The man and woman who took those photographs."

For a few moments Salito was silent. "Come back to London," he said. "You did your job. We can get Crimins whenever we want him. Come back today. On the first plane you can get on."

"You must be joking."

"No. I want you back here."

"Listen—"

"No, Groggins. Get back here. You have twenty-four hours. After that—"

"What about Dissel?"

"You were sent to find the people who killed Ortega and Paula. You found the connection. We'll do the rest. In our own way. In our own time."

Groggins pulled the phone away from him. Looked at it; then dropped it back onto its cradle. "Screw you, Salito!" he exclaimed aloud. "I'm going all the way on this, no matter where the hell it goes."

The rest of the day was uneventful. Groggins spent a leisurely morning in the Vatican Library reading sect-ions of old books on Francesco Sforza, the *condottiere* who became the Duke of Milan in the year 1450. He had often thought about writing a historical novel about the Duke, but hadn't done anymore than read about the man. Perhaps when he returned from this mission, he'd do some serious thinking again about the book.

In the afternoon Groggins made his way back to the hotel and enjoyed a light lunch in the rooftop restaurant that gave him a splendid view of the Villa Borghese. Then he went to his room. After reading awhile, he napped.

By four o'clock Groggin had showered again and left the hotel. He went to Romolo.

"I didn't expect to see you again," Bruno said, coming up to the table.

Ignoring the comment, Groggins asked, "Where's the woman who answered the phone?"

"She'll be here later."

"Did you take care of the funeral for Rinata?"

Bruno nodded.

"And the other matter?"

"Yes."

Groggins lit a cigarette and asked for a glass of Campari on the rocks.

Bruno called over to the barkeep for the drink. "I thought you were being followed."

"They pulled my tails off," Groggins said, taking the glass of Campari in his hand. "I stopped by to make sure everything was taken care of."

"Everything has been," Bruno answered.

"Good," Groggins said. "I wouldn't want to come back someday and find something was left undone. If that were to happen, I'd be very angry."

Bruno flushed. "I know that. Believe me, my friend, I know that."

Groggins finished his drink. Paid for it and left a tip for the barkeep. He shook Bruno's hand. "I just wanted to be sure," he said.

"Yes. I understand."

"By the way your sister wanted to know if I was as dangerous as you said I was."

Bruno flushed. "I told her—"

"It's all right," Groggins said. "I told her I was." Then he left and walked around until it was time to go back to Carlo.

Once again they went through the sign and countersign ritual. But this time when Groggins questioned Carlo, he answered, "Two o'clock the day after tomorrow at the Da Vinci Airport. Main concourse. Join a group of archeologists on their way to a dig. Wear this." He handed Groggins a name-tag from the Society of Christian Archeologists of America. "Bring your clothes."

"Anything else?"

"Not that I can think of, except that you don't have to be back here tomorrow night unless you want to."

Groggins looked at the customers. There were fewer than the previous night. "Any of them going?"

"Some. You'll meet them at the airport," Carlo said. Offering his hand, he said, "Good luck."

"Thanks," Groggins responded. He left without drinking. This time no one was following him.

Groggins paced back and forth, moving no greater distance from the phone than the length of the cord. "Listen," he told the operator on the other end, "find Salito. I don't care how long it takes. I'll hang on."

"I'm sorry, but he left word he's not to be disturbed," the operator answered.

"Listen, you disturb him. Tell him it's Groggins in Rome."

"Will you please wait," the operator responded.

Groggins stopped pacing. Fished out a cigarette from

a pack and lit it. The smoke made his eyes tear. Some-day he intended to quit smoking.

"Go ahead," the operator said.

Salito spoke first. "Are you out of your fucking mind? Goddamn it, you can't be trusted to do anything right. You had a cover name and—"

"Listen," Groggins said, "I don't have much time for chit-chat. I'm leaving tomorrow for a dig."

"What the hell are you talking about?"

"Me and some two hundred other guys have become members of The Christian Archeologists of America. We leave from the Da Vinci Airport at two o'clock in the afternoon."

"Hold it," Salito said.

There was a long pause.

"Salito are you still on," Groggins asked, pacing again.

"Goddamn it, will you hold!"

"Yeah, yeah," Groggins said, though he didn't think Salito heard him.

After a few moments, Salito came back on the line. "We'll have some of our people there to photograph the group."

"So you think it's important?" Groggins chided.

"Don't be smart. You might be putting yourself in the lion's mouth."

"I've been there before," Groggins answered, stub-bing out his cigarette in an ash tray. "Any more on Dissel?"

"Big with the PLO. And very chummy with a few Krauts who made it to Switzerland before the curtain came down on the Third Reich. What about Wagner?"

"Forget about him," Groggins said. "He won't be around to worry about in a few days."

"You have to do things your own way, don't you?"

Groggins didn't answer. He wasn't about to defend his actions. He put out a contract on Wagner because it had to be done.

"All right," Salito said, "we probably would have taken him out in a little while, anyway."

"Then give me brownie points for saving you the trouble."

"I said all right." And then he added, "Good luck."

"Thanks," Groggins answered. He put the phone down and went to the window and looked out. A burnished moon hung over the city. He wondered what color the moon would be when he saw it again.

XI

Salito put the phone down. He glanced at the three other men at the table: Mr. Thomas Wyler, his counterpart from MI-6; Colonel Louis Sides, from the United States Air Force; and Mr. Richard Hook, from Comapny Headquarters in Langley, Virginia.

Hook had come from the States on a supersonic jet, crossing the Atlantic in less than two hours. He looked somewhat disoriented.

Mr. Wyler, on the other hand, was in complete control of himself. The discussion they were having was routine, almost to the point of being boring. Like Salito, he smoked a pipe, but one with a hooked stem and a very large bowl.

Colonel Sides was the chief liaison officer between the Air Force's Global Weather Group, a cover for U-2 operations, although everyone in the international intelligence community knew exactly what the mission of the Global Weather Group was. It hadn't changed from the days when Francis Gary Powers brought the U-2 operations to the attention of the press and the people of the world.

Salito took a few moments to light his pipe before he commented, "There's a 'Peck's Bad Boy' in every organization. The man on the other end of the line happens to be mine. I'm sorry for the interruption. Shall we continue where we left off."

Hook placed his right forefinger on one of the dozen 8 x 10 flat-finished color photographs on the table. "These came from a NASA satellite. As you can see, the color and resolution are of high quality. To the north is the Mediterranean and Italy, as far north as Rome; and to the east, all the way across to the Black Sea. But our interest today is the area marked by the white circle in southern Libya. Something there that wasn't ten days ago, during our last photograph overflight. You can see truck marks going into an area, then vanishing completely, which means that some activity is taking place that is being totally obscured from our satellite observation."

"Are there any educated guesses as to what the activity might be?" Salito asked, puffing gently on his pipe.

"The only educated guess is that Qaddafi is allowing the Russians to build a missile base," Hook answered.

Removing the pipe from his mouth, Wyler said, "There's no hard proof of that." His voice was nasal.

"None," Hook agreed.

"What do the infra-red sensors indicate?" Salito asked.

"Streaks, showing the movement of equipment, and a very large cool area."

"How large?" Colonel Sides asked.

"One hundred yards wide and half as long, running

in an east-west direction. Several of our people think it's a body of water of some sort. Perhaps a lake?''

''But there isn't any lake in that part of the country,'' Sides responded. ''It's twenty-eight degrees, sixteen minutes north latitude and twenty-three degrees even minutes east latitude. Nothing should be there but mountains. It's like the moon out there.''

''That's right,'' Hook said. ''And it leads to the second possibility, which is as serious as the first. Namely, that the Libyans are building a facility to manufacture an atomic bomb.''

Everyone at the table moved uneasily in their chairs.

''Does the radiation level show an increase?'' Salito asked.

''No. But it wouldn't until they moved the nuclear material into the processing plant,'' Hook explained.

Wyler leaned forward. ''Have you anyone who could get close to the area?''

''Negative,'' Hook answered. ''The people we have in Libya are too close to Qaddafi to venture out into a remote section of the country without arousing suspicion.''

''We might be able to drop a few chaps into the area,'' Wyler said, ''to have a look around. But it would take them awhile to walk out. And if they were captured, well, we'd have the makings of an embarrassing flap.''

''That's exactly why I took the liberty of having Colonel Sides with us for this discussion,'' Salito said. ''One of his aircraft should be able to give us sufficient information on the activities down there.''

''We do not fly over Libya,'' Colonel Sides explained. ''But we do fly over the Mediterranean and over Egypt.''

"Suppose one of your planes was taken off course by a storm," Salito suggested. "It most certainly would be taken south if it was over the Med, or west, if it was over Egypt."

"That could happen . . . but only if it couldn't get above the weather because of some mechanical problem. And we don't have storms when we want them."

"But you can arrange mechanical difficulty," Salito said.

Sides nodded.

"What about Libyan fighter planes?" Hook asked. "They'll scramble as soon as the U-2 is picked up on the radar."

"If the U-2 is brought down," Wyler said, "you chaps are going to have the Powers' situation all over again. But Qaddafi might take it all the way to a public execution. He's capable of doing something like that."

"We've got to take the risk," Salito responded. "A missile base or an atomic bomb assembly plant are unacceptable realities."

"If everything went off perfectly, we might get away with it," Sides said. "If our plane develops flap trouble, sends out a May Day and fighters from the Sixth Fleet are scrambled to protect it, then the Libyan jets would have to decide whether or not they wanted to fight. If they fight, we might lose a few aircraft and they might lose a few. But the U-2 would get to the target area, take its pictures, and then suddenly find its flaps are functioning normally."

"How close to the actual area would the U-2 have to be to get the kind of information we need?" Wyler asked.

"Fifty miles at sixty thousand feet should be fine," Sides answered. "It would be better if it could go over it directly. But we could get enough from fifty miles away.''

"If such an overflight were to take place, when would you have the results?'' Salito asked.

"Four o'clock tomorrow afternoon,'' Sides answered. "The flight will take place immediately after dawn.''

"Better let the Sixth Fleet commander know what will be happening,'' Salito said.

Sides nodded.

"Then gentlemen,'' Salito said, "suppose we meet here at five tomorrow evening.'' He walked to the door and shook hands with the men as they left the room. Then he returned to the table, gathered up the photographs and went back to his office to make arrangements to have Groggins and the other members of the Society of Christian Archeologists of America photographed at the Da Vinci Airport the following afternoon. Salito didn't like what Groggins was doing. He didn't like it one bit. He didn't need a Peck's Bad Boy mucking up things when he had real problems to deal with, like this Libyan situation.

Major Phil Hawks was at the controls of the U-2, designated number 369 by the Global Weather Group. A half moon was below him in the western sky, and off his port wing, he could clearly see the lights in southern France all the way up to the west coast of Italy. Naples and Rome looked like puddles of light from over 15 miles up.

He checked his watch. Within three minutes the first light would begin to show across the eastern sky, illuminating first the snow-covered peaks of the Caucasus Mountains and then later spilling westward over the Black Sea, Turkey, and the entire Middle East.

He glanced to his starboard, slowly easing the stick over so that he could look at the northern coast of Africa. He had exactly fifteen minutes before he'd send his first May Day. The 369 was the latest model of the U-2-type aircraft. Not only was it equipped with high resolution cameras capable of photographing a golf ball from eighty thousand feet, but it also had special infra-red sensors that fed information to an onboard compu-ter, which processed the information into visual images that were then stored on video tape for later viewing. In addition to the most advanced state-of-the-art photo-grammetry devices, the plane was powered by four dual-mode jets. For take-off, landing, and operations below the forty-thousand-foot level, the normal jet mode was used. But for any flying above forty-thousand feet the ram-jet mode automatically took over, allowing the pilot to fly at a maximum speed of Mach 3 and cruise at Mach 2.5. Very few fighter planes would be capable of approaching its speed or operational altitude.

Hawks was a short, compact blond with a boyish face and ready smile. The previous Sunday he turned thirty. He was married four years and lived off base in the Spanish village of El Rio Blanca with his wife and two-year-old son.

He had been briefed by Colonel Davidson, the Wing Commander. He had been told to fly the mission in a routine manner up until the moment he experienced trouble with the ailerons, devices on the wings that controlled its rolling. At that point, he was to break radio silence and send out a May Day; then he was to make a ninety-degree turn and fly south for exactly ten minutes, descending to an altitude of 45,000 feet. All cameras and sensors were to be turned on the moment the ninety-degree turn was completed.

"When you get below fifty thousand feet, you can expect Libyan fighter planes to be waiting for you," Davidson said. "But by that time you'll be in visual and radio contact with the Navy flyboys."

It wasn't an ordinary mission and Hawks knew he had been chosen to fly it because he had a good record and was known to be cool in a tight situation.

"We don't expect any problems," Colonel Davidson told him. "But should you have to eject, do it over Egypt or the Med, if you can turn toward it. We don't want any part of the ship to fall into Libyan hands."

Hawks didn't see any difficulty reaching Egypt, should the necessity arise. He wasn't more than a hundred miles from the border. Even if he'd lose all power, he'd be able to glide the distance from 45,000 feet with another hundred miles to spare.

Five minutes before Hawks was to execute a ninety-degree turn and fly south, he began to monitor his instruments. His radar was free of blips. All systems were functioning normally.

He watched the minutes tick off. Two minutes to go.

"One minute," Hawks said aloud. The seconds raced by. He began counting. "T-5 . . . Four . . . Three . . . Two . . . One . . . Mark!" He turned the ship ninety degrees, switched on all cameras and sensors; then began easing the plane down, losing altitude a thousand feet a minute.

Hawks switched on his radio. "May Day . . . May Day. . . . This is number three-six-nine from the United States Global Weather Force. . . . May Day . . . May Day. . . ." He called out his coordinates as they came up in green numbers on the rumb-line computer.

"Three-six-nine," a voice responded. "Three-six-nine. . . . Do you read me?''

"Loud and clear.''

"This is Floating Island,'' the voice said, using the code name given to the aircraft carrier *Enterprise*. "We have you locked on our radar. What is your problem?''

"Malfunction of port aileron. . . . Unable to hold assigned altitude.''

"Can you remain airborne?''

"For awhile,'' Hawks repeated.

Suddenly a great many lights below him came on. Hawks knew they were on various Libyan military installations.

"We're sending sheepdogs,'' the voice from the *Enterprise* said. "Advise position at one-minute intervals.''

"I read you,'' Hawks answered. He glanced out on the port side. The sun was well over the horizon, and some distance below him, he could see three Libyan jets. They couldn't make his altitude or speed and were waiting for him to come down to their positions. He checked the altimeter. He was down to sixty-five thousand feet. He radioed his new position, ran his eyes over the instruments. Everything was functioning perfectly!

"Three-six-nine,'' another voice said. "This is Sheepdog. I have you in sight. There are three wolves below you at nine o'clock.''

"Saw them,'' Hawks answered.

"More coming up at two o'clock,'' the voice said. "We'll come around you as soon as you reach our altitude.''

Hawks looked at his altimeter. He was at sixty thousand. His long underwear was soaked with sweat.

"Three-six-nine,'' the voice said, "those wolves are following close. . . . How far down have you gone?''

Hawks looked at his clock. He still had two minutes to fly before changing altitude.

"Can you change course?" the voice asked.

"Negative," Hawks responded. He was down to fifty-eight thousand feet. The Libyan fighters were wiggling their wings, signaling him to drop lower. "No way, José," he said aloud. His heart was beating very fast.

He had one minute to go before he'd lift the nose of the ship and zoom back up to the safety of eighty-thousand feet. He watched the second hand and wished he could remove his helmet to wipe the sweat from his eyes.

"Three-six-nine," the voice said.

At that precise moment, the second hand passed twelve. The mission had been completed. Ten minutes had passed. Hawks reached out with his left hand and switched off the cameras and sensing device. With his other hand, he eased back on the stick. The nose swung up.

"Sheepdog," Hawks said, "aileron now responding. Heading back upstairs."

"Three-six-nine, you're being fired on," the voice said. "Air-to-air birds."

Hawks heard him. But the next instant the metal around him began to disintegrate. A piece struck him in the abdomen. He screamed. Then he began to fall. Hawks was dead long before his body struck the earth.

At ten o'clock in the morning, Salito received a phone call from Colonel Sides. "There was an accident."

Salito leaned forward, resting his elbows on the desk. Suddenly he was sweating. "Details?" he asked.

"Sketchy," Sides answered. "Our plane was pulling up when a Libyan jet accidentally fired an air-to-air, heat-seeking missile.''

"Any other accidents?" Salito asked.

"None. . . . Our boys flew back to their carrier.''

"The pilot?"

"Never had a chance.''

Salito took a deep breath and exhaled loudly.

"It was a gamble," Sides said.

"Any fallout yet?"

"None. I don't expect any. The Libyans aren't about to admit they're hiding something. . . . And as far as we're concerned, flight three-sixty-nine went down over the Med as a result of mechanical difficulty. We have planes searching for it now.''

"What about the jets from the carrier?"

"The mission was never flown. That's the way the men who flew it will remember it. No record of it exists.''

"Does that include the radio intercept?"

"Yes.''

Before Salito leaned back, he wiped his brow. "Whatever the Libyans have out there, they sure are making sure that no one sees it.''

"More than by just having accidents," Sides said.

"I don't understand.''

"We can't see anything because they've covered it.''

"Now tell me something I don't know," Salito said.

"Just a wild guess, but suppose they knew the transit times of our satellite?"

"Sure, that would enable them to pull a cover over the area. But that's supposing the Libyans even know there is a satellite up there.''

"Suppose they were told," Sides said.

Once again Salito put his elbows on the desk. "The Russians?" he questioned.

"That's the way I would read it. They're buddies with Qaddafi and they would certainly know the transit times."

"How many transits does the satellite make each day?"

"Four. And I'll answer your next question before you ask it. Our overflight took place when the satellite was eight thousand miles away. Or to put it another way, to prevent us from knowing what was going on, there had to be an accident. The area was probably uncovered at the time three-sixty-nine was over it."

Salito was impressed with Sides' thinking and said as much.

"Thanks," Sides responded. "But now you're the guy who's going to have to do some hard thinking about it. You're going to have to figure out a way of finding out what the Libyans are doing and why."

"If you come up with any possibilities, I'm just a phone call away." Salito tried to sound light and airy about the situation. But he wasn't. Langley would soon be on his way back for answers.

"I'll notify Wiley," Sides said.

"Better tell him that the mission was aborted," Salito said. "No need to let M.I.-6 gloat over our problem. I'll brief Hook later today."

"Then that wraps it up," Sides commented.

"Yes. And thanks again for the help," Salito said, putting the phone down. He filled his pipe and lit it. He leaned back into the chair and puffed vigorously at his pipe. As things stood, he didn't have a ghost of an idea how to get close enough to identify whatever was out there. And then, if need be, neutralize it. . . .

XII

Da Vinci Airport, when Groggins arrived, was pandemonium. People screamed, others fainted from the heat caused by air conditioners turned off by maintenance personnel sympathic to striking baggage handlers, air controllers, and fuel-truck drivers. To add to the confusion, the bus and cab drivers refused to drive. The bus drivers supported the strike, while the cabbies were against it. Arguments became shoving matches. These—unless the participants were quickly separated—became fights, which required the intervention of the police. Groggins worked his way through the crowds of milling people. He was sweating profusely. Luckily, he carried only a shoulder bag. Had he been foolish enough to take a suitcase, it probably would have been torn out of his hand more than once.

Just as Groggins passed the cocktail lounge in the main concourse, a man came hurtling through the glass window. Police whistles shrilled above the tumult. A half-dozen carabinieri dressed in riot gear and armed with sub-machine guns charged toward the cocktail lounge. Groggins didn't wait to see what happened. He pressed forward, looking for someone holding the placard of the Society of Christian Archeologists of America.

All around the concourse there were dozens and dozens of signs for various tourist groups. Some of them took the form of an opened multicolored umbrella. There were several Kewpi dolls, held aloft on poles. There was even a crosier, topped with a small, stuffed panda. And all of them tried to hold to their small space. But the surge of people around them was too much to resist, and they constantly changed their positions as if they were doing a kind of demented ballet.

Suddenly a loud speaker blared: ''The Baggage Handlers thanks its brother workers for their support in the struggle against those who'd deny the workers their rights. We have won.''

A wild cheer sounded all around Groggins.

''The strike will be over at three o'clock,'' the voice announced.

More cheering erupted.

Groggins looked at his watch. Three o'clock was fifty minutes away. The shouting and jostling did not abate one iota. If anything it seemed to have increased. He gave up trying to find his group and began to make his way toward the side of the concourse when he spotted the placard.

The name was printed in big red letters on a large piece of white cardboard nailed to a six-foot-high pole. It was held aloft by a man dressed in the black suit of a cleric: white collar and black wide-brim hat.

Groggins scanned the people close by. Several of the

men were holding small overnight bags. A few, like himself, had shoulder bags. He saw Nelson Boyce, the cowboy, whom he had put down in the alleyway. Two of the other men seemed familiar. But Groggins wasn't sure whether he had seen one of them in London, at the Dolly, or somewhere else. The other he was certain he had seen in Carlo's place the night he ate there.

Groggins eased his way toward the man holding the placard. He wondered if Salito's cameraman had located it. By the time he reached the signholder, several other men joined the group.

Groggins went to Boyce. "How's your arm, Cowboy?"

"Okay now," Boyce answered.

"Good," Groggins said. "I didn't want to do any permanent damage."

"That's damn hard to believe."

"Believe it, Cowboy," Groggins said flatly. "If I had, you'd be a one-arm merc and there's not much call for them."

Boyce's cheeks reddened.

"But to show you I have no hard feelings," Groggins said, "I'm willing, if you are, to forget the whole incident. What about it, Cowboy." And he offered him his hand.

Boyce cocked his head to one side questioningly.

"What about it?" Groggins pressed. "Friends?"

"Friends," Boyce finally answered, extending his hand.

"Who's the dude holding the sign?" Groggins asked.

"Don't know," Boyce answered with a shrug. "But he sure looks the part."

Groggins agreed.

More men gathered around them. A few spoke English. The rest French or Italian, with a smattering of Spanish and German.

Suddenly it was much cooler than it had been.

"The air conditioners have been turned on," Groggins said. Looking at his watch, he added, "A little ahead of schedule."

Within minutes activities in the terminal began to return to normal. The jostling and shouting stopped. People moved to wherever they were going. Now there was a great deal of laughing.

"These Italians are as changeable as the goddamn weather," Boyce commented.

"But they enjoy their inconsistencies more than we enjoy being steadfast," Groggins answered.

By now there were well over a hundred men.

"Know him?" Boyce asked, gesturing with his thumb at a man coming toward him.

It was Dissel. Groggins played dumb. "Never saw him before."

"According to some of the other guys, he's one of the guys bankrolling this operation."

Groggins nodded.

Suddenly another man fell in alongside of Dissel. He was a tall, straight-backed individual with a weather-beaten face, light brown hair, and the bearing of a soldier. His eyes were almost yellow. He came directly up to the man holding the placard.

Dissel followed him. "Gentlemen," he said, "you will have the honor of having Professor Alexander Storzzi with you on your dig. He will act as your advisor and second to the man in charge of this expedition."

The men said nothing. They knew that Storzzi was one of the top commanders.

Dissel fished out two sheets of paper. "When I call

your name, please step to the right. Your plane is waiting.'' And he began to call off the names of the men.

By the time Dissel finished, Groggins counted one hundred and eighty men. There were a few young men in the group. But most of them, like himself, were experienced merc's. And a few were what writers of western novels always referred to as ''hard cases.'' These were men whose facial expressions betrayed their love of violence.

Dissel handed the list to Storzzi. ''They're all here.''

''Our plane is waiting at gate fifty-five,'' Storzzi said. ''Follow the placard.''

''Not much of a talker,'' Boyce commented to Groggins.

''Don't be fooled, Cowboy,'' Groggins said. ''When he has something to say, he'll say it. And you better listen.''

The man with the placard started toward the gate.

''C'mon, Cowboy,'' Groggins said, ''let's join the gang.''

Boyce looked back at Storzzi, who was talking to Dissel. ''What do you suppose they're jawing about?''

''Life, maybe sex.'' Groggins answered.

''What?''

''Cowboy, how the hell would I know what they're talking about?'' Groggins laughed.

''Yeah, I guess it was a dumb question,'' Boyce said.

''It sure was,'' Groggins answered, still laughing. But he also wondered what Storzzi and Dissel were talking about.

''What kind of jet is this?'' Boyce asked, as he and Groggins went up the boarding stairs.

"An Aerobus. Manufactured in France. But the markings are Swiss," Groggins answered, ducking slightly to go through the door.

A dark, intense-looking young woman greeted them and said in Italian, "Take any seat you wish." She wore blue slacks, a blue bolero jacket, a white mannish blouse, and a blue beret.

"Anything you say sweety," Boyce responded.

Her smile turned to an icy stare.

"Better take a seat," Groggins counseled in English.

"Just tryin' to be friendly."

"Don't. There's more than a little bit of Arab in her," Groggins said, ambling after Boyce.

"I never made it with an Arab chick. But I heard they're somethin' else in the sack. The guy who told me that said they don't get lovin' from their men."

Groggins stopped just forward of the port side wing. "You want the window seat?" he asked.

"How'd you know?"

"You're still young enough to want to look out on the world," Groggins answered, waiting for Boyce to slide into place. Even with one hundred and eighty men, there was room to spare. He followed Boyce into the aisle and sat down next to him.

"She's got nice boobs," Boyce said, looking at the woman who greeted them at the door.

"Take your mind off her," Groggins said. "You put your grubby hands on her you're just liable to find a knife in your stomach; or worse, your balls cut off."

"A pretty little thing like that wouldn't know what to do with a knife."

"I wouldn't bet on it," Groggins said. He looked around to see who was sitting nearby. And he spotted two of the men he had seen in the Dolly. One was the American; the other, the German.

It took fifteen minutes for everyone to board the plane. Storzzi was the last man. He paused at the door and waved to Dissel.

The door was closed and the boarding steps were rolled away.

Storzzi said something to the young woman. She nodded, picked up a hand microphone, and said, "Gentlemen, you will please obey the usual rules about no smoking during takeoff and landing. Once we are airborne, sandwiches and coffee will be served."

"What about drinks?" one of the men asked.

"Only coffee," the young woman answered.

A groan went up from the men.

Boyce called out, "C'mon, sis, we're all old enough to drink."

Several of the men agreed with him.

"Then you should be old enough to abstain for a few hours," she answered. "Now please fasten your seat belts." She switched off the mike and looked at Storzzi.

He nodded and sat down at the front of the ship.

The jet engines began to whine. The plane began to roll, turn, and lumber toward the runway.

"Man, it must be hot out there," Boyce commented. "I can see the heat comin' off the macadam. It's a wonder we don't sink into it."

Groggins didn't bother answering. He was more interested in what was happening at the front of the cabin. The young woman had disappeared behind a door, probably into the cockpit, and Storzzi was busy poring over papers.

The plane joined a line of aircraft waiting to take off.

"I count nine planes in front of us," Boyce said. "And there are several behind us."

"Everyone is late because of the strike," Groggins

commented. He leaned back. He closed his eyes and wondered what he had gotten himself into. His feelings of indestructibility had vanished long ago in Nam. He wanted to live as much as the next man. But he wasn't afraid of dying either. Death—usually violent—came with the job. He had seen it too many times to think it extraordinary. He had caused it too many times not to be aware that his might be caused by some act of violence, since violence in one form or another was the destructive instrument he and his opponents used against each other.

"We've movin' up," Boyce said.

"That's fine," Groggins answered, suppressing a smile. "Tell the truth, Cowboy, how old are you?" He opened his eyes and turned toward him.

"Old enough."

"Maybe to play soldier. But this is a very different game. You don't wear a tag that says you're dead, or wounded. You're either alive, or you're dead. There's no in-between."

"Look at me, I'm tremblin'!"

"Even if you are, it wouldn't do you much good. You're on this plane and you're not going to get off until it lands at the other end. By then it'll be too late."

The plane lurched forward, swung around, and raced down the runway and into the air. The earth fell away. The ship went into a tight left turn. Within moments it was over the Tyrrhenian Sea. Heading south.

The No Smoking sign was turned off. Many of the men unbuckled their safety belts and began to walk around.

Groggins stood up. He decided to introduce himself to the American and the German he recognized from the Dolly.

Boyce looked up questioningly.

"I see a couple of old friends," Groggins said.

With a shrug Boyce turned back to the window.

Groggins walked aft, where the two men were sitting. The American's eyes were closed, and the German was reading the latest edition of the *Corriere Della Sera*.

Groggins stood over them.

The American opened his eyes, the German looked up from the paper.

"Didn't I see you guys in Dolly's a couple of weeks ago?" Groggins asked, speaking English.

"Dolly's?" the American asked.

"A pub in London. In the West Indian dock section," Groggins said. "You and your friend were there and two other guys. Are they on board also?" The American was built like a linebacker, with a square jaw and a fighter's nose. He squinted up. His eyes were brownish-yellow and truculent.

"Never been there," he answered.

The Kraut was lean, blue-eyed, and blond-haired. "Vee never been dere," he echoed.

Groggins' lips formed a smile. "You may not want to remember but you were there." The smile left his face. "You were there with a guy named Bucky. He was an Englishman. He would have been on this plane. But he got himself taken out."

The American's jaw began to move. He looked very much like a fish gulping water.

The Kraut spoke first. "You got zee wrong men."

Then the American said, "Let me handle this, Peter." He looked up at Groggins. "Listen, Mac, I told you we weren't in Dolly's. Now fuck off!"

"The name isn't Mac. It's Groggins. The two of you have bad memories. Maybe they'll improve. And as for telling me to fuck off, if you ever say that again to me,

I'll kill you. Do you read me?" He spoke softly. Hardly moving his lips. His gimlet eyes were riveted on the American. "I asked if you read?"

The Kraut nodded first.

"I want to hear it from your friend," Groggins pressed.

"We read you," the American said.

"Good," Groggins answered with a smile. Then he turned and went back to his seat. He felt their eyes on his back.

"What was all that about?" Boyce asked.

"Just a chat with a couple of friends," Groggins answered.

"If they were your friends, I'd sure hate to meet your enemies."

Groggins laughed. "They come in all sizes and shapes," he said. The Cowboy was a lot more perceptive than he would have thought.

"Friends or enemies?"

"Both," Groggins answered, closing his eyes. There wasn't any doubt the American and the Kraut had known Bucky. Their reaction to his name proved it. Groggins was almost tempted to look back at them and do something foolish, like wave. But he didn't.

A half-hour after take-off sandwiches were served. They were made of pita bread and filled with a variety of vegetables.

The dark-skinned woman told each man, "You may have coffee, tea, or Coke."

"You sure that's all you have, honey?" Boyce asked, when she came up the aisle.

She repeated, "Coffee, tea, or Coke."

"Shucks, I was thinkin' about somethin' that doesn't come in a bottle or a cup," Boyce said.

Groggins concealed a smile with his hand.

"You make one more indecent remark to me," the woman said, "and I will inform Colonel Strozzi."

"Ah, so that's who you're givin' it to!" Boyce exclaimed. "Now listen here, I'm a lot younger. And even if he is a colonel, I got a lot more to give."

A blush suffused the woman's dark skin. She glared at him and, lifting her head, moved on to the next aisle.

Groggins dropped his hand. "Cowboy, you did that real well."

"Did what?"

"You don't have to play dumb," Groggins said.

"A man has the right to know who's going to be up front," Boyce answered. Then pointing out of the window, he added, "Hey, Groggins, looky down there. Italy sure as hell does look like a boot and Sicily, like a football that's been kicked around too much."

"I've seen them before," Groggins said. Twice now in the space of a very short time the Cowboy surprised him. He found himself wondering about their first meeting. What if Carlo didn't send him? But if Carlo didn't, who did?

Groggins turned toward Boyce.

"What are you lookin' at?" Boyce asked.

"You know, sooner or later I'll find out what your game is," Groggins said.

"My game? Shit man, I don't have a game. I'm just like you, a merc."

"Sure," he answered, facing front. "We're just a pair of happy-go-lucky mercs out for the big bucks."

Groggins dozed. He dreamed he was a boy again, growing up in Brooklyn. It was a strange dream, full of familiar faces. Some of the faces belonged to friends who were killed in Nam. The dream became uncomfortable and Groggins forced it away. Just as he opened his eyes, someone was blowing into the P.A. system.

Then Storzzi said, "Gentlemen, my name is Storzzi. But not Mr. Storzzi. It's Colonel Storzzi. Since this is to be a military operation, we will follow all the rules of military discipline and courtesy. My rank is not arbitrary, or self-decreed. It was conferred upon me by two governments. My own and the one for which all of us here work. In awhile a list of rules will be given to you. But to make it easy for you to understand, anyone who disobeys an order from a superior will be shot. Anyone caught attempting to leave the training area will be shot. Anyone communicating with the "enemy" will be shot. The enemy will shortly be defined. Are there any questions?"

There were none. Everything Storzzi said was very clear.

"Now I'm going to introduce you to your commanding officer. Abu El Forti."

The door to the cockpit opened. A tall, dark man emerged. He wore desert brown camouflage battle fatigues. Jump boots. A typical Arab headdress. His beard and eyes were black. A Luger rested on his right hip and a canteen on his left.

Two men followed El Forti into the cabin, flanking him. They too wore battle fatigues and jump boots. Each one carried an AK-47.

"Gentlemen," El Forti said, speaking in English, "we will begin training tomorrow morning. At the end of the first two days Colonel Storzzi and I will choose officers from among you. Once we land, we will be at our training ground. All supplies are flown in, and no one will be permitted to leave. Near the end of your training, you will be provided with women. These women will be inspected for VD before they are brought to you."

"Are there any questions?"

"What's our mission?" one of the men asked.

"I'd prefer not to answer that now," El Forti said.

"Where're we going?" Boyce asked.

"Libya," El Forti answered with a thin smile.

"Whoee!" Boyce exclaimed. "Now that's a place I never counted on visiting."

The smile evaporated from El Forti's face.

"He didn't like that," Groggins whispered.

Boyce moved slightly forward. "It's not that I wasn't countin' on any other place. It's just that Libya wasn't on the top of my list."

"Quit while you're ahead," Groggins said. "Your explanation did bring back his smile."

Boyce slid back and faced Groggins. "I didn't mean—"

"Listen, Cowboy, don't tell me what you meant. Tell the man up there." Groggins wanted to laugh. But he figured that would be rubbing the proverbial salt into the wound. El Forti didn't seem to have much of a sense of humor. The Cowboy looked miserable. Like a school boy made to stand in the corner with a dunce cap on his head.

Storzzi took a step forward. He spoke to El Forti in a low voice. Then he said to the men, "Try to confine your remarks to the business at hand. Those of you who are Americans and English please remember that what you might consider humorous, El Forti and his men might consider insulting. If you must play the wit, do it among yourselves."

"In case you don't' know," Groggins told Boyce, "you've just been told off."

"Yeah, I know. I know," Boyce said, trying not to laugh.

El Forti took hold of the mike again. "Gentlemen,

our training will be difficult, but it will provide you with the expertise needed to successfully carry out our mission. Now until we land, enjoy the remainder of the flight.'' He set the mike back in its wall bracket and reentered the cockpit, followed by his two guards.

''Which one of them calls the shots,'' Boyce asked, ''the Arab or Storzzi?''

Groggins shrugged. His guess would have been Storzzi, even though El Forti would appear to be running the operation. But he answered, ''We'll find out soon enough, won't we?''

''Man, your answers are always questions!'' Boyce exclaimed.

''That's just my style,'' Groggins said, closing his eyes.

Groggins looked at a large cloud that made him think of sand castles he built when he was a child. They were elaborate structures with walls and towers. Some even had a moat surrounding them.

Suddenly Groggins was aware of two black specks against the white of the cloud. Thoughts about the past dropped away from him. Within moments he realized that he was looking at two fighter planes.

''We've got company,'' Groggins said, glancing at Boyce.

The Cowboy had fallen asleep. His head lolled off to the left. He was breathing slowly.

Suddenly the PA system crackled. Storzzi was standing up front with the mike in his hand. ''Gentlemen, there are two Libyan fighter planes coming in on our port side. They will escort us to our destination.''

Boyce straightened out. ''Did the man say fighter planes are escorting us?''

''That's right, Cowboy,'' Groggins said.

Boyce turned to the window. "MIG 21s," he commented. "Hey, I can see the pilot!"

Groggins looked. The MIG was just a few feet off the tip of the wing. "I'd feel much more protected if he'd put more distance between his wing and ours."

Boyce looked out of the window again. "Yeah, you might have a point." Then he settled back and closed his eyes. "At least there's some class to the operation. I never had a fighter escort before."

Groggins said nothing.

"Have you any idea what we're goin' to do?" Boyce asked.

"None."

Boyce made a low humming sound. "Whoever is bankrolling this operation must have real big bucks. Just the men on this plane cost—"

"Cowboy, stop asking me questions," Groggins said. "I want to relax. You heard Storzzi. The training is going to be hard, so why don't you relax and enjoy the rest of the flight."

"I was only makin' conversation."

"Don't," Groggins answered. "You're just spinning your wheels." Groggins expected Boyce to say something else. But he didn't. Groggins dozed until the change of the sound of the jet engines and the pressure in his ears awoke him. The plane was descending. He opened his eyes and looked toward the window.

"The fly boys left about five minutes ago," Boyce said. "I waved to the guy off our wing here."

"Did he wave back?" Groggins asked, rubbing his eyes.

"Nah. He made like he didn't see me."

Groggins clicked his tongue sympathetically.

The Seat Belt and No Smoking sign flashed on. The young woman took the mike and repeated the instructions. The ship banked suddenly to the left.

"Hey, if you think that MIG was close to our wing, you should take a look at these damn mountains," Boyce said.

Groggins leaned forward to look out of the window. The plane was between two walls of rock, and it was dropping fast. Within moments it was on its glide path. Then it slammed down onto a sunbaked landing strip. Rushing forward, it sent a huge curtain of yellow dust high above the plane. With a roar the engines were reversed and the ship slowed.

"There's nothin' out there!" Boyce exclaimed.

"There must be something," Groggins answered, "or we wouldn't be here."

The plane continued to roll.

Boyce's face was glued to the window. "If we keep goin', we're goin' to go off the landing strip."

Almost as he spoke the aircraft came to a halt and then turned around.

The PA system came on. Storzzi was on his feet. "Gentlemen," he said, "you will deplane in groups of twenty. Once you are outside, you will follow the two men assigned to your group. They will lead you to a tent, where you will exchange the clothes you are wearing for battle fatigues, boots, field jackets, and the like. Your own clothes will be placed in boxes and stored. All wallets and letters will also be stored in the boxes with the clothing. This is an order. Should it be disobeyed, the punishment will be severe. All personal jewelry, such as rings and/or religious medallions will also be stored. Once you are dressed, you will follow your guides to the trucks. Ten men to a truck. The trucks will transport you to your training site. Unfortunately the strike at the airport in Rome delayed us. But there will be supper waiting for you at the training site. Are there any questions?'' Storzzi waited a moment. Then he ordered the doors opened. The hot desert air rushed in.

Groggins and Boyce were in the third group of men to deplane. The heat seemed to scorch their lungs and the sun was difficult to look at. They were in a bowl, with mountains all around them.

''Man, this is really the boonies!'' Boyce commented.

Groggins looked around. He spotted the road that led from the landing strip to a pass in the mountains to the east. He estimated the pass to be at least ten miles away, maybe more. It was hard for him to make a good estimate because the sun was low enough in the west so that its light blurred whatever it touched in the east.

Inside the tent the heat was worse, and it smelled. Arabs behind long tables gave them boxes for their clothing and personal items, and black markers with which to write. At another table they were handed their battle fatigues, boots, web belts and caps.

There was hardly any talking among the men as they moved along the tables. Almost all of them had similar experiences on other missions. And those who didn't remained silent for fear they'd betray their innocence—and it was innocence, of a kind. Whatever they imagined about being a mercenary would soon be proven false.

Groggins watched Boyce, trying to decide whether he was one of the innocents, or one of the experienced ones. But he couldn't decide.

''How do I look?'' Boyce asked as soon as he was dressed. He wore the cap with the peak low down on his forehead.

''Like John Wayne,'' Groggins answered.

The men were led out of the tent to the waiting

trucks, which were the Russian version of the U.S. Army's "deuce-and-a-half."

Groggins and Boyce sat next to each other halfway into the truck. The two men who had been escorting them were the last to board. One of them shouted to the driver in Arabic and the truck began to roll. The second truck followed close behind.

"I'm glad I'm not in that one," Boyce said, gesturing to the other vehicle. "Those men are goin' to eat our dust all the way to wherever we're goin'."

"You've got a point," Groggins responded.

The truck bounced along the dirt road. To prevent themselves from falling off the bench, the men were forced to grab onto the side.

"My coccyx is sure as hell takin' a beatin'," Boyce complained.

"As long as it's not your cock," one of the other men said, "you have nothing to worry about."

Suddenly the roar of jet engines filled the bowl and a huge curtain of yellow dust rose along the landing strip. In less than a minute the plane was in the air and the dust dropped back to the ground.

The shadows grew out of the west and spread toward the east across the bowl's floor as the sun slipped lower and lower in the sky. When it disappeared everything was cast into twilight, with the exception of the tops of the mountains in the west, which glowed with the reddish yellow light of sunset.

Almost as soon as the sun was gone, it became cold. They put on their field jackets and turned up their collars. The pass was very narrow and didn't lead, as Groggins thought, out of the mountains. It was nothing more than a passageway between the bowl and road that hugged the side of the mountain.

The stars began to show. In a short time the sky was filled with them.

Groggins didn't know enough about the constellations to pick out any one of them from where he was sitting. Had he been up front with the driver, he would have been able to find the Big Dipper and from it, Polaris. That would have told him if they were still moving south. But as it was, he didn't know.

Three hours after boarding the truck, they rolled through a large gate and into a well-lit camp. They stopped in front of a long wooden building. The two Arabs at rear jumped down, opened the tailgate and said, "Come."

Groggins waited his turn to leave the truck. When he was finally on the ground, he felt stiff, tired, and hungry.

But almost immediately they were escorted into a large mess hall.

"I sure hope the cook knows how to cook western style," Boyce said, taking one of the plastic trays from a large stack.

"My advice to you," Groggins said, "is don't ask what you're eating and don't think about what you're eating. Just eat it."

After dinner the men were led to another building and assigned bunks, toilet articles, and additional clothing. Then they were left alone.

Just before ten o'clock, Rome time, Colonel Storzzi's voice came over a public address system. "Gentlemen, on behalf of the UDAR wing of the PLO, I welcome you to Base One. Tomorrow and thereafter your day will commence at zero four-thirty. Lights out will be at twenty-three hundred. Goodnight."

"Who the hell are the UDAR?" Boyce asked.

"An extremist group within the PLO," Groggins answered, leaning back in his bedroll.

Boyce rolled his eyes.

Groggins didn't know what Boyce's action was supposed to mean and he wasn't about to ask him. He lit a cigarette. Blew smoke rings. And wondered if he should have listened to Salito and returned to London.

XIII

Salito was in a small room in the basement of the shop that served as his cover. He studied the video screen, while speaking to John Ramano, his field man at the American embassy in Rome. "I don't see Groggins," he said. "At least not in the three shots you've transmitted."

The picture on the screen changed. Salito stared at it. "I spotted him," he said after several moments.

"Where?" Ramano asked.

"Area A-Eighteen."

An instant later that portion of the picture filled the entire screen.

"Yeah, that's him," Salito commented.

"Which one?" Ramano asked. "There are four men in that segment."

The video grid lines shifted and Salito said, "D-eight." Almost before he finished speaking, Groggins' face filled the screen.

"Is he as mean as he looks?" Ramano asked.

"And twice as mean, if you happen to be his enemy. Okay, send me a half-dozen blow-ups, just in case I need them."

"Sure."

"Let's go through the rest of the pics," Salito said.

In rapid succession two more photographs came up on the screen. Salito didn't recognize any of the men in them but when he looked at the third picture, he exclaimed, "Holy Christ, that's Colonel Grachev!"

"Wouldn't know him if I fell over him," Ramano quipped.

"I want a half-dozen shots of him," Salito said. He was genuinely upset. Grachev's presence meant that Russians were probably directing and financing the operation.

"I need sets of coordinates before I can give you what you want," Ramano responded.

"L-Twenty."

The lower right hand portion of the original photograph filled the screen. Salito waited for the grid lines to shift before he read out, "P-fourteen."

"Got it! Who's the guy next to him. He looks familiar."

"Hans Dissel."

Ramano repeated the name. Then said, "Rings a bell. Swiss, with a Nazi past and a present association with the PLO."

"You got him!"

"What about Grachev? Who the hell is he?"

"KGB. He ran operations in Angola and in a few other places before that. His full name is Aleksandr Fedorovich Grachev. He and Groggins tangled in Angola, only Groggins never saw him."

"Is there any chance of Grachev knowing Groggins?"

"If he does, Groggins is dead now," Salito answered.

"Do you want me to keep watch on Dissel?" Ramano asked.

"Yes," Salito answered. "No, let's go through the remainder of the pictures. I hope there aren't any more surprises." There weren't. Thirty minutes later, Salito was back in his office on the phone with the Company Director in Langley, Virginia.

After Salito explained the situation, the Director asked, "What are our options?"

"We don't have any," Salito responded. "We have to wait until Groggins finds some way of contacting us. He's our only hope of finding out what Grachev is up to."

"And a damn slim one," the Director said. "That's not the man I want where I know there's going to be trouble. When I authorized his use I specifically stipulated that it be on a limited basis. He was supposed to find out who took Ortega out. That's what he was supposed to do, and now he is our only man in a priority situation."

"I ordered him to return to London," Salito replied. He was sweating now.

"You should have sent a couple of men to put him on a plane."

Salito remained silent. Had he done that, either Groggins or the men he sent would have wound up dead.

"Have you any idea where the plane went?" the Director asked.

"I checked Sixth Fleet Surveillance. They picked up

the plane but didn't bother tracking it because it was flying on its preposted flight plan." He could hear the Director sigh. And he said, "It's normal procedure for the fleet surveillance to track only those planes whose courses cannot be verified."

"Where was the plane heading?"

"Syria, according it its flight plan."

"The Syrians wouldn't give us the right time, let alone tell us if a plane with Swiss markings carrying one hundred and eighty mercenaries landed at one of their airports."

"We've got men there, who—"

"No, we better keep what we know to ourselves. There's no sense in alerting Grachev's people that we know something, even if what we know is damn near nothing." The Director sighed again. "We've got a bad situation and a bad apple right in the middle of it. But whatever we've got is what we have to live with. Okay, we'll wait. But in the meantime I'm assigning an eight priority to it. If anything comes out of Groggins, or from any other place, let me know immediately.

"Yes sir."

"Let me tell you this, Salito, if Groggins fucks up, it's your head that'll roll and he'll be taken out. I don't need a spook like him playing double-oh-seven."

There was nothing Salito could say to that. Essentially he felt the same way about Groggins.

"Do you read me on that?" the Director asked.

"Yes."

There were no goodbyes. The line went dead.

Salito put the phone back in its cradle. Leaned into the chair and anguished over his inability to have told Groggins off. But he liked Groggins and he had let that sway his judgment and that was dumb. Because of it his own head was on the chopping block.

But there was another side to the situation, which he saw and the Director was completely overlooking. If Groggins wasn't there, who would be? No one. The Company wouldn't even be aware that Grachev was up to something again. And Groggins wouldn't be with Grachev, if he wasn't Groggins. He knew that something more was going down and wasn't willing to call it quits until he found out what it was.

Salito reached across the desk for his pipe. The problem wasn't Groggins—regardless of what the director thought—Groggins was in the right place at the right time. The problem was how to get hold of the information Groggins got. Unless he found a way to send the information out, or bring it out himself, the Company would be totally ignorant of what Grachev was going to do. It would be caught off guard again and forced to react rather than act.

He finished filling his pipe, lit it and realized that if the Company was caught with its pants down, so to speak, the Director would have to answer to the President and the Congress. But that fact didn't give him any feeling of satisfaction. There was nothing to do but wait. Wait until either Groggins made contact, or Grachev made his move.

Salito stood up and began to pace. . . .

Using a line anchored with a grappling hook to the top of the rock cliff, Groggins climbed hand over hand up the stone face. Despite the low humidity, sweat streamed into his eyes and soaked through his combat fatigues. Every muscle in his body ached.

And it was hot. The rock face was hot. The air was hot. The sun was a prolonged incandescent flash that tortured Groggins and the other men.

For three days, from 0430 to 2200, Storzzi put the

men through the most rigorous exercises Groggins had ever experienced. His training for the Green Berets was easy compared to what he and all the others were going through.

The first day Storzzi force-marched them twenty miles, after which they had to swim across a large lake. After that they were divided into assault teams and spent five hours in simulated combat with real ammunition and Arabs firing at them, as they stormed a village, a bunker, or just a fortified position on the crest of a hill.

The second day was a repetition of the first, with the exception that they did underwater demolition at night.

This morning they began with hand-to-hand combat, followed by a 'copter assault and now, just before noon, they were making their way up the face of a rock cliff with full battle gear, which included an American M-16 rifle, four bandoliers of ammunition, a loaded .45 with two spare clips, three grenades and a U.S. Marine Corp-issue trench knife.

Groggins was the lead man on his line. There were four other lines. Boyce was behind him and there were three more men on the line after him.

About five feet from the top, Groggins suddenly realized that if he were Storzzi, he would have a surprise waiting on top of the cliff, something to keep the men on the ropes until they fought their way off of them.

"Hey, Mac," he shouted to the lead man on the line nearest to him. "Hey, Mac, ease up. There's going to be trouble up there." Even as he spoke Groggins realized he was looking at the American who he had recognized from the Dolly. Like himself, the man was sweating profusely.

"Yeah, could be," the man said, squinting up at the top of the cliff.

"Pass the word to the other front men," Groggins told him.

Suddenly Storzzi came on a bull horn. "What's going on up there, Groggins?"

Groggins was surprised Storzzi knew his name.

"Keep moving," Storzzi urged. "Woods, Peters, Valdez, Gunter move."

"Not before we throw a few grenades," Groggins shouted back. "We're not going to be caught hanging on these lines, while El Forti's men shoot at us." Groggins slipped a grenade free from his web belt. "Toss it as far as possible onto the ledge," he told the American.

The man nodded and passed the word to the other lead men.

"Groggins," Storzzi said, over the bullhorn, "I've ordered the men not to fire."

"Order them to withdraw," Groggins said. "We're going to throw the grenades."

"Done," Storzzi answered after a few moments.

Groggins braced his feet against the rock face. Pulled the pin from the grenade. Holding the line with his left hand, he hurled the grenade with his right.

Within moments, there were five explosions on the top of the cliff. Some rock debris came down.

Groggins quickly climbed the last five feet. He scrambled onto the top of the cliff. Less than ten feet from the edge, there were the torn remains of two sandbag emplacements, where El Forti's men would have been waiting for them.

"You saved us a lot of trouble," Woods said, coming up to Groggins. "Thanks."

Groggins nodded.

Boyce scrambled onto the ledge. "You're a pisser, Groggins. You sure as hell are a pisser. . . . Those Arabs would have had us dangling on the line 'till Storzzi or El Forti called them off."

Groggins shrugged. "There's probably another way up to the top. Some of the guys would have been caught on the lines, but once the other way was found, there'd be no reason to keep any of the men on the lines."

"I wouldn't bet on it," Boyce said. "Storzzi is a mean motherfucker."

"I'm with you," Woods commented.

"He's just doing his job," Groggins said, "and he is doing it damn good." He moved back and sprawled out on the rock surface, leaning against what was left of one of the sandbag emplacements.

Boyce settled down next to him.

Groggins offered him a cigarette and he took it.

"What do you think Storzzi is goin' to do to you?" Boyce asked, blowing smoke.

"I don't think about it," Groggins answered, closing his eyes and letting the cigarette dangle from the right corner of his lips. And he didn't. He did what the situation called for.

"Don't you ever think about anything?"

"Cowboy, I think about why the lights in our camp go out every few hours. I think about where we are and I think about where we're going. Now tell me what you think about?" He opened his eyes and looked at him.

Boyce grinned. "I guess I could tell you now."

"I'm all ears," Groggins answered.

"The book I'm going to write about when I'm back in the States."

Groggins pushed himself up. "You're joking."

Boyce shook his head.

"You told me that because you knew I write," Groggins said. He ground the remainder of his cigarette against the rock.

"Hey man, are you here for the same reason?"

Groggins was no longer sweating. But his throat was dry. He opened his canteen and drank before he said, "You've got to be crazy."

"Listen. There's this writer, Hank Carter—"

"I'm Hank Carter," Groggins said. "Hank Carter is my pen name."

"Then you're here to get material for another book."

Groggins shook his head. "I wish the hell I was. I'm here because of the pay," Groggins said. He wondered how many other men read his books and thought they could become a merc and write about it. It had never occurred to him until now that anyone would be crazy enough to believe there was a real Hank Carter or want to follow in his footsteps.

"When I was in the Corps," Boyce explained, "I did a few pieces for the battalion newspaper and got to like writing. I even had a piece in—"

Groggins was on his feet. "You're a loonybird. I told you before, this isn't Marine Corps training shit."

"That's why I'm here. I wanted to get real experience."

"What if you get yourself wasted getting that experience?"

"It's not goin' to happen," Boyce answered with conviction. "I'm goin' to make it and write about it."

Groggins was about to tell him again he was nuts. But the expression on Boyce's face stopped him. He looked like a college boy waiting to be told he was going to win the big Saturday afternoon football game. "Yeah," Groggins finally said, "with luck, maybe you'll do it."

"Sure," Boyce responded. "Think positive thoughts and positive things happen. I mean people make their own lives. Hey, maybe we could collaborate. Think about it before you say no."

"I'll think about it," Groggins said. Settling down again and lighting another cigarette, he was having trouble dealing with what Boyce had just told him. If Boyce was telling the truth, it didn't jell with their first meeting in the alleyway.

"Now I've got a question for you, Cowboy, and I need a straight answer," Groggins said.

"Shoot."

"Who told you to follow me the night we met in Rome?"

"No one," Boyce answered. "I saw you jawin' with Carlo, figured you were a merc and wanted to see what would happen if I followed you. Man, you were so fuckin' angry, you didn't make any damn sense."

"That's the truth?" Groggins asked.

"Sure as hell is," Boyce smiled.

Groggins shook his head. "What if I had wasted you?"

"But you didn't. The *what if's* don't count."

Groggins took a long drag on the cigarette and let the smoke rush out of his nose. "Listen Cowboy, I know you were in the Corps. But while we're here, stay close to me. And maybe we will get to collaborate on a book."

On the morning of the fourth day while the men were still at breakfast Storzzi and El Forti entered the mess hall and walked to the center of the room. They waited for conversation to stop.

When it was absolutely silent, Storzzi said, "During

the past three days your performance has been evaluated, and while all of you are professional and experts in the use of small arms and explosives, some are more capable of leadership than others. El Forti and I have chosen four men to be given the rank of captain, four to be their lieutenants and four to be sergeants. The remainder of the men will be divided into groups of nine-men squads with a total of forty-four men including officers and lieutenants under the command of each captain.

As your name and rank is called out, you will fall out and form up into units Able, Baker, and Charley. There will be no transfers from one unit to another. Now are there any questions?''

There were none. But Boyce leaned close to Groggins and whispered, ''What happens if we're separated?''

''Remember what you said about thinking positive thoughts,'' Groggins answered.

''Yeah, but how do I know those Arabs think positively about anything?''

''Only one of them is an Arab.''

Boyce didn't answer.

''I'll read the list in order of the ranks assigned,'' Storzzi said. ''Captains: Robert Wood, Jurt Rugger, Juan Valdez and Jack Groggins. Gentlemen, fall out.''

Groggins stood up. He put his hand on Boyce's shoulder and squeezed it. Then he joined the other captains as they walked toward the door.

Wood nodded to Groggins. Rugger and Valdez shook his hand. Since the day they arrived, he hadn't spoken to either one. From the name, he guessed Rugger was a Kraut. And Valdez was one of Castro's volunteers.

The lieutenants started to come out of the mess hall.

Boyce was one of them. He was smiling. "Works all the time," he said, coming up to Groggins.

"Positive thinking, right?"

"Right, man. Right!"

Storzzi and El Forti were the last men out of the mess hall. They positioned themselves in front of the units and for a few moments spoke to one another in low tones.

Then El Forti took three steps forward and said, "Today we begin training for our mission. We will leave this camp and go to our actual training site. After six weeks, we will be ready to attack the target assigned to us. Are there any questions?"

"What's our target?" one of the men asked.

"You will find that out at the training site," El Forti answered.

Storzzi stepped alongside of El Forti and said, "Just so there is no confusion about the privileges of rank, there are none. Each officer is there to lead in training and combat situations. He will be respected in that capacity only. In all other ways his privileges will be the same as the other men. There will be no saluting and no insignia of rank. We are a small enough unit for every man to know its officers. Are there any questions?" He waited for a few moments before adding, "You have twenty minutes to pack your gear and be back out here, ready to board the lorries. Dismissed!"

"What do you think the target is?" Boyce asked, as he and Groggins walked back to the barracks.

"Whatever it is, it's high priority," Groggins said. "My best guess is that we'll be going after some sort of military installation."

"I thought of that, but how big could it be? We're a

hundred and eighty men, say, two hundred with El
Forti's Arabs. Even with the element of surprise on our
side, we still couldn't tackle anything too big. I'd say
we could handle a thousand guys, and if that's so, the
kind of base we'd hit would be limited to an airstrip, or
a radar site.''

"I'm impressed," Groggins said. "You really can
think.''

"It would make it a lot easier to figure out if we knew
where the hell we are. And don't tell me we're somewhere in North Africa.''

"I was going to agree with you.''

"About what?" Boyce asked.

"About the probable target and about knowing
where we are," Groggins laughed.

Groggins sat in the cab with the driver. The man was
armed and had a sour smell.

The road they took was familiar to Groggins. It led to
several of the training sites around the camp. But as
they continued to drive through the mountains, nothing
was familiar. He knew they were going in an easterly
direction because dawn was beginning to break in front
of them.

He offered the driver a cigarette.

The man took it and smiled.

Groggins tried to speak to him in the dialect he had
learned in Angola but the driver looked at him blankly.
He tried English and received the same blank look. He
said a few words in Spanish and scored.

The man had originally come from Spanish
Morocco. He joined the PLO four years before.

Groggins considered whether it was more important
for him to know what the target was than where they

were. But when he asked the question, the man shrugged. He said he didn't know.

Groggins knew he was lying, but he didn't pursue the matter. To pass time, he continued to speak to the man about Spanish Morocco.

After four hours, they reached the shore of a lake. Groggins had no way of knowing whether it was the same lake they had used previously for their training.

The road continued to climb. They came suddenly to an enormous canopy of canvas stretched above the road. Up ahead of them, Groggins saw the massive structure of a dam, most of which was constructed of earth and stretched across the lake.

The convoy of trucks rolled up to an area of barracks and other buildings made of wood. Like the dam, they were concealed under the canvas canopy. The trucks pulled into a large square and stopped.

Storzzi and El Forti were there to greet them.

The driver turned to Groggins and explained that El Forti and Storzzi were brought there by a 'copter.

Groggins nodded. He gave the man another cigarette and asked, "Are we still in Spanish Morocco?"

Shaking his head, the man said they were in Libya.

"I thought it looked familiar," Groggins said.

The man gave him a questioning look. Then he started to laugh.

Groggins swung down from the cab. He ordered his men off the trucks. "Form up in four ranks of ten men each. I want a lieutenant on the right of each rank and a sergeant on the left."

The other units fell to in a similar manner, though Valdez positioned his lieutenants four steps in front of the first rank's center. And the Kraut, Rugger, put the lieutenants on the right and the sergeants on the left in front of the first rank. Woods ordered his men into a formation with the officers on the left of the ranks and the noncoms on the right.

El Forti smiled. "It would be better if all units formed up the same way." He preferred the way Valdez's men were positioned and ordered the captains to reform their units that way. Then he said, "That dam you see is an exact replica of the one we will destroy. No detail has been omitted. Our training will consist of three parts: familiarization, participation and destruction. Familiarization means just that. You will learn every detail of your role and how it will be applied to the dam. Participation means that you will spend a great deal of time simulating your attack. And the final test will be the destruction of this replica when it is defended by seasoned troops."

As he stopped speaking, the canopy was rolled back automatically. The stagnant air was instantly replaced by a rush of furnacelike air from the surrounding sunparched mountains.

"I was going to ask if there are any questions," El Forti said. "Are there any?"

"Yes sir," Boyce said. "Why the cover?"

El Forti glanced at Storzzi.

"We must keep this operation secret if it is to be successful," Storzzi answered. "This area is watched but only at certain times. When we know it is going to come under observation, we activate the canopy."

Groggins realized the lights were turned off in the other camp for the same reason. But the UDAR couldn't possibly know when an American spy satellite was passing overhead. They would need someone with very sophisticated astronomical equipment to tell them when to shut the lights and pull over the canopy over.

The Russians were the only ones who could do that, which meant it was either done by radio or there was a prepared schedule.

"Each unit will occupy its own barracks," Storzzi said. "Each barracks is designated by either A, B, C, or D. Captains, move your men to their respective barracks and fall out here again at," he looked at his watch, "eleven-thirty. We will lunch before beginning the first part of our training. Dismissed!"

Groggins marched his men to the wooden structure with the large red D painted on the door. The inside was no different from the one they occupied at the previous camp. There were two rows of cots set up under a window on opposite sides of the rooms. Every man had two shelves of his own, a place to hang his clothes, and a special stand for his rifle. The bedding was rolled. It consisted of a thin mattress, mattress cover, a sheet, a pillow and pillow case, and two dun-colored blankets.

Boyce chose the cot to the right of Groggins. "Interestin' about the canopy," he said. He leaned back against the bedroll and placed his booted feet on the metal springs.

"Very," Groggins agreed.

"So now you know why the lights went off a few times during the night," Boyce commented.

"We also know that we're not going after a military installation," Groggins said, settling down on the cot. "What we don't know is the name of the dam and why the UDAR wants to knock it out."

"If any of the other guys around here were in a gamblin' mood I'd lay odds it was the Aswan."

Groggins sat up, swung around and planted his feet on the floor. "I'll gamble," he said, testing Boyce.

"How does nine-to-five grab you?"

"Make it double," Groggins said, "and I'll go for it."

"You've got it," Boyce said, reaching across to shake Groggins' hand. "We start with five C-notes. You get a grand if it's not the Aswan. But if it is I get five C's from you."

Groggins shook his hand. "You're that sure?"

"Yeah, I'm that certain."

"Why?" Groggins asked. He was still not convinced that Boyce knew what he was talking about.

"I went to see the Aswan when I was at the Embassy. If that dam out there ain't a replica of the 'Swan. . . ." He smiled. "I'll give you one big one."

Groggins lit a cigarette. He leaned back. Took several deep drags. He knew enough about the Aswan Dam to know that if it were blown, it would cause havoc in Egypt. Was the accord between Israel and Egypt sufficient reason to blow it? And why would the UDAR want to do it?

"The waters behind that dam," Boyce said, "will drown most of the lower part of the country."

"I was thinking about that, too," Groggins said.

"What'll be left of the Egyptian army will sure as hell come lookin' for us."

"Storzzi and El Forti know that," Groggins answered.

"I sure as hell hope they do more than just know about it. I hope they have a damn good plan to get our asses out of there."

Groggins looked at his watch. "Two minutes before assembly time. Better get the men moving." Boyce nodded and left the cot.

Groggins stubbed out his cigarette in a small tin can next to the cot. That the Aswan Dam was the target was enough to knot his stomach. But knowing he had no way of getting the information to Salito made him break into a cold sweat, despite the heat.

Groggins walked outside to the assembly area. The sun was almost directly overhead. His shadow was close to him.

He walked to where his unit had formed up and took his place in front of it. Neither Storzzi or El Forti were there yet. It gave him time to think of what he bought when he had decided to track down Ortega's killer. For openers Paula's death. Most certainly Rinata's and Arturo's. And soon maybe his own. The odds for survival were certainly against him. He figured they'd lose seventy to eighty percent of their strike force. He had to find a way of getting the information to Salito. If the Aswan were blown, then several million people would die.

He stopped thinking when he saw El Forti and Storzzi coming out of the headquarters building.

XIV

Salito was in his office, ruminating on his upcoming vacation scheduled to start in a few days. Ordinarily, he would have gone back to the States to visit with his mother in Boston; then his older brother, Vincent, in Chicago, where he taught mathematics at the University. Finally, all his family obligations completed, he'd go to New York and live it up until it was time to return to his post in London.

But this year was different. He had decided to spend his time in Europe with Christy Johnson, a woman he had met just two weeks before at an art show.

Salito had one bad marriage behind him and several affairs, some of short duration and others lasting a year or more. But until he had met Christy, Salito kept his interest in women on a strictly physical basis. With Christy it was a great deal more than that. He enjoyed

189

being with her and found that they had a great many
interests in common, including a delight in sex.

Though he had not as yet asked Christy whether
she'd accompany him to Europe, he was certain she
would. So certain, in fact, that he started to call her
now, when the phone rang.

He picked it up. "Salito here."

"We have an advisory from the Israeli Shin Beth,"
the man from communications said.

"Go ahead," Salito answered.

"El Forti has dropped out of sight and there's an
unusual amount of PLO movement."

"What the hell does that last statement mean?"

"The elements of the UDAR have begun intensive
training."

"Where?"

"The advisory doesn't contain that information,"
the monotone voice said.

"Thanks," Salito said.

"Do you want a copy of this advisory?"

"No. And thanks again," Salito said. He put the
phone down and filled his pipe. What he didn't need
was the UDAR doing something to make the Middle
East more tense than it already was.

El Forti was a very dangerous man with a
psychological makeup that was part sadist and part
killer. Otherwise he was a delightful human being. In
several of the UDAR raids organized and led by El Forti
against Israel, he killed men and women alike. The
bodies of the dead men were mutilated. Their penises
were stuffed in their mouths. All of the women were
raped before they were shot.

Salito puffed on his pipe, wondering if there was any
connection between the UDAR activity noted by the

Shin Beth and the activity of Dissel and Grachev. There didn't seem to be any, though Dissel was connected in various ways to the PLO.

The UDAR was a highly organized, well-trained fighting group and had enough men in its own ranks without having to hire mercenaries. Yet there was always the possibility that Russia might be financing an operation that required the use of mercenaries and units of the UDAR.

Salito stood up and began to pace. That possibility began to take on a certain feeling of validity when he considered who was in command of the mercenaries. Grachev would be just the man to handle El Forti.

He returned to his desk and relit his pipe. He had put Groggins on the back burner of his brain, so to speak. But now he wasn't so sure it belonged there. The only way he'd ever get information on Grachev and his mercenaries would be after they struck their target, or if they needed something from the outside.

"Need," he said aloud. "What the hell would almost two hundred mercs need?" He was sure all their food, clothing, arms and ammunition was being supplied.

Women. The mercenaries would need women, especially if they were going to be involved in an extended mission. Knowing Grachev's thoroughness, Salito was certain the Russian would supply his men with women. And those women would have to come from somewhere.

Pleased with himself, Salito puffed gently on his pipe. He picked up the phone and dialed. In a moment a man on the other end answered, "Center." The voice belonged to the same individual who gave him the advisory.

"This is Salito." There was a few moments silence, while the voice analyzer checked out his voice pattern.

"Go ahead," the man said.

"To all field agents, request info on recruitment of prostitutes in large numbers. Suggest use of own female personnel to acquire said information. Matter has class-ten priority and a ten sensitivity. Advise this office if contact is made. Signed, Euro One."

The man on the phone reread the message.

"Send it," Salito said. "And thanks." He pressed down on the button switch to break the connection and dialed Christy's number.

"Are you free for dinner?" he asked.

"If we make it an early night," she answered. Her voice had a slightly deep timbre.

"I was hoping we might spend it together," he said directly.

"That's why I want it to be an early evening," she laughed.

"I'll pick you up about six," he said, feeling a sudden warmth in his groin.

"Fine."

He put the phone back in its cradle. He'd talk to her about the possibility of going to the continent with him sometime in the near future. The less specific he'd be about exactly when they'd go, the more flexibility he'd have. Maybe he still would be able to go on vacation by the middle of September, but if he couldn't, she wouldn't feel disappointed. Salito didn't want anything to upset their relationship. He had the feeling he might be falling in love with Christy and might want to make another try at marriage. Moving from woman to woman was no longer as appealing as it once had been. Now he wanted a woman who belonged to him, and who he belonged to, in the old-fashioned way.

Lately he was beginning to think in terms of having something resembling a normal life and not necessarily with the Company. But if he were offered a decent desk job in Langley, he'd most certainly take it!

The phone rang.

Salito picked it up.

"We have another advisory from Shin Beth," the man said.

"I'm listening."

"Asgar Krudi is training several of the UDAR Units in Lebanon. Krudi was second-in-command under El Forti on three different raids into Israel by the UDAR. We now believe El Forti has been assassinated and Asgar Krudi has assumed total command of the UDAR. . . . End of advisory."

"Request a full dossier on Krudi," Salito said.

"Anything else?"

"No, thank you," Salito answered, knowing the Shin Beth must be very concerned about the activities of the UDAR if they sent two advisory notices within the space of an hour. No doubt they hoped that his people might have picked up something about the UDAR and would send it to them.

Thus far he hadn't informed them about mercenaries under Grachev's command, or even about the loss of a U-2 over Libya; though doubtlessly they knew about it through their own monitoring stations.

The Company was generally not too keen about sharing information with the Shin Beth. But he had worked with several of their agents in the past and found them to be highly trained and even more highly motivated.

Salito decided to wait a few days to see whether his own people picked up anything about the hiring of prostitutes in any significant numbers before he spoke to his Israeli counterpart in London about the mercenaries and Grachev. The more information he had, the better position he'd be in to get the Shin Beth to cooperate with him.

Salito emptied the ashes in his pipe. He took a few moments to give a special operator the number of the restaurant where he and Christy would dine and that he'd be at home after nine o'clock. Then he left the office, passed through several security doors and into the outer area of the antique store.

Asgar Krudi was an avuncular-looking man—except around his eyes. They were coal black. They had a lidded look, hinting at something sexual. But when angry, their lidded appearance gave way to a hard brightness that changed again when he was in combat to the wild look of a man totally caught up in the ecstacy of killing.

Because he was a short man, Krudi wore custom-made boots that added two inches to his height. He enjoyed the contrast of white robes and black headdress or the reverse. In combat he wore no special uniform or insignia. When he moved about the streets of the various cities in Israel or Lebanon he looked very much like a successful merchant rather than one of the leaders of the UDAR.

Using the name of Nikros Popondopulis and a Greek passport, Krudi occupied a luxury suite in the Hotel Dan in the city of Elat. The hotel was on the waterfront. All of the windows of Krudi's suite looked out on the busy port and the Gulf of Aqaba beyond. Krudi had made several visits to Elat before choosing the Hotel Dan for this visit and for eventual target of his UDAR raid.

On this particular afternoon, he wore blue slacks and a white sport shirt. He was seated near the pool at a small table. He drank a frozen daquiri enjoying the many bikini-clad women in and around the pool. They wore such skimpy coverings that he could easily see the nipples of their breasts, and the lips of their vaginas, especially when the material was wet. In such an environment he found it difficult to concentrate on his work. He was there to develop a plan that would enable his men to seize the hotel, hold it for as long as it would take to kill all its guests and then escape, sustaining as few casualties as possible.

Krudi had shifted the date of his attack, moving it to September 12, from the sixth. He had made the change because on September 12 the hotel would be occupied mainly by American tourists. Some two hundred of them, according to his sources, would arrive about eleven o'clock in the morning and depart the following afternoon, at about two.

Krudi thought it was about time the United States paid in blood for its support of Israel. And what he liked most about the change of plans was that the Americans his men would kill would be Christians on a religious pilgrimage to the Holy Land. The killing of Christians would most certainly have repercussions in the United States, particularly among certain elements , who already believed the Jews were responsible for most of the trouble in the world. Killing Christians would only serve to inflame that view, especially since it would be fed by well-placed propaganda stating that if the Jews did not steal Arab territory, then there would be no need for terrorist raids. That, coupled with the strike at Aswan, would most certainly put Israel and Egypt at each other's throats. Most probably the rest of the Arab nations would finally attack Israel, forcing the United States to choose sides or remain neutral and allow Israel to be destroyed.

That prospect so excited Krudi, that he finished off his frozen daquiri too fast, feeling the cold in his sinuses. He was forced to rub the area above his eyes to ease the pain. When it was gone, he ordered another and continued to think about his plan.

Krudi had three men inside the hotel. One was a maintenance man. The second an elevator operator. And the third wasn't a man. It was a young woman who worked in the kitchen. Of the two men, the maintenance man, Aben Fraker, was the more dependable.

He and five of his men would take rooms for the twelfth of September. At some time around eleven at night, a fishing boat would approach the hotel. It would develop engine trouble and run aground on the beach. Some twenty men would be aboard. Once the fishing boat was aground, the hotel lights would go out, giving the men on the boat a chance to land and set up their machine guns. There would be four guns in all, arranged with intersecting fields of fire.

At the same time two large lorries would pull up to the front of the hotel. One would be loaded with explosives and the other would carry another twenty men. As soon as the lights in the hotel went out they would storm the lobby; at the same time the elevator operators would stop the elevators. While all this was happening, he and his four men would seize the switchboard and destroy all the coin-operated phones. By the time the lights would come back on, the hotel would be completely in the hands of his men.

The explosives would be removed from the lorry and placed in and around the hotel, making it impossible for the Israelis to storm it from any of the sides facing land. As for the one side open to the water, any men coming up the beach would either be cut down by the machine guns or by the mortars set up near the pool.

The guests would be killed in groups of ten by the pool. He would allow his men to rape the women before shooting them. He would not communicate with the Israeli authorities, and when the killing was done, the hotel would be set afire. That would be the signal for three high-speed torpedo boats to run into the harbor to take them off the beach. This withdrawal would be synchronized with an air raid alert, though of course there wouldn't be an air raid.

Exactly eight hours after the conclusion of the raid on the hotel, the Aswan Dam would be attacked.

Krudi sipped at his drink. He had already mapped out the various routes his men would take through the blacked-out hallways of the hotel. Every detail was in place. He had drawn diagrams showing the placement of machine guns, mortars, even where the explosives would be buried. Now he was reviewing each detail of the operation before he'd return to his men and give them the plan.

He was slightly amused by how easy the entire operation appeared to be. He expected the Israelis to attempt a 'copter assault, but some of his men would be on the roof armed with heat-seeking missiles. He also figured that a nerve gas might be used against them. Should that be done, he would change his method of killing from shooting, to throwing his victims out of the windows, one by one. But he did not think this would be necessary. The use of nerve gas would most certainly anger the United States, to say nothing of the rest of the world.

Krudi looked up at a woman in a very skimpy wet bikini. She was tan, with long blond hair and gray eyes. About thirty, he guessed.

She was smiling at him.

He smiled back. "Would you care to join me for a drink?" he asked in English.

"Yes," she answered. "I'd like that." She spoke with a French accent.

Krudi stood up as she came to the table. He took hold of her hand, kissed the back of it, and said, "I'm Nikros Popondopulis."

"Renne Villagais," she answered, sitting down.

"What would you like to drink?" he asked.

"A glass of white wine."

He nodded and, summoning the waiter, Krudi gave him the order. Then he looked across the table. And he knew—just as he knew that this life was guided by Allah—that before the afternoon passed, he would be in bed with the woman.

Krudi felt Renne move off the bed. He watched her, pretending to be asleep.

She padded into the bathroom.

He could hear her urinate, even though the bathroom door was closed. He expected her to return to bed. The prospect of having her small bare buttocks close was beginning to excite him again. She was extremely good.

Renne did not come back to the bed. She walked past the half-closed venetian blinds. Paused so that her naked body was alternately stripped by bars of sunlight and gray. She looked at him.

Krudi still feigned sleep. But he was alert.

Renne turned and moved to the desk and eased the drawer open. Her hand reached down.

Krudi was out of bed and across the room before she could turn. A chop on the back of the neck dropped Renne to the floor. He went to her bag. A driver's license in her name. No passport or other identification. And in a zippered section an Israeli .32 caliber automatic.

He looked down at her. It would be a while before she'd come to. He dressed and lit a cigarette, wondering whether or not he should kill her. He could take her up to the roof and throw her off. But if he did that, he'd attract attention to the hotel. And just possibly to himself. She might have had someone else working with her who saw them together. There were other guests at the pool who must have been aware of them, and he couldn't risk having one of them make any connection between her and himself. The longer it would take for anyone to say that they saw them together, the less likely they would be to remember what he looked like.

Krudi took several long drags on the cigarette and considered the problem. He had no doubt that she was a Shin Beth agent. But it was unlikely she knew who he was. If she had the slightest suspicions, he'd be in the hands of the Shin Beth at that very moment, instead of looking down at her naked body and calmly smoking. Killing her was out of the question. But he had to make sure she would not return to her employer, and the only way to do that was to have her taken out of the country and kept out.

Krudi smiled. Luckily there was a way to do that and even be paid for it.

He squatted down on his haunches. Rolled Renne onto her back. His hand moved over her breasts, down her taut stomach and over her tufted, honey-colored mound. For a moment he thought about taking her again. But it would be nowhere as pleasurable as what he had already experienced with her. She'd remain motionless. Having sex with a woman who couldn't move would be like masturbating.

Krudi shook his head. Then he stood up and reached for the phone. He dialed for an outside line, then the number he wanted.

A man answered. He spoke in Arabic.

"This is Krudi," he said, also speaking in Arabic. "What's the going price for a blonde Jewess?"

"Virgin?"

"Hardly," he laughed, looking down at her.

"In all other respects healthy?"

"Yes."

"Then I should say she could bring as much as five thousand dollars at an auction."

"Have your men pick her up at the Dan Hotel, suite eighteen ten. Have them use one of those canvas carts. She will be nude and have them bring a hypodermic syringe with something to keep her out."

"Yes. Any other instructions?"

"I will come for the money in a few weeks."

"It will be here."

"One more thing," Krudi said. "I suggest her tongue be removed before she is sold."

"That might decrease her value," the man suggested.

"Not if the buyer is wise," Krudi laughed.

"By Allah," the man on the other end said, "I think you're right."

"How long before the men come to take her?"

"A half hour at the most."

"Excellent," Krudi said. He thanked the man. Put the phone down and lit another cigarette.

Storzzi was in a rage. He paced back and forth

making the wooden floor of the Headquarters building creak.

From time to time the man at the desk glanced up at him. But fearing the colonel would catch him, he immediately returned to his work.

Storzzi looked at his watch and stomped over to the radio operator. "Are you sure El Forti received the message?" he asked.

"Yes Colonel," the operator answered. "Do you want me to contact the 'copter?"

Even as the man spoke, the sound of the incoming chopper sould be heard clearly.

Storzzi went to the window to watch the 'copter land. Its rotors sent up a cloud of yellow dust that completely obscured it. Within moments he saw El Forti run out from under the cloud in a low crouch.

Storzzi drew away from the window. And faced toward the door.

El Forti entered the room. He looked straight at Storzzi. "Your message came just as we had begun our underwater—"

"I received this message from my people," Storzzi broke in. "Krudi has sold a woman Shin Beth agent into slavery."

El Forti blanched.

"According to the information I have he took her up to his room before he made arrangements to have her sold at auction."

El Forti wiped his brow. "Does the Shin Beth know?"

"Know that we have an idiot in charge of a major operation!" Storzzi shouted. "I don't know what they know. But I tell you this, I know that we can't afford to have a man like Krudi running around loose. It was foolish enough for him to be at the hotel, when he could have sent other men to diagram the place, but it was even more foolish for him to have become involved with a woman—any woman.''

El Forti shifted his weight from one foot to another. "There is nothing I can say that would change anything that has been done.''

Storzzi took a deep breath. He knew El Forti was losing face in front of his own men. But he didn't really care. This operation was too damn important for him to worry about Arab sensibilities. "First he changes the day for the raid and now this. Hasn't he any idea that within a matter of days, if not hours, the Shin Beth will have a description of him. They might even know what he did with the woman, or worse, they might even be able to get her back.''

"I can assure you that will not happen,'' El Forti said in a low, very tight voice.

"It can happen,'' Storzzi shouted. "The Shin Beth have their agents wherever we have ours. There isn't a slave auction held where they don't have someone there to see who the buyers are and who they're buying.''

"I will order the woman killed,'' El Forti said.

Storzzi threw up his hands. He was too angry to continue speaking. He took several deep breaths before he said, "Order her killed.''

El Forti looked toward the radio operator. "Contact Krudi, order him to retrieve the woman he sold to the slave dealer in Elat and have her killed. Have it go out under my signature.''

The radio operator immediately began to call Krudi's code name.

"Is there anything else, Colonel?'' El Forti asked coldly.

"Until this operation is complete, I don't want

Krudi, or anyone else from the UDAR in Israel. Is that clear?''

''Yes.''

''Any man who disobeys that order will be shot,'' Storzzi said.

''Yes,'' El Forti said.

Storzzi felt emotionally and physically drained. He would have liked very much to go to his bunk and sleep for a few hours. But he couldn't afford to let El Forti see how tired he was.

''I will be returning to the dam in a few minutes,'' El Forti said.

''Good. I'll go with you,'' Storzzi responded. ''I want to see how well the underwater teams are doing.''

Groggins sat on a huge rock overlooking the dam. Eight days had passed since he had left Rome. Four days had been spent in the first camp and the rest at the dam. In that time the men got to know the dam as if it belonged to them.

Each unit was assigned its individual task. His men would blow up the hydroelectric plant on the east end. Wood's men were to blow the outlet channel on the east bank. Valdez's group would cause a series of explosions at the base of the dam on the west end. Rugger's force would cover the other three. All units were expected to have to fight their way to their prime target and then fall back on the east side, where the choppers would be waiting to carry the survivors back into Libya.

Groggins went over every detail of the hydroelectric plant in his head many times. And then with his men many more times. Not only did they have the replica to work from, but each captain was provided with exact scale models of the dam that could be taken apart and reassembled. He and his men knew every stairway, every door, every power switch of the plant. Even where the electric lights were located.

Groggins wiped away the sweat from his forehead with his arm. The canopy was up, and the heat and humidity were unbearable. He glanced at the canopy. He still hadn't figured out a way of sabotaging it. But even if he had, he wouldn't have been able to do anything about it. When he wasn't training, he was always under the very watchful eyes of El Forti's men.

He looked across the earthen dam to where Storzzi was sitting. Suddenly he realized Storzzi and El Forti weren't spending as much time with each other as they previously had. He looked for El Forti and found him with Valdez.

"Interesting," Groggins commented aloud, knowing he'd get a response from Boyce. He had become genuinely fond of him, even though he still thought his reason for being there was insane.

"Okay," Boyce said, "tell me what's so fuckin' interestin'."

"I didn't say it was fucking interesting. I just said it was interesting."

"Okay, I withdraw the fuckin', now will you tell me?"

"Have you noticed anything different about our two chiefs?"

"Neither one is in drag," Boyce laughed. "And even if they were, neither one is my type."

"Okay my writer friend, there's something different about them. Tell me what it is."

Boyce scratched the stubble on his chin. "They're as mean as ever and—they don't hang out together. Right?"

"Right."

"Can't be over a woman because there isn't a sniff of muff around here," Boyce said.

"Probably right again."

"Then it's somethin' about the operation," Boyce said with a smile.

"If I had a gold star, I'd give it to you," Groggins answered.

"Any ideas?"

Groggins shook his head. "Wouldn't even begin to guess. But I'd give a month's pay to know."

"No way you're ever goin' to know," Boyce said. "Looks like El Forti is getting up."

Groggins got to his feet.

El Forti blew a whistle.

"Okay men," Groggins called, "saddle up."

Storzzi summoned the men toward the middle of the dam. "Can everyone hear me?" he asked and waited a few moments. Then he said, "The explosives you will be using on the real target will be new. They look and handle like plastique, only the kind you'll use are a thousand times more powerful and can be detonated with a fuse, electrically or with a round fired from a revolver or a rifle. For those men planting explosive devices at the base of the dam, the plastique will be set off by a timing device. The purpose of the explosions is not to destroy the dam. The purpose is to weaken the structure so that when the rains come, the pressure behind the dam will rupture it.

"Captain Groggins' force will cause sufficient damage to flood the land below the dam. His men will handle the largest amount of the new explosive."

"Any questions?"

"Where's the real dam located," Boyce asked.

"You'll be told in due time," Strozzi answered. "But I'll tell you this. All but the last phase of your training will end in four days. The following day you will be taken to a seaside resort where you will have the opportunity to enjoy the company of lovely and accommodating women."

A cheer broke from the men.

"Didn't you tell me it was the Aswan?" Groggins asked.

"Yes, sir. But I wanted to hear it from him."

"Cowboy, you're nuts!"

Storzzi put up his hands. "You'll have two full days for, for whatever please you. And you'll be able to eat, drink, and be merry."

Another cheer arose.

"Now let's get back to the 'copters," Storzzi said, "and practice our assault."

Groggins ordered his men to form up in a column of threes. Then he turned to Boyce and said, "We're going to have to be faster once we're inside the powerhouse. I don't want anyone caught inside because this new type of plastique starts to go off before they're out."

"Don't you trust it?"

"Sure. But I'd trust it more if we could chop thirty seconds from our inside time."

Boyce nodded. Then he asked, "What kind of woman would you like?"

"Haven't given it much thought."

"God damn, I'd like one with boobs that stick straight out and a cunt that fits like a glove."

"You might get the boobs that way," Groggins laughed. "But you can count on the cunt being somewhat less than glove fit."

"You mean it's probably been used before?"

"Probably," Groggins answered. "Very probably. Now before you cream your pants, get our guns loaded onto the choppers."

Boyce high-balled him. And walked off grinning.

"She was found naked in a drainage ditch behind a warehouse," Mordechi Richter, the chief of police, said. "Her tongue had been cut out and, according to the coroner, she had been sexually abused just a short time before she was killed."

Joseph Ben Gershom listened carefully. He was thirty-six years old. Since the end of the 1967 war, he had been with Shin Beth and now he was second-in-command of the organization's southern district. He was a tall, muscular man with black eyes and close-cropped hair.

For several moments Ben Gershom said nothing and stared at the form under the sheet. The harsh light from the ceiling was made harsher by the white tile of the morgue. There weren't any shadows. The scene reminded him of a painting he had once seen in which the central figure was a sheet-draped corpse. Even with a sheet over the body, the mound of her breasts was clearly defined.

"Naturally," Richter said, "there wasn't any identification on her. But from her fingerprints and teeth we were able to establish her identity and that she belonged to your organization."

Ben Gershom nodded. Reaching over to the sheet, he eased it down until her face was completely uncovered.

"She is one of yours, isn't she?" Richter asked.

Gershom nodded. "She was assigned to the Hotel Dan," he answered in a low voice. He looked at the police chief. "We sometimes spent the night together and now and then a weekend." Tears streamed down his cheeks. "I could never make up my mind if I loved her. Now I don't have to."

"I'm sorry," Richter responded.

Ben Gershom nodded. He used his handkerchief to wipe his eyes. After he took a deep breath, he said, "I'm all right." Then he asked, "Do the police have any leads?"

"We only know she was in the hands of slave dealers," he said. "There's a small mark under her left breast that was put there by a tattoo pen."

"How long had she been dead before you were notified?"

"Not more than five or six hours."

"She was at the Dan the day before yesterday," Ben Gershom said. "I think you better have your men question the guests. I'll have her photograph sent down to you. Somebody might remember who she was with."

Richter nodded.

"Slaves," Ben Gershom exclaimed savagely. "Goddam filthy slavers! I tell you, no matter how you cut it, those people are still living in the twelfth century, and that's if they're modern."

"We'll do our best to get the bastard who did it," Richter said.

Ben Gershom kissed the dead woman's forehead. Then he gently moved the sheet back over the face. "Her real name is Sharon Gotfried. I'll notify her parents. They live in Jerusalem. I don't think they have any idea she worked for us."

"Did you ever meet them?"

"Yes," Ben Gershom answered. "Sharon told them I was a clothing manufacturer." He shook his head and started toward the door. "I want the man who killed her. I want him and when I'm finished with him, I'll give what's left of him back to you. Do you understand what I'm saying?"

"Yes," Richter answered. "He's yours when we get him."

Ben Gershom nodded and again the tears started to flow and streak his cheeks. . . .

XV

Salito lit his pipe and puffed at it several times while he looked at Luise Talbert seated on the opposite side of the desk. She was twenty-five. High breasts, visible through her white blouse. Direct, brown eyes and honey-colored hair. She lacked a couple of inches to be considered tall.

"If you're through with the examination," she said, "we might be able to have a meaningful conversation."

Taken aback, Salito swallowed some smoke and began to cough. He wasn't expecting her to be so direct. She was, in the particular situation, much more self-possessed than he.

"I'm sorry," Salito said. "I didn't mean to stare."

"Translated that means you're wondering how I can do what I do."

He tried to deny it. But he never felt comfortable about working with female agents. Maybe he was old-fashioned but it was easier to take someone like Ortega being offed, than Paula Bennet.

"I'll tell," Luise said, "I do what I was trained to do. And if you're wondering if I enjoy my work, the answer is sometimes. Oh yes, there's one more thing you might be wondering about and that is whether or not I have an orgasm when I'm on assignment. The answer to that is: yes, frequently. It's just part of the perks that comes with the job."

Salito flushed. He put his pipe down and cleared his throat. She'd be just the right kind of woman to work with Groggins. As tough and straight forward as he was.

"Are there any other questions?" Luise asked. "If you'd like to know my sexual preferences, I'd be more than willing to tell you."

"I'm sure you would," Salito answered. "But that will not be necessary. According to the cable I received from our field man, you were contacted by a George Sommers."

"Yes."

"How did he know you were available?" Salito asked.

"I met him at, at one of those parties. There were several women there beside myself."

Salito nodded. "Were any of them asked?"

Luise shrugged. The sudden motion slipped the nipple of her left breast between the opening of her blouse. "I really don't know."

"Just what was the deal?" Salito asked.

"An all-expense-paid trip for two days to a seaside resort and a fee of two hundred dollars."

Salito cleared the ashes from his pipe into an ashtray. "Did Sommers tell you where the resort was located?"

"No. I was just told we would leave from Athens."

"And just how many men would you be required—"
He was going to say *service* but stopped himself.

Luise smiled. "One man for each woman," she
answered.

"Then you could assume there would be more
women there," Salito said.

"Yes."

"According to the information I have, this Sommers
is about six foot tall. Has light brown hair. Brown eyes
and is about forty."

"That's the description I gave to your field man,"
she said. "And he is presently staying at the Hotel
Maurice in Paris. Oh yes, he has a friend named Dissel,
German or Swiss, I think. Sommers has a put-on English accent but my guess is that he's from the States."

Salito raised his eyebrows. Dissel's presence just
about made it certain his guess that Colonel Grachev
would provide women for his men was right.

"You know what I mean," Luise said. "They
wouldn't look at a woman the way you looked at me a
few minutes ago."

"Did you meet any more of Sommer's friends?"
Salito asked.

"No."

"When are you supposed to be in Athens?"

"In two days," Luise answered.

"Were you given any money in advance?"

She shook her head. "But I was told that any money I
laid out would be reimbursed."

Salito refilled his pipe. "You'll be going on that
two-day outing." And opening the top drawer of his
desk, he removed four 8x12 photographs. "These are
enlargements of pictures taken a few weeks ago at the

Da Vinci Airport in Rome." He pushed the photographs across the desk.

Luise quickly scanned the pictures. Then she looked at Salito.

"There are two white circles on each of the photographs. The one marked A is a picture of Groggins. Jack Groggins. He's our man. He's the one you'll have to get to."

"And who's the B circle?" she asked.

"Colonel Aleksandr Fedorovich Grachev. He's about the best the KBG has. All those men are mercs. We don't know where they are and what they're supposed to do."

"And you're betting Groggins knows?"

Salito nodded. He wasn't going to tell her how Groggins became involved, or anything he knew about Dissel. He was having Dissel and Crimins shadowed. When the time came he'd have them taken in and sweated for the information they had. But for him to do that without knowing what Grachev was up to might blow the opportunity to take Grachev out, ruining a major covert Russian operation.

"The man next to Groggins is Marine Sergeant Nelson Boyce," she said.

Salito worked at looking disinterested. He couldn't get an ID on him. There were only three other men in the group who couldn't be identified by the Company specialists at Langley.

"I met him in Egypt about two months ago. He was with the Marine detachment at the Embassy."

"That's him," Salito lied.

"What the hell is he doing with that bunch?" she asked.

Salito gambled. "His tour was up. I guess he was

looking for good pay and plenty of excitement. To change the subject, did Sommers tell you what kind of men you'd be meeting?''

"A mixed bag. He said they're working in the oil fields.''

"Interesting,'' Salito commented.

"How do I identify myself to Groggins?'' she asked.

"Tell him you're a Hank Carter fan and—''

"But I am,'' Luise laughed. "His books have a sense of reality about them that so many others of the same genre lack.''

"Tell him that when you meet him,'' Salito said, feeling for the first time since she entered his office that he surprised her. And it was a good feeling, a very good one. "Use my name and,'' he continued with a smile, "give him his own ID number.'' He jotted it down and passed the slip of paper across the desk.

She looked at the number for a few moments, nodded and passed it back to him. "I have it.''

"How many other women are going to Athens?'' he asked.

"I don't know.''

For a few moments neither of them spoke; then Salito said, "I can't think of anything else. Can you?''

"You don't have any idea what your Russian Colonel might be up to?''

"Not even a hint of an idea,'' Salito said.

Luise stood up. "I'll get back to you as soon as I can.''

Salito came around to the front of the desk. "Take care of yourself, Luise,'' he said. "If Colonel Grachev discovers what you are, he'll—''

Luise cut him short. "I know what he'll do, and if he's with Arabs, as no doubt he is, they'll do the same

thing to me that they did to one of the Shin Beth women
in Elat a few days ago.''

Salito's brow wrinkled. ''I didn't know anything
happened there.''

She nodded. ''It's being kept quiet. Nothing went
out to the press about it.''

''How did you find out?'' he asked. The woman was
full of information. First she IDs an unknown, and now
she comes up with something the Shin Beth has taken
pains to keep under wraps.

''I'm part of a small sisterhood. When something
happens to one of us, the rest of us generally know soon
after. There must have been some pillow talk about it in
Israel. But I found out in Paris.''

''From a good source?''

''Good enough so that I can tell you that the Shin
Beth agent in charge of the investigation is Joseph Ben
Gershom. You have ways of checking that out, I'm
sure.''

''Yes,'' he answered. And escorting her to the door,
he shook her hand.

Luise smiled. ''See you in a few days,'' she said and
left. For a few moments Salito watched her. Even her
walk was sexy. Unquestionably she was a beautiful,
sexually provocative woman.

Salito took the photographs from his desk. He went
into the communications room and told the communications chief: ''Hook me up with the officer in
charge of the Marine detachment at our embassy in
Egypt. As soon as you have him, set up a video ID
circuit. I want to show him a few photographs.''

''It'll take about ten minutes for the people in the
embassy to connect up their video display screens,'' the
communications chief said.

Salito nodded. "I'll wait," he said. And dropping into a chair, he lit his pipe. His gut feeling was that Boyce had been a Marine the way he had been a Sunday school teacher.

He puffed vigorously at his pipe. He could understand a man claiming to be a Marine or anything else, if it would get him into the sack with a woman, especially a woman like Luise. Though she didn't say that they had gotten it on together. He was just assuming that they had.

"I have the embassy," the communications chief said.

Salito left the chair and entered a small cubicle where the video sending and receiving equipment was located. He sat down at a console and pressed a red button.

"Captain Anderson here," the man on the screen said.

Salito identified himself. He held up one of the photographs in front of the camera. "Captain, there are two circles on the picture. Do you see any man you know near the men who are circled?"

"No sir," Anderson answered.

"Are you absolutely sure?"

"Yes sir."

"Look at the man speaking to the individual in circle A. Was he a member of your detachment?"

"No sir."

"How long have you been at the embassy, Captain?"

"For the past eighteen months."

To be absolutely certain Anderson couldn't identify Boyce, he held up the other photographs. Asked the same questions and came up with nothing.

Anderson was smart enough not to ask questions.

Salito thanked him. Pressed a button and the screen went black. His gut feel had been right. Only he wished it hadn't been. Now he'd check with his French, British, West German, and Italian counterparts to find out if Boyce belonged to one of them. But he knew he'd be running the check to play it safe. He was sure that Boyce didn't belong to any of them. Then he began to sweat! Boyce could be a Russian plant. One of Grachev's men. All Salito could do was hope that Groggins wouldn't give Boyce any reason to suspect he was something more than a merc. That he was doing what he was doing for the money and the adventure, nothing else.

Salito left the communications room, returned to his desk and began to contact the counterparts of the few foreign governments who might have sent Boyce to shadow Grachev. After six hours of faint hope, he had come up with nothing.

By the time he was finished it was going on eleven-o'clock. He remembered he was supposed to call Christy at eight to tell her if he'd be spending the night with her. He dialed her number, while drumming on the desk with his fingers.

The phone rang six times before Christy answered.

"I couldn't call because something came up," he explained. "I had a prospective buyer in for that terra cotta Greek statue, the one in the glass case." Christy hadn't any idea of his real work. She believed what she saw, and she saw an antique dealer.

"I cooked dinner but I guess I could reheat it," she said.

"I'll be there in about forty minutes," he told her. "And thanks for not being angry."

"Oh I'm angry. But that doesn't stop me from wanting to spend the night with you."

"I love you." The words were out before he could stop them. He put the phone down. "Well I'll be goddamned!" he exclaimed aloud. He leaned back. Put his hands behind his head and looked at the phone. "I meant it," he said.

A few minutes later Salito was on his way out of his office, when the phone rang. He returned to his desk. The call was coming in on the security number. He pursed his lips and picked the phone up.

"A woman Shin Beth agent was found murdered in Elat. Agent last seen at the Dan Hotel in the company of Krudi. Shin Beth involved in the police investigation."

The message was signed by the Company man in Elat.

Salito put the phone down. But didn't move away from the desk. Maybe the time had come to let the Israelis know about Grachev and his mercs. Maybe Krudi was buying women too. Decided to try the merchandise and discovered he was making it with a Shin Beth agent? End of agent!

Salito was torn between wanting to leave and contacting his Israeli counterpart. He took two steps away from the desk, returned, picked up the phone and dialed a special number.

He identified himself but it took several minutes before he was connected to Yitzhak Fishbine.

"I have something that might interest you," Salito said. "Will you be able to meet me tonight?"

"Yes. Where and when?"

"Say in about thirty minutes in front of Foy's Bookstore on Charing Cross Road?"

"I know the place."

"See you," Salito said. He cut the connection and called Christy. "I'll be much later than I thought. But I'll be there."

"So will I and so will your dinner," she answered.

"Thanks again." He put the phone down. Gathered the photographs together and slipped them into a leather carrying case.

Fishbine arrived at Foy's a few minutes before Salito. He looked at the window display of books. He hadn't read any of them. He had all to do to keep up with the reading required by his work. And when he returned home at night, he much preferred to watch TV. It required absolutely no thinking on his part and he could relax.

Fishbine was a tall, lean man, with a long face. He had gray eyes and thinning hair that was beginning to gray. Some morning he'd look in the mirror and wonder whether he'd lose his hair first, or turn gray? Though he wasn't a vain man, he hoped he'd turn gray. He wouldn't look well bald. Something like a cue-stick with a distorted billiard ball perched on its thick end.

He turned around facing the street. That Salito had called him was unique. Company men usually avoided contact with Shin Beth agents, either out of pride, or the old anti-Semitism that manifests itself in peculiar ways. More than likely a combination of both.

Fishbine saw Salito. He was coming across the street.

"Waiting long?" Salito asked, shaking Fishbine's hand.

"Not more than three or four minutes."

"Let's find someplace where we can sit and talk," Salito said.

Fishbine nodded. "There's an all-night place just a few streets from here in Soho."

"Fine," Salito answered.

The two of them walked side by side. For a few moments neither one of them spoke. Fishbine enjoyed the silence, and out of the corner of his right eye he looked at Salito.

The man appeared unperturbed, at least that was all that could be read from the expression on his face. Fishbine knew Salito was a professional. And he admired him for that.

They passed a couple embracing.

"They're having a much better time than we are," Fishbine said.

Salito laughed and agreed.

The all-night place was in Carl Street, off Soho Square. Fishbine led the way to a side table. "We can talk here," he said. The two tables on either side of them were empty. There was a couple at a table in front of the window. A man at the counter.

"I'll just have tea," Salito said. "I have dinner waiting for me."

"This place makes marvelous pastry," Fishbine said. "The baker is an Arab from Tel Aviv."

Salito smiled. "I understand; next time I'll take you to a place that serves Texas-style chili dogs. It's run by a guy from El Paso."

"You said you had something that might interest me," Fishbine said.

"Let's order first," Salito responded, summoning the waitress.

Fishbine waited until they were alone. "I don't have time for games. Don't stall and think you're playing with me."

Salito flushed. "One of our U-2's was shot down over Libya," he said.

"That happened about three weeks ago," Fishbine

said. "We have recordings of the conversation between the U-2 pilot and planes of the Sixth Fleet."

"The plane was sent there because satellite photos show that something is out there that shouldn't be."

"We know that. We have been trying to get men into the area but their security is too tight."

"It would be," Salito said. Then he went on to explain how one of his agents joined a group of mercenaries in Rome. "On the day that group left the Da Vinci Airport, we managed to photograph them. We came up with our old Russian friend Colonel Aleksandr Fedorovich Grachev."

Fishbine ran his hand across the rough stubble on his chin. He was impressed and worried. "If Grachev is leading those men, it's something big."

"You can bet on it," Salito said. "My guess is that Grachev and his mercenaries have something to do with whatever is being hidden in Libya."

"That could be," Fishbine agreed.

"A day ago a man named Sommers was on the buy for women," Salito said. "One of our agents will be among those who will go on a two-day trip to keep some men happy. Men from the oil fields, so she was told."

The waitress came with their orders.

"Are you sure you don't want a piece of pastry?" Fishbine asked.

Salito shook his head. "The tea will be fine."

"The Ruskies are the only ones who'd be able to tell their Libyan friends when one of your satellites is overhead," Fishbine said.

"Exactly. And when we sent up a U-2 to take a look it was shot down."

"Who do you have with Grachev?"

"A man named Jack Groggins."

Fishbine raised his eyebrows. "He was in Angola with you, wasn't he?"

Salito nodded. "We took him back into the fold," he said.

Fishbine didn't make any comment. Groggins could be the best or the worst. No matter which, he was Salito's problem.

"Tonight I received word a woman agent of yours was found murdered in Elat," Salito said. "Some days ago I was informed that El Forti had been wasted and Krudi was no longer top dog at UDAR."

"I'm really impressed," Fishbine said.

"I want to know if there's any connection between the killing in Elat and—"

"We don't know," Fishbine said. "And that's the truth. The only thing we do know is that Krudi was definitely identified as the man who was last seen with our agent. But we don't know why he was at the hotel. I don't suppose you know the woman had been sold to a slave dealer and had her tongue cut out and that she was repeatedly raped before being killed."

Salito had a fleeting image of the same things being done to Luise. And shuddered.

"Our agent in Elat has been with this thing since it has happened," Fishbine said, "and he hasn't found out anything more than what I have already told you."

Salito sipped his tea. It was tepid. He drank it anyway.

"Is there anything else?" Fishbine asked. He was beginning to feel very tired. The fact that Grachev was leading those mercenaries worried him.

"So you can tell your boss that you've seen the photographs, I brought four of them along," Salito said. He opened the leather case and handed the 9x12 envelope to the Israeli. "Open it."

Fishbine looked at the first picture. "That's Grachev, all right. And I take it the other man is—"

"Who's the man with Groggins?" Salito asked, filling his pipe.

Fishbine glanced up at Salito. The man had been playing with him. All he wanted was the identity of the man next to Groggins. "He's one of ours," Fishbine said. "His name is Nelson Boyce. His father is Irish. He came to fight against the British in 1948 and stayed to marry an Israeli woman. Boyce transferred to us while he was still in the army. The last I heard about him, he was in Egypt. I don't know what he was doing there."

"Posing as a Marine sergeant part of the time," Salito answered, blowing smoke rings from his pipe.

"What's this 'bit of luck' you mentioned on the phone?" Gershom asked, settling down into the chair in front of Richter's desk and checking his watch against the clock on the wall. The two read two-thirty-eight and six seconds. Satisfied, Gershom fixed his eyes on the Chief of Police.

"There was a hit-and-run accident," Richter said. "Happened just past midnight, about a mile from the Dan Hotel."

Gershom rubbed his unshaved chin. It was past two o'clock in the morning. He hadn't slept for about thirty hours. He uttered a deep sigh and said, "Get to the 'bit of luck,' " he said.

"The man who was struck down had just finished his shift at the Dan Hotel. His name was Aben Fraker."

Gershom shook his head. "The name doesn't ring a bell."

Richter took a cigarette from a pack that was lying on the desk and offered Gershom one. Then he said, "Fraker wasn't badly hurt but he was thrown some fifteen feet from the point where the car struck him and he landed against a tree. His head apparently struck the tree and he was knocked unconscious and is now suffering from a concussion. For a time he was delirious. That's where the 'bit of luck' comes in. He spoke about Krudi and how he would be willing to die for him."

Gershom was on his feet. "Where's Fraker now?"

"In the city hospital under guard," Richter said.

"Not uniformed men, I hope?"

"No. A couple of plainclothes are in the corridor. Two hospital attendants are going in and out of the room constantly. And one of the nurses is really a policewoman. I also have men in vans outside the entrance."

"Good," Gershom said with a nod. "Now we've got to move him without anyone being aware that he has been moved. The longer he stays in the hospital, the more chance there is of him slipping through our fingers, or being killed by his friends because he has suddenly become a bad security risk."

"Can you arrange to move him?"

"May I use your phone?" Gershom asked.

Richter pointed to it.

Within minutes Gershom made the necessary arrangement to transfer Fraker from the hospital to a private house. One of the Shin Beth men would take Fraker's place in the hospital bed for the next twelve to twenty-four hours, depending upon how long it would take for Gershom to get the information he wanted. After that Fraker would be returned to the hospital.

Even as Gershom was talking on the phone, he decided to hurry the process along by using what was usually referred to by the press as a "truth serum." The use of drugs would hasten the interrogation process and when it was finished there wouldn't be much left about Fraker that he wouldn't know.

"Is there a door in the room beside the one leading into the corridor?" Gershom asked, looking at Richter.

"Yes. There are doors between each of the rooms. Like those between adjoining hotel rooms."

Gershom repeated what he was just told and said, "Evacuate three rooms to the left of where Fraker is. Move him into the third room and take him out of there wrapped as a corpse. When the stand-in for Fraker is brought in, have him taken to the third room to the right and then brought into the room where Fraker was. I want this done within the next hour. Yes, I'll be waiting at the house for Fraker. Have Doctor Raban at the house. Thank you. We can use all the luck that comes our way." He put the phone down and helped himself to another cigarette. "You were right. 'We do have a bit of luck going for us."

"That's what I said," Richter responded.

"I'll let you know what happens," Gershom said, going to the door. "Fraker may help us understand why Krudi was at the hotel. Ever since we identified positively that Krudi was the man with Sharon, I've had the uneasy feeling that the UDAR is going to do something here in Elat. Something big. Something that will focus world attention on Krudi."

"Let's hope you're wrong," Richter said.

Gershom shrugged. He knew he wasn't. His intuition told him he wasn't. "Thanks," he said to the Chief of Police and left the office.

Gershom took time to return to his own apartment to

shave, shower and dress in clean clothes. Then he drove to the house, which was located in a well-to-do section of the city. The house was owned by a retired, wealthy American Jew by the name of George Appleman. But in reality Appleman was neither wealthy nor American. He was in fact a Shin Beth agent, approaching his retirement age.

Gershom turned the corner of the street where the house was located and saw that a tan car was just backing out of the driveway. He slowed, giving it enough time to reach the far corner of the street before he resumed his normal speed. A few moments later, he turned into the driveway.

The door was open before Gershom was out of the car. He walked quickly into the house.

Appleman said, ''The doctor is with him now.''

Gershom nodded and walked through the kitchen, into the dining room, and down a flight of steps into a finished basement, where a bed had been set up.

Dr. Raban was there. So was Moses Luban, one of Gershom's agents. The doctor was a gray-bearded man with a pleasant manner. Luban looked like a truck driver, or prize-fighter. His nose was broken. He had a square jaw and the heavy brow of a Neanderthal man.

Gershom stayed back and motioned to Luban. ''Does he know what's going on?'' Gershom asked.

''Not yet. We had to put him out when we moved him,'' Luban explained.

''How long before he regains consciousness?'' Gershom asked. He removed his jacket and rolled up his sleeves.

''He's coming around now.''

''We're not going to waste any time on this one,'' Gershom said. ''I want everything he knows.''

''Raban said he'd have to go easy on the juice because of the concussion,'' Luban said.

Gershom nodded. Then he moved toward the bed.
He nodded to Raban and looked down at Fraker. More
boy than man, Gershom thought. Possibly twenty years
old. The top of his head was bandaged.

Fraker's eyes suddenly went wide with fear. He
looked around him and began to moan.

"Do you know who we are?" Gershom asked.

Fraker nodded. Wet his lips. And with difficulty
said, "Shin Beth."

Gershom nodded.

"Better start," Gershom told Raban.

The doctor turned away and picked up a hypodermic.
"Hold him," he ordered.

Luban took hold of Fraker's arms. In a moment the
shot was administered and he released him.

"Listen, Fraker," Gershom said. "Everything is
going to be all right. You just relax. . . . I'm going to
ask you some questions and after you give the answers,
you'll be moved back to your room."

Fraker took several deep breaths. His eyes lidded.

"Do you know what happened to you?" Gershom
asked.

"I was hit by a pickup truck. Then I was taken to the
hospital."

"Very good. Yes, that's what happened to you. . . .
Now tell me about Krudi."

Fraker began to wave his hands and shake his head.

"We know you saw him. We know the two of you
are friends."

"Friends," Fraker repeated.

"Tell me what Krudi was doing at the hotel?" Gershom asked.

"No. No," Fraker answered in a low voice. "Too
important to tell."

Gershom moved away from that question and began to ask Fraker things about himself. Then suddenly he said, "You killed the woman in the hotel room."

Fraker shook his head. "I've killed no one yet. But I will kill many, many."

"When will you kill many?"

"When the time comes," Fraker answered. "Krudi will say when."

"Where will you kill?" Gershom asked, wiping the sweat from his brow with a handkerchief.

Fraker was quiet for a moment.

Gershom repeated the question.

"At the hotel," Fraker said. "At the hotel. Krudi and many others will be there to see it."

"At the hotel where you work?"

Fraker nodded.

Gershom glanced up at the doctor. "Is he drifting off?"

"Better let him rest for a few minutes," Raban said.

Gershom nodded and walked away. He lit a cigarette and paced back and forth. He had made some progress. Something was going to happen at the hotel. Dan and Krudi would be there either to see it or command it. Now he needed a date.

The phone rang. Luban answered it. "It's for you," he told Gershom. "Headquarters."

Gershom took the phone. The Deputy Chief was on the other end. "We are alerting all our people to the possibility of a large UDAR operation taking place in the very near future involving some two hundred mercenaries under the command of Colonel Aleksandr Fedorovich Grachev."

Gershom looked at Fraker. He took a deep breath and said, "I have reason to suspect that the Hotel Dan will be the target."

There was silence on the other end.

Gershom realized that the Deputy Chief had put his hand over the mouthpiece and was probably talking to one of his aides. After a long pause he was back on the phone, asking for an explanation.

Gershom told him what Fraker had said. "I'm going to try and get the date out of him."

"Get back to me as soon as you have it," the Deputy Chief said.

Gershom put the phone down and resumed his place next to the bed.

"He's asleep," Dr. Raban said.

Gershom reached over and shook Fraker until his eyelids rolled open. He began by asking if Fraker had a girlfriend. He didn't, although he was interested in a young woman who worked in the kitchen.

"Will she be there to watch you kill?" Gershom asked.

Fraker suddenly became frightened.

Gershom ran his hand over his face. He was aching for sleep. "You know what will happen to you if Krudi finds out you spoke to us?" he asked.

"I will prove to him I'm loyal," Fraker wept. "I will prove it."

"When will you prove it?"

"The day he and his men come."

"What day will that be?"

Fraker shook his head, the tears streaming from his eyes.

"I need the date," Gershom said to Raban.

"We can wait four or five hours and try a different drug," Raban answered. "But I don't think you're going to get much out of him now."

"Listen, Fraker," Gershom said, "I promise nothing will happen to you. I'll make it possible for you to leave the country. You'll have enough money to do whatever you want. Tell me the date.''

''I don't know. . . . I don't know.''

''You must know!'' Gershom exclaimed in exasperation. ''Goddamn it you must know!''

The phone rang again. Luban went for it. ''It's Headquarters,'' he called out.

Gershom left the bedside and took the phone.

''There is a large group of Christian Americans coming to the hotel on September twelfth,'' the Deputy Chief said. ''If I were Grachev, that would be the time to strike. The UDAR could claim that none of it would have taken place if the Jews hadn't done something to provoke the attack. The blame would be put on us and in the United States that would be picked up by every anti-Semitic organization. And God knows there are many.''

''Sounds reasonable,'' Gershom answered. ''How did you find out the Americans were scheduled to stay at the Dan?''

''I remembered reading about it in one of our daily bulletins. Try the twelfth of September out on the man you have.''

''Will do.''

''I'll be in touch,'' the Deputy Chief said. ''The matter will be turned over to the military. It'll be their responsibility to protect the hotel.''

Gershom agreed and replaced the phone in its cradle. He lit another cigarette and came back to the chair by the bed. ''Fraker,'' he said, ''I know the date. I know it's September twelfth. Is that the date when you will kill? Tell me.''

Fraker nodded, closed his eyes and uttered a low moan.

XVI

This morning they were to leave the training site for a weekend of fun and games at the seaside resort. The men under Storzzi's command fell out at 0530 and in the usual formations.

Groggins was bleary-eyed. He hadn't slept very well during the night. He had many dreams, all of them replays of how he saw Ortega and the woman, complete with the rats looking at him when he entered the room. Rats with blood all over their snouts. Then he dreamt of Paula. That wasn't any better. Under the sheet in the morgue she was so small. Even in the dream he found it difficult to realize that the body he was looking at had given him so much pleasure. . . . After the dreams he lay awake for a while staring at the ceiling until he turned toward Boyce's cot. It was empty. He thought Boyce must have gone to the head. But when Boyce didn't return after awhile, he became worried and went to find him. Boyce wasn't in the head. He wasn't in the rec room either. Groggins went back to bed. But he didn't sleep. Boyce returned to his cot an hour before formation.

El Forti and Storzzi came out of the Headquarters building. They took their usual place in front of the formation, going through the formalities of roll call.

"Immediately after breakfast," Storzzi said, "you will be flown by 'copters back to Camp Number One, where you will change the clothing you are now wearing for your own. Once that is done, you'll be flown to a village some twenty miles from the coast. Buses will take you from the village to the resort area. Because of the nature of our operation, we must maintain strict security. To the women you will be men who work in the oil fields. Should any one of them ask you questions about your work, tell them that it's dirty, hard, and pays well. Is that understood?"

The men were quick to answer in the affirmative.

"There is one other matter to tell you about," Storzzi said. "The resort will be well guarded. Every inch of the perimeter will be covered by El Forti's sharpshooters. I don't want any accidents. The resort is very large. There are all sorts of activities other than the one you are mainly interested in. The perimeter is clearly marked. I will be there, and I don't want my weekend ruined. That's all. See you at the resort. Dismissed."

Within an hour they were in the air heading toward Camp Number One.

Groggins was aware that Boyce was very quiet. He said very little at breakfast and nothing in the last few minutes, although it was difficult to talk over the engines. But silence wasn't one of Boyce's traits.

When they finally landed, Groggins made it a point to pull Boyce off to one side as they walked toward the building where they'd change their clothes.

"Cowboy, something bothering you?" he asked.

"Naw," Boyce answered. "I just get all moody whenever I start thinkin' about pussy."

"I know what you mean," Groggins said. Keeping his response in the same vein. "Especially when it's going to be strange pussy."

Boyce nodded but didn't continue the conversation.

The village they eventually found themselves in was hot and dirty. But air-conditioned buses were waiting to transport them on the last leg of their journey.

The men were boisterously obscene. Some didn't hesitate to describe in vivid detail what they intended to do with the woman they'd team up with.

"What I'd like to know," a man nicknamed Sharky asked, "is what's goin' to happen if two guys go after one woman?"

"Or two broads after one man?" another man questioned.

"Hey, Captain, have you ever had two broads at the same time?" Sharky asked.

Groggins laughed.

"Sure he has," a third man said. "What the hell do you think, he's wet behind the ears?"

"Well, have you Captain?" Sharky pushed.

"A few times," Groggins admitted.

"See, what the hell did I tell you," the third man said.

The buses rolled down from the hills and approached the sea.

"Smell that tang!" Groggins said.

"I'd rather smell something else," Boyce commented.

"You'll have your chance to do that," Groggins told him. It was the first time Boyce had spoken since boarding the bus. And though he said the right thing, the way he said it was wrong.

Groggins began to wonder if all Boyce's talk about women was just so much smoke to hide his real desires. There were a lot of guys who swung the other way and still were damn good soldiers. If that was the case with Boyce, he'd have every right to clam up. This weekend of fun and games would only be hell for him.

Suddenly Groggins saw the sea through a break in the hills. The water was azure blue and very still.

Boyce saw it too and said, "It looks like a picture postcard."

Groggins agreed.

"You think the rooms are bugged?" Boyce asked.

This possibility never occurred to Groggins. But he had to admit that it was a possibility. But not probable.

Boyce leaned back into his seat and put his cowboy hat over his eyes.

A short while later the bus was moving parallel to the sea. Far out at the horizon, Groggins saw a smudge of smoke against the blue sky. But there was absolutely nothing along the road.

The half-hour drive along the coast brought them to a cove and a huge white building surrounded by a lush lawn and shaded by olive trees. The bus rolled up the driveway and stopped.

The house had once been a private villa or a small hotel. It was two stories high and looked more like a plantation house in the South before the Civil War, with Corinthian columns, a large portico, and a great many windows.

Each man was assigned his own room by a very efficient desk clerk, who told them that their guests would soon be arriving and that there was a nine-hole golf course on the grounds, a large swimming pool, bowling alleys, and billiard tables.

Groggins went up to his room. It was simply furnished with a bed, a chair, and a dresser. A door led to the bathroom, which also had a bidet. A blue-curtained window overlooked a patch of red and yellow flowers.

He tested the bed. It was a lot more comfortable than the cot he had been sleeping on. Suddenly he realized the entire place was centrally air conditioned. He didn't remember having seen any power lines along the road. He decided the place must be equipped with its own electric generating plant. Probably a diesel or gasoline engine was used to drive the generator.

He was about to go down to the bar, when someone knocked at his door. "Cowboy?" he asked.

"Yeah."

"Come in," Groggins said. "I was just about to go for a drink."

Boyce waved the suggestion aside. "Listen, Groggins," he said, "I've got to talk to you."

"Talk," Groggins said, sitting down on the bed. He expected something like this to happen.

Boyce pointed to the bathroom.

Groggins followed him.

"Just a precaution," Boyce said, turning on the shower.

"Okay, talk," Groggins told him.

"I'm not what you think I am," Boyce said. "I'm a Shin Beth agent. I've got to get away from here. Almost every night for the past two weeks I've been doing some night prowling. Last night I discovered Israeli army uniforms and now this whole thing adds up. I've got to get out of here."

Groggins gave a long, low whistle. His mind was racing. He had Boyce pegged all wrong. And it did add up. "Why lay this on me?"

"Because of all the men here, you're the only one I

trust. The only one who has something else going for him than just being a merc.''

"Thanks for the compliment but you're all wrong. I'm no better or worse than the rest of the guys here.''

"If we hit the Aswan in Israeli uniforms, the Egyptians will think we're Israeli soldiers and they'll sure as hell do some hitting of their own. Then what we'll have is another war between Egypt and Israel.''

Groggins nodded. He had to be absolutely cool in his actions as well as his words if he wanted to maintain his own cover. "You heard the Colonel. El Forti's men have this place covered.''

"Got to chance it,'' Boyce answered.

Groggins shook his head. "Look Cowboy, I'm being paid by these guys.''

"Don't you give a damn what happens?'' Boyce asked.

Groggins shook his head. "I don't have any particular feelings for either side. I do what I'm paid to do.''

"If the dam is blown, twenty million people will die, and God knows how many more millions will die in the war that follows.''

"I won't stop you from going,'' Groggins said. "But I sure as hell won't help either.''

"I don't believe you,'' Boyce said.

"Believe it, Cowboy. Believe it, because if you're looking to me for help, you're going to run out on the short end of the stick,'' Groggins told him. He reached over and turned off the shower. "I still want that drink.''

They walked out of the bathroom.

"You're going to do something crazy,'' Groggins said, "and my advice to you is to stop sending out signals that something is wrong with you. Act natural, or Storzzi will pick up your signals and become jumpy. Now come on down to the bar with me and bend your elbow until the ladies come."

Boyce was about to object.

"Don't be a damn fool!" Groggins told him angrily. "Don't risk getting yourself stopped, even before you start."

"Okay, I'll go down to the bar with you."

Groggins didn't bother saying anything more. He left the room and headed downstairs with Boyce in tow. "Remember," he cautioned. "Act natural."

They bellied up to the bar, and Groggins ordered a vodka and twist. Boyce asked for a bourbon on the rocks.

A few other men were at the bar, including Woods.

"To the women," Boyce toasted.

"To the women," the men echoed and drank up.

Groggins had another vodka. He liked Boyce and didn't want to see him die. But there was no way he'd be able to stop it from happening. The way things were he wasn't in any position to stop what would probably become the third and last world war.

The talk at the bar was about other places and other times. Some of the men had been mercs most of their adult life.

Groggins was glad to see that Boyce joined the conversation. When the talk turned to restaurants, Woods seemed to possess a specialized knowledge of places that would never be listed in the Michelin Guide or in any of the gourmet magazines. But from the way he spoke about them, Groggins was sure the food would be unique.

After the third drink, Woods turns to Groggins.

"What do you think our chances are?"

Groggins made a fluttering motion with his right hand. "If we catch the opposition with their pants down and if we get out quickly, most of us will live to talk about it."

Woods nodded.

Groggins sensed that Woods wanted to say something else but changed his mind. Was it possible that Woods and some of the other men might not like the two *ifs?* If there was more than the usual trepidation about a mission, could something be done to render it ineffective or stop it altogether? But if he miscalculated the mood of the men, he would very likely get himself killed. Or if Woods was feeling him out for El Forti or Storzzi, he already had said too much. At least enough to make the two commanders jumpy about having him in a key position.

Groggins saw that Woods was giving him an eye signal to move away from the bar. He picked up his drink and walked to where french doors opened on to a sun-drenched terrace, which overlooked a lawn and the sea beyond it.

Woods came up alongside. "I was going to talk to you before this. But the time never seemed right."

"Talk about what?"

"London," Woods said.

"Why now?"

"Just in case we get into a tight spot," Woods said, "I'd like to know there's no hard feelings between us."

"Tell me about London," Groggins said, looking at the empty sea.

"Your friend was asking too many questions. Bucky was paid to kill him."

Groggins nodded.

"I don't know who killed Bucky," Woods said.

"What about Paula Bennet?"

Woods shook his head. "I don't know anything about her."

"Did Bucky ever mention any names?"

"Crimins is the only one I can remember. Crimins was the man who paid our expenses to Rome."

Groggins extended his hand. "I'll have to pay Crimins a visit when I get back to London."

"He's a hard man to get to," Woods answered, shaking Groggins' hand.

"Don't worry, I'll get to him."

"No hard feelings?"

"None," Groggins answered. And he didn't have any. Crimins was the man he wanted.

"Another drink?" Woods suggested.

Groggins held up his hand. "I want to remain sober for the ladies."

"I guess that's a good idea." He offered Groggins a cigarette. "I'm seriously thinking of packing it in after this mission. Sooner or later my luck is going to run out, and I'll wind up dead or a prisoner. And that could be worse than dead. Imagine winding up a prisoner of some of El Forti's men?"

"That's the stuff that nightmares are made of," Groggins said, blowing smoke.

Just as they started back to the bar, one of the men came running into the room. "The women are coming!" The men ran from the bar to the front of the building. The buses were turning into the long driveway.

Boyce came up behind Groggins. "What was the pow-wow with Woods all about?"

"Later, Cowboy," Groggins said. "Now it's time to meet the ladies."

Luise sat in the third of five buses. She wore a simple white linen suit, no bra, and a thin gold chain around her neck. The previous day the women were flown from Athens to a small village on the coast, where they spent the night and were examined for VD.

The village, she guessed, was perhaps no more than ten miles away. There was absolutely nothing between it and where they were going. She had seen the hotel from the road a few minutes before, and it probably was the only place with grass and trees for miles around.

The women in the buses were from every nation in Europe and a few were from the States. Some were prostitutes. Others were there for the money. A few for excitement. And no doubt there were some who just couldn't get enough cock.

Luise closed her eyes. Had she not been picked up by the Company, she wondered, to which category she would belong? She had started out as a surrogate wife, teaching sexually frightened men how to make love to a woman. One of these men happened to be a top Company man. He was so grateful to her for what she had taught him that he offered her a job with the Company. The pay was very good and she lived very well. Actually she didn't do anything she hadn't done before, or that most women don't do for less of a reason. She went to bed with a man because he wanted her and she needed information. Sometimes it was military or political information. Very often it was whatever she could pick up in the course of the liaison, whether it was a one-night stand or a couple of weeks on the Côte d'Azur.

"Do you think the men are there?" the woman next to her asked. Her name was Cybil. She was a blonde from Scotland.

"Probably," Luise answered, opening her eyes.

"They must be as randy as the devil."

"You can be damn sure you're not going to get too much sleep," Luise said.

"I don't mind that as long as there's no rough stuff."

Luise agreed.

"That Mr. Storzzi who spoke to us last night seemed nice enough," Cybil said. "I wouldn't mind having him in my bed, would you?"

Luise smiled. "One of us will have to take him on."

The bus slowed, swinging into the driveway.

"The men are in front of the place waiting for us!" one of the women shouted.

Luise leaned out in the aisle, trying to get a better view of the men.

"Well, we're here!" Cybil exclaimed, taking hold of Luise's hand. "Good luck!"

"Good luck!" Luise answered.

The bus doors opened. And the men began to cheer.

Luise swept up to the door. She paused. Even with sunglasses the sunlight was intense. She took a moment to scan the men, hoping to spot Groggins.

"May I help?" a man asked.

Luise lowered her eyes. It was Storzzi. She hadn't realized he was aboard one of the buses; although, of course, there wasn't any reason why he shouldn't have been. After all, these were his men; he was training them, and when they went off for a weekend of fun and games, so did he.

"Thank you," she answered. She gave him her hand.

Storzzi held her small valise. "Unless you have some objection," he said, "I would enjoy spending the weekend with you."

Luise smiled.

"Am I to interpret that smile as a yes or a no, or

perhaps a maybe?'' Storzzi asked, as they walked toward the house. ''Before you answer, let me tell you that I am ordinarily a blunt man. But in these circumstances where there isn't much time to play the usual man-woman game, I prefer to be even more direct. I want you.''

Luise's smile broadened. ''I have absolutely no objection to spending the weekend with you,'' she said.

Storzzi grinned. ''Would you care for something to drink?''

''Something tall and very cold,'' she answered.

''For the next two days, anything you want is yours.''

''Now that's something I haven't been told before,'' Luise said. ''You could tell me where the hell we are.''

''On the coast of Libya,'' Storzzi answered, as they walked up the four steps that led to the portico.

''That's why it looks familiar,'' Luise responded with a straight face.

Storzzi gave her a questioning look.

Luise didn't offer any further explanation. She waited for him to react.

Finally, he understood and began to laugh.

She paused and turned around. All of the men seemed to have found their partners. She spotted Groggins. He was with Cybil, the blonde next to her on the bus. Not too far away from Groggins was Boyce. And he was looking at her with an unmistakeable expression of surprise and recognition on his face.

Groggins got a big kick out of Cybil's Scottish accent. He was in no hurry to bed down with her, knowing it would eventually happen, and when it did, it would be very good because they would have begun to relate to each other as individuals, rather than just bodies.

When they went to Groggins' room to change into swimsuits, he saw that she was a real blonde, although the hair on her love mound was a darker shade of honey than the hair on her head. He joked about the difference, telling her "Most blondes I've known weren't really blonde on the bottom. But you're two-tone."

"I touch up the top a bit," she admitted. "But I don't like to use that stuff on my muff. I tried it once and it burned like hell."

"It's just fine as it is," Groggins said, patting it.

"If you'd rather stay here and—"

"We're going swimming," he said. "Now get into that thing you call a bikini and let's go."

They reached the pool a few minutes later. There were a few other men and their newly acquired girlfriends in the water; others lounged around the poolside, sipping cool drinks.

Boyce was there with a brunette named Alyce. "I thought you'd come down for a swim," he said after the introductions were over. "I recommend you try one of these white drinks. Has coconut milk and something else that makes everything seem aces."

"First I'll get myself wet," Groggins said, "or the sun will do a job on me." He turned to Cybil. "With your milk-white skin, you better put on some lotion and keep something over you besides."

"Aren't we the considerate one!" Boyce exclaimed in a mocking voice.

Groggins ignored him and climbed up to the high diving board. He jumped up and down twice. At the third jump, he launched himself into the air, somersaulted and plunged into the water. He arched his body. The sudden rush of cool water felt wonderful. He almost touched the bottom of the pool, then shot to the surface. An instant later, Cybil surfaced behind him. He turned and took her around, pressing her body against his. The flimsy material of her white bikini was no covering at all.

Groggins was excited. "Listen," he said, "if you don't swim away from me, I'm going to rape you here in the pool."

"Above or below the surface?" she teased.

He released her and dove to the bottom.

She came down after him.

He grabbed her again and kissed her. They came up together, breaking the surface with their lips still pressed together.

"Let's get something to drink," Groggins said.

"You sure you can risk getting out of the pool?" she asked.

He laughed. "Not a trace of a hard-on."

When they came back to where Boyce and Alyce were sitting, their drinks were waiting for them.

"I took the liberty of ordering them," Boyce said.

Groggins nodded, realizing that Alyce looked totally bored. Almost grim. "Will you ladies please excuse me and my Cowboy friend?" he said.

The two women nodded.

"Okay, Cowboy, let's talk," Groggins said, walking away, toward the shallow end of the pool. When he was sure they were out of earshot, he said, "You must be out of your fucking mind!"

"The woman with Storzzi," Boyce said. "I know her."

"So you know her."

"I met her in Egypt. I was posing as an American Marine."

"Okay, Cowboy, you tell me what you're trying to tell me, only tell it to me in simple language. See, I'm dumb. So spell it out for me."

"Maybe she's Storzzi's girlfriend?"

"She's a call girl, just like all the others. Come on, Cowboy, start thinking again. And start acting like the rest of us. Go fuck that woman you're with."

"She told me they spent the night in a village east of here."

"That's a beginning. Now take her up to the room and bang her."

"I'm going to try for the village," Boyce said. "Listen, I walked around this place. I can knock out all the electricity—"

"I don't want to know," Groggins said tightly. "I don't want to know." He started to walk away.

Boyce came after him. "I've got to get word back to my people."

Groggins stopped. There was no way he'd be able to stop him. "Okay," he said. "I understand. You do what you must do. I won't stop you."

"Will you help?"

Groggins took a deep breath and exhaled slowly. "What do you want me to do?"

"Start a fire?" Boyce said.

"Where?"

"In the hotel. I want everyone busy while I go into the water."

"When?"

"About one-thirty would be fine."

Groggins nodded. "You got one fire about one-thirty. What will you do with Alyce?"

"She'll sleep through it all with the sedative.

"Just don't give her too much."

"Don't worry, I won't." Boyce smiled. "Now I think I'll have me some sex. That woman sure looks glum."

Groggins did a racing dive into the pool and swam the length.

Boyce jumped in after him, but in a matter of moments pulled ahead. "All right," he said to Alyce, when he reached the other side, "let's do some fancy swimming before we go to lunch."

Alyce was out of her chaise lounge and into the water before Groggins climbed out of the pool. He flung himself down in a chair next to Cybil. He picked up his drink and said, "He must have given his father on hell of a bad time."

Cybil laughed and said, "But you like him, don't you?"

"Yeah," Groggins said, "I like him but I wish the hell I didn't."

She reached out and touched his hand. "Is he giving you a hard time?"

"You wouldn't believe how hard," Groggins answered. "But let's forget about him. Now, how about going upstairs and changing for lunch?"

Luncheon was served buffet-style in a very large dining room. There were platters of fried chicken, cold roast beef, and salads, although most of the food was Middleastern. Groggins and Cybil sat at a table with Boyce and Alyce.

Alyce was no longer glum. She laughed easily and said, "Nelson—I mean Cowboy—is off the wall."

"That's me," Boyce said. "I do it off the wall, anytime."

Groggins looked toward the doorway. Storzzi and his lady made their entrance. The Colonel looked like a goddamn peacock with his tail feathers spread. Only it wasn't his tail feathers he was showing off. It was the woman on his arm. The woman he had probably just screwed.

"That's Luise," Cybil said. "I sat next to her on the bus. She is beautiful."

Groggins nodded. She was beautiful. She was very tan and wore a white shorts and a halter.

Storzzi visited his captains at their tables. When he came to Groggins, he introduced himself and Luise Talbert.

"I hope everyone is enjoying themselves," Storzzi said.

"Oh absolutely," Boyce answered.

Groggins agreed.

"Tonight we'll have a band here so that we can dance," Storzzi said. "And we will have several very good belly dancers. Just to put everyone in the right mood."

"There goes a man who's happy at his work," Groggins said, as Storzzi led Luise toward the buffet table.

"Is he your boss?" Alyce asked.

"So much so," Groggins answered, "that the men usually call him Colonel."

"Anyone want more food?" Boyce asked.

Groggins looked at Cybil.

She shook her head.

"Nothing for us," Groggins said. "I feel like taking a walk. What about you, Cybil?"

"Why, yes, of course I do."

"Sex rears its lovely head," Boyce laughed. "Go ahead and enjoy."

Groggins took Cybil by the hand, left the table and guided her across the room.

Storzzi and Luise were at the door of the dining room when they passed. Luise flicked her eyes toward Groggins.

He looked straight at her. There was something challenging in those brown eyes of hers. Something that said: *I'm available, if you want me*. Groggins looked away. But the challenge in her eyes and the thrust of her breasts stayed with him. Trying to take her from Storzzi would be the same as asking for a bullet between the eyes.

When they reached his room he opened the door and followed Cybil inside.

"Why the frown?" she asked.

"Something real stupid just crossed my mind," he answered, taking her in his arms.

She closed her eyes and kissed him.

Their mouths opened; their tongues met. . . .

Groggins undid the buttons of her blouse. His hand moved over her breasts. He bent down and kissed each erect nipple. Then he slipped the blouse off.

"I better do the slacks," she said. "They're snug." She stepped away from him and unzipped the fly.

Groggins undressed, dropping his clothes where he stood.

Cybil was naked before him, and she padded over to the bed and turned it down.

Groggins dropped onto the bed, taking hold of Cybil, pulling her down to him.

"Let me work on you a bit," she said.

"Work on me?"

"Turn over on your stomach," she told him.

"Okay, I'm on my stomach. Now what?"

"Just relax," she said softly. "Relax." And settling between his legs, she began to massage his neck and shoulders. She used the balls of her fingers, exerting a very light pressure. It felt good and Groggins told her so.

"Don't think about it," she said. "Just let it happen!"

Groggins agreed wordlessly. He closed his eyes, but he was finding it hard not to think about Boyce. The fire would help him. But Storzzi wasn't stupid. Once he discovered Boyce was gone, he'd put everything together and come up with the conclusion that someone had to help Boyce. As Groggins saw it, the finger would point to him. Everyone in the unit, including Storzzi and El Forti, knew he and Boyce were thick. . . .

Cybil's fingers moved down his flanks. Then over his buttocks.

"You don't have any fat here," she said. "You've got a good body."

"Yours isn't bad either," he responded. Her fingers slid between his buttocks, teasing.

Cybil bent over him. She pressed her lips to the back of his neck.

Groggins felt her muff against his right thigh, while her nipples just touched the broad of his back. He was completely aroused. And though he wanted very much to be inside her, he was curious enough about what she would do next to wait. As soon as he felt her tongue between his shoulders, he knew she would lick his whole body. He had experienced that on several occasions with various women; once when Paula was slightly drunk.

Cybil's tongue flicked over his ears. Down his back. Over his buttocks, and then between them.

Groggins sighed with delight.

She started at his neck again and worked her way down. But this time, her right hand eased itself under him.

Groggins rolled slightly on his side to give her greater access to his penis.

Then she said, "Now turn over completely."

When he was on his back, she began to lick his nipples.

Groggins reached down and, lifting her face to his, kissed her on the lips. Their tongues met. He could taste himself. Rolling Cybil on her back, he pressed his mouth against her breast, teasing the nipple with his tongue.

"I like that," she said in a throaty voice.

He kissed the hollow of her stomach and moved his hand on the insides of her thighs. They were warm and silky.

She took hold of his hand and put it down between her legs. "That's where it should be," she said.

He played with her until she moaned softly. He pressed his mouth against her, using his tongue on her clit.

Cybil made sounds of pleasure. She opened her thighs as wide as she could, and with her hands, reached down and separated the lips of her sex for Groggins.

"I want to do you at the same time," she said in a low, breathy voice.

Groggins shifted, turning on his side, while she did the same. In an instant, he felt the warm, wet pressure of her lips circle his shaft. He rested his head on her thigh, tonguing her.

Cybil licked his penis and his balls, moving all the way back.

Groggins was completely enveloped by wave after

wave of sensuous delight. The world shrank to the ecstacy he felt in his body and the musky scent in his nostrils.

By some secret communication between them, they moved again, only this time Cybil lay flat on her back, with her thighs splayed, Groggins between them. She arched slightly toward him, guiding his penis into her.

"That feels so good," she sighed. "So very good."

Groggins tongued her nipples again and began to move. The contractions deep in her gave him the delightful sensation of many lips moving along him. He eased his hand under her buttocks slowly easing his finger into her cheeks.

She ran her hand under his scrotum lightly caressing him.

He quickened his movements.

Cybil thrust herself against him. Her head thrashed from side to side. She wrapped her legs around his back.

Groggins could feel her tense. The heat in his groin was exquisite.

Suddenly Cybil cried out, "Oh now. . . . Noww. . . ." Her body slammed against his. She raked his back with her nails, and her body shook.

Groggins exploded. He growled with delight and spun off into endless moments of ectacy. . . . Slowly, he came back to the real world. He was already thinking about giving Cybil a message for Salito. . . .

XVII

El Forti and Krudi sat in a walled garden in the town of Al Aqabar, Jordan. The small house served as Krudi's headquarters. There were guards at all of the windows, at the door to the garden, and in a car across the street.

El Forti had come to make a last check on Krudi's plans to hit the Dan Hotel. He didn't particularly like Krudi or admire his methods, especially his involvement with slavers. Even the women who served them coffee were purchased from slavers. Except for the black Ethiopian woman, all the women were Arab.

"I think I should signal you," Krudi said, "as soon as we begin the attack. That way you and your men will be on your way while the attack is still going on. It would hasten your attack and make it seem as if Israel didn't hesitate. Perhaps the claim could be made that they struck first."

"But you shouldn't meet with any opposition," El Forti said, sipping the strong, sweet coffee.

"The fighting will come later," Krudi answered, lighting a cigarette.

"Then send the signal as soon as you begin to move on the hotel," El Forti said. "I will tell Storzzi of the change. He will not like it but he will accept it." Then he looked straight at Krudi. "He told me to tell you that the next time you do something stupid, you'll be shot."

Krudi threw back his head and roared with laughter. "These Russians are so serious that if you fart at the wrong time, they want to shoot you or send you off to Siberia."

"This operation is very important to him," El Forti said. "I wouldn't be surprised if he is made a general."

"It's important to us—"

A man appeared in the doorway of the house. "Message from Elat," he said.

"What is it?" Krudi asked.

"Fraker has disappeared," the man said.

Krudi was on his feet.

El Forti followed. "What do you mean he's disappeared? No one just disappears."

Krudi hurried into the house, El Forti following close behind. They crowded close to the radio operator.

"Ask for details," Krudi ordered.

"I already have," the radio operator replied. "There are none. Our people have checked his room, and our friends at the hotel where he works have not seen him for the past forty-eight hours."

"What about the hospitals?" El Forti asked.

"Nothing," the radio operator said, shaking his head.

El Forti tapped Krudi on the shoulder and gestured toward the door with his head. Then he walked out of the room. "We have a problem," he said, as soon as they were back in the garden.

"A possible problem," Krudi answered.

"We must assume the worst," El Forti said. He took a cigarette from a gold case and offered one to Krudi.

"Suppose Shin Beth or MOSSAD has him. We must then suppose that he gave them enough information for them to know that we attack on the twelfth of September."

El Forti leaned slightly forward and placed his elbows on the table.

"Then we must not disappoint them," Krudi said. He sent a cloud of smoke out of his nostrils.

"You know of course that units of the Israeli army will be waiting for you, that none of the Americans will be there, and that none of you stand any chance of surviving?"

Krudi smiled. "What is Allah's will is Allah's will. The men who die at the Dan will become martyrs for our cause. Their deaths will bring others into our ranks."

El Forti saw the light glowing in Krudi's eyes. He knew it would be useless to continue the discussion.

"Maybe our deaths will finally unite the entire Arab world in a holy war against Israel. Should that happen, then dying would have been worth it. . . . No, we will leave things as they stand. I and my men will attack the Dan, as planned."

"Allah be with you," El Forti said. He stubbed out the cigarette in an ash tray and stood up. It was time to go. He still had many things to do before he returned to the training site.

The dinner was sumptuous, with a choice of several different lamb and veal dishes, broiled fish, and a bouillabaisse, which Groggins enjoyed. During dinner, all of the captains and their women sat at the same table with Storzzi and Luise.

Groggins was eager to see if Luise would signal him again with her eyes. But she didn't. She spent all of her time attending to Storzzi and making small talk with the other captains. Luise was by far the most beautiful woman in the room. She wore a royal blue gown, with a plunging neckline that went to her midriff.

Storzzi couldn't keep his hands off her. He continually stroked her bare arm or held her hand.

Groggins found himself wondering what she was like in bed. Whether she did to Storzzi what Cybil did to him. He guessed the other men at the table were also fantasizing about what she might be like in the sack.

After dinner the tables were pushed off to one side. There was more drinking before the band set up. And Storzzi did a great deal of talking about "bringing in gushers" and opening a new oil field that would be the largest in the world.

Luise looked impressed. She clung to Storzzi's arm, giving it the benefit of her ample breasts.

Now and then Groggins looked over to Boyce. He seemed to be having a good time.

The eight-member band set up their amplifiers and electronic paraphernalia. Strobe lights turned the room into a disco.

The dancing actually began with a very tame fox trot. Groggins started off with Cybil in his arms. The next dance was a tango, and from there on it became disco.

It didn't take long for everyone to change partners. Within moments, Groggins faced Luise. She crouched down in front of him and smiled.

He gyrated down.

"I need two minutes to speak to you," she said, keeping the smile on her face.

Groggins glanced around, saw Storzzi and said, "You're being watched." He came up facing her. From dancing, color had come into her tan cheeks, suffusing them with a lovely glow.

"Bring me in close," she told him.

Groggins took her in his arm. Her firm breasts came up against his chest. "I wouldn't try to make Storzzi jealous," he said.

"I like the books you write, Hank Carter," she said.

He almost stopped moving.

"Salito sends his best," she said. "Now let go of me."

He pushed her away. They circled each other. When they were facing one another she said, "Your ID is zero-two-four-five-forty four."

Again they moved around each another.

"I'll manage to see you," she said.

Then she moved off with another man, leaving Groggins facing Alyce, Boyce's woman. "How's it going?" he asked.

"Your friend is something else," she laughed.

"Good, eh?"

"Very," she answered and spun off with another man.

Groggins left the dance floor. He went to the bar. Despite the air conditioning the room was very warm. He was hot and sweaty. He drank a tall glass of orange juice and a splash of vodka.

A few of the men had gotten hold of pot and were smoking joints. He was offered one. He took it, lit up and took a few drags before passing it on. He was feeling better than he had in days. Salito, he had to admit, was one smart-ass guy. He looked for Boyce. When he spotted him, he waved him to the bar.

"What's up?" Boyce asked, coming up to him.

"Get something in your hand," Groggins said.

Boyce asked for a scotch on the rocks.

Groggins moved closer to Boyce. He looked around and decided that no one was close enough to hear what he was going to say. "Listen and listen carefully. Don't ask questions and don't give any indication of surprise. . . . Now listen. I'm CIA. There's someone here who'll take out the information."

"No shit!" Boyce exclaimed.

"Drink," Groggins said. "I don't want you to do anything to foul up—"

Boyce started to laugh. "That's very funny. I'll have to remember that."

"No fire," Groggins said.

Boyce drank.

"You've got to stay put, or you'll blow the whole operation."

Boyce turned back to the bar. "Give me another one," he said. When he was close to Groggins again, he asked, "Who's the courier?"

"Your lady from Egypt," Groggins answered. "Now go back on the floor and dance."

"What are you going to do?"

"Exactly the same thing that everyone is doing," Groggins answered.

"If you're trying to bluff—"

"I'm not, Cowboy, I'm not," Groggins said. He placed his empty glass back on the bar and walked out on the floor dancing with the first woman he found.

Boyce passed him. He smiled and said, "It's your dance, man."

Groggins smiled broadly. He was relieved that

Boyce didn't need a lot of pressure. It was obvious that Boyce's plan was a real long shot.

Eventually Groggins was dancing with Cybil.

"Was that a joint I saw you smoking?" she asked.

"Sure was," he answered.

"Does pot make you horny?" she asked.

"Only sexy, beautiful women make me horny," he said.

"Are you horny now?"

"You?"

"Horny as hell," she answered, pressing herself to him.

"Then let's go upstairs and fuck," Groggins said. "It's the only real way I know of that puts an end to being horny." He circled Cybil's waist with his arm and led her off the dance floor.

Groggins was dreaming. . . . He was crouched in the thick undergrowth. Everything was wet from the heavy dew common in the jungle at that time of year. From his position he could see the road without any difficulty. . . . "Remember," he told the men behind him, "we want those trucks."

"What the hell is so important about them?" a voice asked.

"Stop the convoy," Groggins repeated. "That was Salito's orders. 'Take the last four,' Salito said, 'and all of us'll be rich.' " . . . Within moments the trucks came. The firefight began. The last three trucks were left behind. Then nothing. The trucks were loaded with sand. Sand that flowed and moved like the waters of the sea. Groggins started to run. He ran until his lungs felt like they would burst. He lost his footing. Just as the sand was about to reach him he awoke.

For an instant, Groggins was confused: part of him

was still in the dream, fighting to escape the sand. And part of him was in a small room in bed with a woman. Quickly, reality took hold. He looked at his watch. Two-fifteen. He had been asleep for the better part of three hours.

Groggins reached over to the night table. Took a cigarette and lit it.

Cybil moved. Her bare buttocks brushed his thigh.

He took a deep drag on the cigarette, blowing smoke toward the ceiling. He was surprised to learn that Luise worked for the Company. Now the problem was how to give her the information for Salito.

Groggins frowned. He thought about the dream again. His heart raced. He had dreamt about that convoy hundreds of times and had gone over the whole sequence of events in his mind hundreds of times. Why was he nailed for it? Why?

Groggins shook his head. He stubbed out his cigarette and lit another one. He was on the verge of coming up with the answer, when the doorknob began to turn.

He eased himself into a sitting position. Carefully left the bed. Slipped on his pants. Then he moved swiftly to the other side of the room. He wanted to be behind the door when it opened, in position to grab the person entering the room. Groggins thought it might be Boyce.

The door swung open.

He tensed.

Groggins picked up the smell of perfume and recognized the scent that Luise wore at dinner. A floral scent with a strong note of heather.

He waited.

She stepped into the room and was caught in the flood of moonlight coming through the window.

Groggins stepped out from behind the door. He put one hand over her mouth and the other around her midriff, pinning her arms to her side.

"I could have broken your back," he whispered to her.

Suddenly he realized she wasn't wearing anything more than a diaphanous negligee.

He let go of her and drew away.

Cybil bolted up. She saw Luise in the moonlight. "Just what the hell is going on?"

"He beat me," Luise sobbed. "The bastard beat me."

Groggins moved toward her.

"No. . . . No, I don't—" She flung herself at Cybil. "I don't want any man to touch me."

Cybil patted her. "It's all right, it's all right."

"I tried to get away but he wouldn't let me go. He started to curse in Russian, I think."

"Maybe we better look at your bruises. Are you sure nothing is broken?" Cybil asked.

"He hit me on my breasts and on my back."

"But why?"

"He drank too much," Luise sobbed. "Drank too much and tried to—"

"What? What did he try to do?"

Luise shook her head and wept even more.

"What's he doing now?" Groggins asked.

"I left him on the floor," Luise answered. "I tried to get him back in bed but I can't lift him." She turned toward Groggins. "I came here for help."

"We'll go back with you," Cybil said.

"Oh would you? Would you really?" Then easing herself up, she said, "Maybe it would be better if I tried to do it myself again. I don't want to cause any trouble for either of you."

"No trouble," Groggins said. "We'll go."

Luise shook her head. "I'm afraid. He's mean. I think it would be better if I went alone."

"But you said you couldn't move him by yourself," Cybil said.

"I can't," she looked at Groggins. "Maybe if you came, it would be okay."

"Go with her," Cybil urged.

"Sure," Groggins answered.

Luise came close to Groggins. "Thank you," she said in a low passionate voice. "Thank you. I'll do something for you. Really, I will."

"It's all right," Groggins answered, aware of how beautiful she was.

Luise turned and headed for the door.

Groggins followed. "I'll be back quickly," he told Cybil.

"I'm not going anywhere," she answered.

Groggins closed the door behind him and hurried to catch up with Luise.

As soon as he did, she stopped. And gave him a big smile. "Not bad, eh?"

He nodded. "I bought it." Then looking toward Storzzi's room he asked, "What about him?"

"Asleep. Slightly drugged," she answered.

"Tomorrow morning he's going to know it," Groggins said.

"I'm counting on him being too sick to remember anything too clearly," she answered. "I gave him a shot of milk. An injection. By morning, he'll have all the symptoms of typhus, including a very high fever for the next seventy-two hours. When he wakes up, he's going to feel lousy."

As soon as they were in Storzzi's room, Groggins

made a quick search. He found nothing, except a Russian version of a .39 caliber special. When he finished, he turned to Luise. "We're being trained to blow the Aswan Dam. There are two hundred mercs. The camp is somewhere in the mountains south of here. It's protected to prevent observation from the air. And on the ground it's heavily guarded."

"Are you sure it's the Aswan?" she asked, handing Groggins a cigarette and taking one for herself.

"Boyce—by the way he recognized you—"

"I met him in Egypt. He was a Marine sergeant then."

"Then and now, he's a Shin Beth agent," Groggins said. "Anyway, he made the identification. He also says there's a load of Israeli uniforms waiting for us when we return to camp."

"Meaning that when you go in to do the job, the Egyptians will think it's—"

"Israeli commandos," Groggins finished. He was standing very close to her. And, crazy as it was, he wanted to take her in his arms. But instead he said, "We're going in by 'copter. Storzzi—"

"Storzzi is Aleksandr Fedorovich Grachev, a colonel in the KGB," she said.

"Grachev? Are you sure?"

"Salito gave me the ID from the photograph," she explained. "You and Boyce were on the same picture."

"Grachev was in Angola," Groggins said. "I never saw him. But he was leading a convoy I attacked." Groggins shook his head. "We were creamed."

"Anyone else I should know about here?" Luise asked.

"El Forti," Groggins said. "He's supposed to be in

command. But it's really Storzzi, I mean Grachev's, game all the way. Lately, there seems to have been something of a falling out between the two."

Groggins killed his cigarette.

"When is the raid to take place?" she asked.

"Sometime between the tenth and the fifteenth of September, if we complete training on time."

"That's less than five days away!"

"If Salito wants to stop the Third World War, he's going to have to act quickly. He can't wait for confirmation. Because the only confirmation he'll get is twenty million dead Egyptians and the atomic war that follows."

Luise trembled. "Suddenly I feel cold."

Groggins took the light blanket off the chair and put it around her shoulders.

"I could use a drink," she said.

"The best I can do is another cigarette," Groggins responded.

Luise shook her head. "Once the dam is blown, the Russians would be in a position to make a pre-emptive strike at Israel and the States."

"That's the picture."

For several moments, neither of them spoke. Then Luise said, "You'll have to be stopped before you hit the dam."

"Yes," he answered.

"What will happen to you?" she asked.

"Maybe I'll be lucky and—"

Storzzi began to move. *"Rodnaya moya,"* he said. *"Milya moya."* His hand moved over the bed.

"He's trying to find you," Groggins whispered.

Storzzi rolled on to his back. His head came up slowly.

"I thought you said he was drugged," Groggins said.

"Lightly," she reminded him.

Storzzi squinted at them. "You Luise?" he asked, his speech slurred.

"Yes," she answered.

"Someone else with you?"

She managed to say, "No one else is here." She waved Groggins to the door. "I'm coming back to bed."

"Sounded like you were talking to someone," Storzzi said.

Luise dropped the blanket from her shoulders. Slipped out of the negligee and dropped down next to him. Immediately his hand was on her breast.

Groggins moved along the wall.

"*Rodnaya moya,*" Storzzi said passionately.

Groggins eased the door open and left the room. He was sweating profusely. And was full of anger. Halfway to his own room, he stopped and took several deep breaths. He wanted Luise. He wanted her badly. She was the type of woman he could fall in love with. He knew that, even without really knowing her. But now, in this situation, there was no way for them to come close to one another.

The anger gave way to sadness. And he walked slowly back to his room.

"I was beginning to worry about you," Cybil said, as he got back in bed with her.

"No need to," he answered.

"Did she tell you what Storzzi wanted her to do?" she asked.

"No," he answered. His brain filled suddenly with the picture of Luise's naked body pressed very close to

Storzzi. It was painful, and he uttered a ragged sigh.

"Are you all right," Cybil asked, moving her hand over his chest.

"Just tired," Groggins answered. "Just very tired."

XVIII

"What happened the next morning?" Salito asked, looking at Luise from across his desk. He was taping her debriefing. And though he was anxious to move on the information she had given him, he wanted to be sure she had given him everything.

"Storzzi—I mean Grachev—was sick. But not as sick as I thought he'd be. He wasn't running any temperature. He asked me about the previous night. He said he was sure someone was in the room watching us. I tried to convince him that he had too much to drink."

"Do you think he'll remember?" Salito asked.

"For Groggins' sake, I hope not," she said. "Anyway, Storzzi slept most of the morning. By lunch time, he was feverish and said he felt as if he was coming down with the flu."

"Did you get any more time with Groggins?"

"Only what you already know about," she answered. "By four we were back on the buses. We landed in Rome last night at six. I called you at six-thirty.''

Salito reached over and switched off the tape. And filling his pipe, he said, ''You've done a remarkably fine piece of work.''

Luise nodded. ''Thanks.'' Then she asked, ''What will happen to Groggins?''

Salito puffed on his pipe. He wanted to tell her Groggins would be fine. But he didn't. Instead, he said, ''He and Boyce are not in the best place to be.''

''The two of them are crazy. But you won't find better men anywhere.''

''Groggins,'' he said, ''was on the Company shit list.''

She shrugged. ''I couldn't care what list he's on,'' she answered. ''He's one man I'd like to get to know better.'' She stood up. ''You know where I'm staying.''

''Yes,'' Salito said. He got to his feet and came around to the front of the desk. ''Did you mean what you just said?'' he asked.

''I meant it.''

''Could I tell him that, if I see him?''

''Tell him. And tell him where I am. The rest will be up to him, if he's interested.''

''I most certainly will tell him,'' Salito answered, walking her to the door.

Salito returned to his desk. Rewound the tape and played it back. Suddenly he remembered the advisory from Shin Beth concerning UDAR activities. There was just a possibility the Israelis had latched on to the same operation as he had. If that was the case then there was a good chance they'd hit the camp. . . . But the advisory came through a few days ago. . . . The lapse of time made it improbable that the Shin Beth knew about what was going on in Libya. The Israelis wouldn't have let so much time pass before they struck.

Salito puffed on his pipe. The only conclusion he could possibly reach was that Shin Beth had picked up on a second UDAR operation.

He left his chair and began to pace. Should the two UDAR operations be coordinated then?

He stopped pacing. He needed to know if the Shin Beth had any more information on the UDAR. This time he had no choice. He had to bring the Shin Beth into the picture.

Salito picked up the phone and put through a call to Fishbine. "I have something I want you to hear," he said.

"Name the place and the time," Fishbine said.

"It's warm enough to meet on the Embankment, where the boats leave for Hampton Court and Greenwich. In about an hour."

"I'll be there."

Salito put the phone down. If his hunch was right, there would be two attacks made somewhere between the tenth and the fifteenth of the month. One against the Aswan Dam by mercs wearing Israeli uniforms and of course one somewhere in Israel by members of the UDAR wearing Egyptian uniforms. It would have to happen that way. And the attack in Israel would have to preceed the one against the dam.

Salito dropped down into his chair. He felt cold, yet he was sweating. He was finding it hard to think clearly. The world was on the brink of another World War.

He picked up his pipe. Knocked the ashes from it and refilled it. When it was lit to his satisfaction, he reached for the phone. Dialed. And tapped his pipe against his teeth, while he waited for the man on the other end to pick up.

"Nathans here," the man said after the fifth ring.

"Pick up Crimins. If there's any trouble, take him out." Salito leaned forward and cut the connection. He dialed a second number and waited for another man to answer.

"Richards here," the man said, after the fifth ring.

"Pick up Dissel. If there's any trouble, take him out." Salito put the phone down. He wiped the sweat from his brow. He never felt any pleasure in doing what he had just done. But he did experience an undeniable feeling of power. That he could order anyone, in any part of the world, killed, sometimes frightened him. But it also made him a more humble man. Something, he knew, that many of his colleagues in and out of the Company did not feel.

After a few moments, his introspection passed. He was ready to leave his office and meet with Fishbine.

Salito watched the crowd of tourists board the boat for Hampton Court. It was one of the places he had been wanting to visit but somehow never got around to. He remembered, suddenly, that he and Christy planned to go to Paris for a few days and then on to Florence, where they had already booked a room at the Hotel Villa Medici for a two-week stay. He would have to call Christy to tell her that their planned vacation would be postponed or possibly canceled altogether. That did not sit well with him. He was looking forward to it and had planned to ask Christy to marry him sometime during their stay in Florence.

Salito pursed his lips. He turned away from the river and looked toward the steps.

Fishbine was walking toward him. He looked like a proper London businessman with his bowler hat and umbrella, even though the sun was shining brightly.

They greeted each other with a handshake and started to walk along the Victoria Embankment.

Salito began by saying, "Before I tell you what I have, I want to know if you have anything more to explain about the heightened UDAR activity?"

Fishbine glanced at him. "If you hadn't phoned me, I was going to call you sometime today. One of our men in Elat—"

"That's where one of your women agents was killed, wasn't it?"

"Yes. We're certain she was with Krudi. But that's not what I was going to call you about. We know that Krudi plans to attack the Dan Hotel in Elat on September twelfth."

Salito stopped. "Are your people certain about the date?"

With a nod, Fishbine said, "As certain as they could be considering where the information came from."

Salito knew then that the date came from an informer or someone who was picked up and sweated. Either way, it was unmistakeably tied to the information Groggins had given Luise. "Let's continue to walk," he told Fishbine. "And whatever you hear, I don't want you to stop." He handed him a micro-miniature tape recorder with an earplug. "Put the unit in your jacket pocket."

Fishbine nodded, fitted the plug in his ear and switched the tape on.

Salito filled his pipe. In a few moments he enjoyed the nutlike taste of the smoke. He began to reason out the UDAR operation. Krudi would hit the Dan Hotel. His men probably would be wearing Egyptian uniforms. The UDAR wanted the Israelis to think Egypt violated the truce, thereby giving them the right to strike back. In the meantime, Grachev and El Forti would lead the mercs against the Aswan. Neither Israel or Egypt would realize what was happening, and when they finally did find out, it would be too late. Most of lower Egypt would have been destroyed and Israel would have been subject to massive retaliation by the other Arab nations and Russia. Once that happened, the United States would be forced to counter Russia's move.

Salito was puffing so hard on his pipe that it became excessively hot. His mouth filled with the bitter taste of tobacco juice and saliva. He spat it out. He knocked the bowl against the trunk of a tree and returned the empty pipe to his pocket.

Fishbine switched off the tape. He removed the ear plug. He handed the tape recorder back to Salito. He was pale. Had difficulty finding his voice. "How have you decided to deal with it?" he finally asked.

"On the highest level. All the way to the White House," Salito answered.

"The attack on the Dan and on Aswan—"

"Part of the same plan," Salito said.

"Is there any part of the tape I can transmit to my own people?" Fishbine asked.

"Wait a few hours," Salito said. "I have to lay it all out for the chief in Langley. He'll take it from there. I'll inform him that you heard the tape and recommend your government be apprised of the situation."

"Thank you," Fishbine said. "It's almost impossible to believe the Russians would be party to such a scheme, let alone fund it."

"It's a gamble, albeit a desperate one," Salito

answered. "But even if they were successful, there wouldn't be much of a world left."

They turned around and headed back toward the steps.

"I'll wait for your call," Fishbine said. "You have my home number."

Salito nodded.

When they reached the top of the steps, they shook hands and went their separate ways.

XVIII

Groggins, like most of the men, was quiet during the flight back to the training camp. He knew that they were locked into the mission, unless it was stopped by outside forces, or he could manage to start something inside. The first depended on Luise giving the information to Salito. There was always the possibility that she had been discovered and killed. Perhaps subjected to torture and forced to betray him. And he was attracted to her. What was she really all about?

The following morning only El Forti appeared at formation. "I regret to say," he announced, "that Colonel Storzzi will be joining us later in the day." Then he said, "Immediately after breakfast, you will be issued new uniforms. And weapons. Both will be Israeli. This brings me to the nature of our mission. The dam we have been practicing on is, as some of you might have guessed, the Aswan. . . . We're going to blow the real dam."

"All right," Boyce said under his breath, "tell me something I don't know."

"Shut up and listen," Groggins responded.

"Our purpose is to destroy the Jewish State and those who have been foolish enough to be its friend. I'm sure I speak for all of you, when I say the world would be a better place without Israel. What you men will do will be to settle the Jewish problem far more effectively than the gas chambers and ovens of Nazi Germany did."

Some of the men broke into a spontaneous cheer.

Groggins glanced at Boyce. He was flushed. His breathing was rapid.

"Easy," Groggins said. "Easy!"

"Because of the nature of the mission and the fact that its execution is so near, you'll notice that additional guards have been placed around the camp, and we have ringed the camp with intersecting fields of machine guns. Naturally it is our fervent hope that none of these measures will have to be used. To show you our good will every man who survives will be given an additional bonus of five thousand dollars."

"That dam is gone!" one of the men yelled.

"I'd blow the goddamn Boulder Dam for that kind of money," another man shouted.

El Forti looked pleased. He dismissed the men, turned and walked back to the headquarters building.

Late that afternoon, after they had completed another 'copter assault on the dam, Groggins decided to have a talk with Woods. He had been thinking about doing it all day. Ordinarily he wouldn't have put his life in someone else's hands. But Woods offered the only chance to stop the mission.

Woods was leaning against a large boulder. He looked beat.

Groggins figured all of them must look that way. A

two day's growth of beard. Everything covered with the light tan desert sand. Weary from lack of sleep and the physical exertion. Even El Forti was tired. Only Storzzi seemed ready to leap up for a twenty-mile hike.

Groggins marveled at Storzzi's recuperative powers. The man should have been out of action with a high fever for at least three days. But he was only sick for twelve hours. After that he was able to train with them. Every time Storzzi looked at him, it seemed as if he was trying to remember something. The look always turned into a frown. If Storzzi should remember, Groggins knew he'd be dead. No, worse than that, he'd wish he'd be dead. He was sure Storzzi and El Forti wouldn't let him die until they got the information they wanted from him.

Groggins walked over to where Woods was resting. Hunkering down, he said, "Can we go somewhere and talk."

Woods nodded. "The side of the hill seems private enough."

Groggins stood up. He held out his hand to Woods and pulled him to his feet.

Neither one said anything as they walked halfway up the hill.

Woods offered Groggins a cigarette, and said, "If you're planning to complain to Storzzi about the training, I'll back you."

Groggins blew smoke out of his nostrils. "There's no way for me to beat around the bush about this. It's got to be straight out."

"I'm listening," Woods said.

"I want you to help me stop the mission."

"What?" He started to stand.

Groggins pulled him down. "It won't work. Most of us, maybe all of us will be killed."

"Some of us will die but—"

"We blow the dam and twenty million people will die. That's just for openers. How about starting the Third World War?"

"You're putting me on," Woods said.

Groggins shook his head. "Your group and mine could stop the rest."

"Listen, do you know how many Arabs are here watching our every move? We'd be dead a few seconds after we fired the first round. I'll take my chances at the real dam. Throwing in with you would be a one-way ticket to winding up very dead."

At least think about it before you give me your answer," Groggins said.

"I don't have to think about it," Woods answered. He scrambled to his feet. "As far as I'm concerned, we didn't have this conversation."

Groggins nodded. And watched Woods go down the hill. He'd gambled and lost. But there was a great deal of truth in what Woods said about the Arabs. They were all over the place and wouldn't hesitate for one moment to fire at them, if ordered, or if they thought something was amiss. They'd shoot first and ask questions later.

He walked down to his own group. He stretched out on the ground with his hand behind his head and his eyes closed.

"Woods seemed in a hurry to get away from you," Boyce said.

Groggins squinted up at him. Motioned him to squat down. "I tried to get him interested in a little mutiny," he said.

"For us a little mutiny is like a woman being a little pregnant."

"He's willing to take his chances at the dam," Groggins said.

"You think he might want to mention your little mutiny to Storzzi?"

Groggins shook his head. "He's not the type to rock the boat. Besides, by telling me he'd rather take his chances at the dam, he was also telling me he didn't want me to rock the boat either."

"Then what the hell are we going to do?" Boyce asked, lighting a cigarette.

"Wait until the Company gets the information."

"You never did tell me who the courier was."

"Luise," Groggins answered.

Boyce smiled broadly. "So that explains why Storzzi was sick."

Groggins nodded. "I think he knows intuitively that he's been had but he can't figure out by whom, although I think I rank high on his list."

"Tricky," Boyce commented.

"Something will trigger the connection," Groggins said, "and then—" He snapped his fingers. "But maybe it won't happen. Maybe I'll be lucky. But I have the feeling time is running out."

The whistle blew.

"Storzzi's bird call," Groggins said, beginning to sit up. "Okay guys!" he called to his men. "Saddle up! We're going to blow a dam!"

The President paced the length of the Oval Office. He wore a dark blue bathrobe over a pair of light blue pajamas. The bathrobe had the Presidential Seal over the right breast pocket. He had spent the previous evening celebrating his sixty-second birthday with his family and friends; now he was facing a crisis of gigantic proportions.

The President was a tall, muscular man with a broad, open freckled face and soft brown eyes. Before going

into politics he had played football for the University of
Delaware and was a halfback for five years with the
New York Giants. For awhile he had been the butt of
many jokes in and out of the media. But that stopped as
soon as the politicians realized he had a way of talking
to the people that made them vote for him, first as a
Congressman, then as a Senator, and finally for President. And now when he was thinking seriously of
running for a second term, the world was about to blow
up.

Suddenly he stopped pacing and looked at the other
men who were seated around a coffee table. "As I see
it, we only have two choices. We can let the Egyptians
stop it at the dam, or stop it ourselves." As he spoke his
eyes rested on the Egyptian Ambassador, Gamel
Ashware. "Naturally we would give them every assistance if we take that course of action." He began to
pace again. "To go it alone would mean that we would
be attacking another country."

"Mr. President," the Director of the CIA began, "I
don't think the other nations of the world would view it
as that. They would understand the situation and our
intent." The Director was a thin, saturnine man who
had a firm grasp of international power politics.

The President stopped. He moved closer to the
group, which included the Ambassador from Israel,
Hershal Ben Nussem; the President's Chief of Staff,
John Bliss; and the head of the Joint Chiefs of Staff,
Admiral Clark Gammell.

All of them had been awakened two hours before and
told to appear at the White House within thirty minutes.
They were unshaven and casually dressed.

"I will be damned if I do and damned if I don't," the
President said.

"Israel will most certainly render whatever assistance Egypt requests," Ben Nussem said.

"The question is whether to let it go that far," the President said. He strode away from the group and went to his desk for a cigar. He didn't smoke them often, but whenever he felt under a great deal of tension, smoking a cigar seemed to take the edge off it. At least for awhile.

"Mr. President," Bliss began, "I think we should bring the entire matter before the United Nations."

"No," the President answered. "No. I don't want it to be used as a forum against us or against Israel or Egypt." He turned around and came back to the group. He had made his decision. "We will need the use of Egyptian airfields," the President said.

"Then we're going to—"

"Stop the fucking bastards in their tracks," the President exclaimed. "We can't allow this kind of thing to take place. Mr. Ashware please communicate my request to your President. Tell him we will need the use of one large airfield close to the Libyan border. Have him issue some sort of a statement that a joint military exercise will be taking place between our two nations and that advance support units are scheduled to arrive within three days. That will give us five days before the attack on the dam is scheduled. We will go in at dusk on the tenth. Admiral Gammell, I want a carrier force detached from the Sixth Fleet to take up a position off the Libyan Coast. Should our first effort fail, we will have to send in the fleet Marines. If that happens, I want maximum air support."

"You might consider sending them in first," Admiral Gammell suggested.

The President shook his head. "We have special

forces trained for this kind of dirty work. Now let's see how well they perform.'' He turned to the director of the CIA. ''I want five hundred men of your Special Forces unit in the air and on their way to Egypt by eight o'clock this morning.''

''Yes, Mr. President,'' the Director answered.

''Is there anything else you will require, Mr. President?'' Ambassador Ashware asked.

''I can't think of anything. But if I do I'll let you know. Gentlemen, from now on anything connected with this operation is classified top secret.''

''We'll need a code name for the operation,'' Admiral Gammell said.

''Groggins' Show,'' the President answered. As an afterthought, he added, ''That son-of-a-bitch Groggins must be one hell of a man!''

Everyone in the room agreed with him.

''Christy, I promise you that we'll go on a vacation together,'' Salito said, adjusting the phone against his ear. He had been talking to her for the better part of half an hour and was getting nowhere.

''But I don't understand why we can't go as we planned,'' Christy answered.

''I can't explain why now,'' Salito answered. Suddenly the signal light began to flash. ''I have another call,'' he told her. ''I'll get back to you as soon as I can.''

''When?''

He was becoming irritated. ''Soon as I can.'' He hung up. Pressed another button and said, ''Salito here!''

''Nathans,'' the man announced. Then he said, ''Crimins killed himself.''

''How?''

"Jumped from the window."

"Thanks," Salito said. He put the phone down and picked up his pipe. Moments after he lit it, the phone rang again. This time it was the Company Director.

"We're going in with our people," the Director said. "Code name Groggins's Show. Better pass the information to your Shin Beth counterpart."

"Anyone else?"

"No. It's top secret."

"I just received word that Crimins killed himself," Salito said.

"What about the Swiss, Dissel?"

"Nothing yet. If he's picked up have our people there sweat him," the Director said.

"Yes. . . . Is there anything else?"

"I want you with this operation," the Director told him. "Leave for Cairo by tomorrow. Our embassy people will get you to the airport."

"Yes, sir," Salito answered.

"By the way, the President thinks Groggins is one hell of a man. When this is over I think he's going to want to meet him."

Salito smiled. "If Groggins makes it out alive, he might just agree to a meeting with the President."

"I'll be talking to you," the Director said, hanging up.

Salito put the phone back in its cradle. He began to laugh softly at first and then very loudly.

Groggins's Show was in the air and on the way to its jump area.

Salito was 'chuted and armed like the rest of the men in his transport. There were five planes. Each of them carried a hundred men. There were two designated jump zones. The first was one mile east of the UDAR

camp. The second, one mile south. Both drops would
be concealed by mountains. The two forces would
converge on the camp simultaneously.

Salito sat next to the commander of the mission, a
lean, muscular man with a hatchet face. His unpro-
nounceable Polish name was abbreviated to Wolk. His
given name was George. He held the military rank of
Colonel in the Marines, but with this group he was
always referred to as "Commander."

The men in the Special Forces units came from every
branch of the service. There were enlisted men as well
as officers among them. But their respective ranks did
not matter in the Special Force units, except for matters
of pay. Though this mission was commanded by a man
holding the rank of Colonel, the next could very well be
headed by a sergeant or even a private. The mission
determined the command, and the command was chosen by a computer at Langley that evaluated each man's
ability and matched it against the prospective mission.

Salito looked at his watch. Seven minutes before
they were over the jump zone. His throat was dry and he
was nervous. He hadn't been in any sort of military
action since Angola. And this, according to what Wolk
had said, "was going to be a rough scrap, especially if
the mercs fight us."

"The Egyptians and Israelis must have just hit the
two radar stations on the border," Wolk said, leaning
close to Salito in order to be heard over the roar of the
aircraft's engines.

Salito nodded. Wolk had initiated that phase of the
operation, after he discovered there were two Libyan
radar stations monitoring the air space along the
Libyan-Egyptian border. He also initiated another action on Libya's western border with Algeria. American

planes from the Sixth Fleet would fly in Algerian airspace within range of Libyan radar installations. That would send their own jets scrambling, and for awhile American and Libyan fighter pilots would be eyeball to eyeball.

The warning buzzer sounded. The red jump-light began to flash.

The jumpmaster stood up.

Wolk signaled his men to kill their cigarettes. Then stand and attach their static lines.

Salito was sweating. Though he had made several jumps into combat situations, he never was able to get over the fear that gripped him and churned his stomach.

Wolk reached over to a PA mike making it possible for him to speak to the men in all the planes. "Remember, the 'copters will come in for us one-half hour after we land. The landing area will be lit by red flares. We will take our dead, wounded, and prisoners out with us. If the mercs fire on us, don't hesitate to return fire. They'll kill you dead just as efficiently as any member of the UDAR. Good luck."

The green jump-light went on.

The first man went out the door. . . . The second. . . . The tenth. . . . The twenty-fifth. . . .

Salito was counting. He would be the one-hundredth man to jump. Wolk would come after him. Because the transport continually descended during the jump time, the first man to jump would be the last man to land and the last man to leave the plane would be the first to touch down.

"How low will we be when we jump?" Salito asked.

"Five hundred feet," Wolk answered.

Salito nodded. And swallowed. Should the static line fail to open his chute, he'd barely have time to pull the rip cord on the emergency chute. Even if he could pull it, he'd be falling very fast. Too fast for him to control the chute. The thought of smashing his legs or breaking his back made him even more apprehensive than before. He suddenly felt the intense need to shit. The pain in his bowels was so intense he didn't realize he had moved up to the door until he felt the cold rush of the air stream against his face. He braced himself against the two sides of the door.

"Go!" the jumpmaster shouted.

Salito took a deep breath and launched himself out of the aircraft. He was falling! Suddenly he felt the jerk. The dark gray chute blossomed out over him. He looked up at it and nodded approvingly. Now he only had to worry about staying alive!

Groggins and the other captains had just ordered their respective units into formation when they heard the planes. They couldn't see them because of the mountains.

Storzzi used his field glasses. But the sky to the east was already too dark.

Suddenly a man appeared at the door of the headquarters building. He shouted something in Arabic.

Storzzi and El Forti raced back into the building.

The men murmured about what was happening.

Storzzi came running out onto the field again. El Forti was right behind him.

"Libya is being invaded by Egyptian forces," Storzzi said.

Groggins glanced at Boyce. "She made it," he said.

The same man who came to the door before was there again. This time he shouted directly to El Forti.

A quick exchange took place between the man, El

Forti, and Storzzi. And just as Storzzi seemed ready to speak, the distant flat-sounding "wamp" of mortar firing filled the air.

"We're being attacked," Storzzi shouted.

There was more firing from the mortar battery. Then a much louder explosion, followed by silence.

"Captains, your units," Storzzi shouted, "will take up defensive positions in the surrounding hills with El Forti's. Every man will draw two extra bandoliers and—"

"Time to act!" Groggins said to Boyce, unslinging his automatic rifle. He moved forward. "Stay where you are!" he ordered Storzzi and El Forti.

Boyce was behind him.

"Okay, Cowboy, let's see who goes where," Groggins said.

Boyce had turned and his weapon was pointed at the other men.

"It was you," Storzzi shouted. "Now I remember. It was you and Luise. You were in my room with her."

"That's right," Groggins answered.

Storzzi started to move.

Groggins squeezed off a short burst. The bullets slammed into the ground in front of Storzzi. Making him jump back.

"Woods," Groggins shouted, "the fucking boat has not only been rocked, it's leaking like a sieve."

"He's coming," Boyce said.

"Any of you men," Groggins said, "can make the same choice."

A burst of small arms fire erupted from the south and east of the camp.

"You guys don't have much time," Groggins told them.

Suddenly some of El Forti's men began to shoot at the formation.

Groggins dropped to the ground.

Boyce was thrown on his back. "I'm hit!" he shouted.

Storzzi raced back to the headquarters' building.

El Forti started after him.

Groggins cut him down.

Then Valdez and the Kraut started to fire at him.

But Woods blew the Kraut away and put a few rounds into Valdez's right shoulder.

"Listen," Groggins shouted, "return that fire. Keep El Forti's goons busy." He crawled over to Boyce.

"Not goin' to make it," Boyce said. He coughed up blood.

Groggins nodded.

Suddenly the whole area was illuminated by flood lights. "Take those goddamn lights out," Groggins yelled.

Several quick bursts from automatic weapons destroyed the lights. The area was locked in the deepening twilight.

"Don't bother about me," Boyce said. "Get Storzzi!"

Groggins crawled away. Motioned Woods to follow him.

There were dozens of grenade explosions around the perimeter of the camp.

"Your people are closing in fast," Woods said.

"Not fast enough," Groggins answered. They reached the building. "You put one grenade through the window. I'll send one against the door. Okay, now!"

The final explosion tore the window out and part of the wall. The second blew away the door.

Groggins ran into the building with his finger squeez-ing the trigger. Two men fell. Two others ran to the far end.

Woods came through the wall and killed both of them.

Groggins stepped into the radio room. Flung a gre-nade. Then darted up the hallway. The radio room blew apart, and started to burn.

The small-arms fire in and around the camp was very heavy.

"We better get back to the men," Woods said.

"You go," Groggins told him. "Make sure they stop firing when my people show up. I want Storzzi."

Woods nodded. And ran out of the building.

Smoke from the radio room swirled through the long hallway. Groggins eyes began to tear. He started to cough.

The sudden pain of a knife slash burned across Grog-gins' back. He dropped to the floor and rolled to one side.

Storzzi flung himself at him. Missed. And drove the knife into the floor!

Groggins smashed his fist against the side of Storz-zi's head. He tried to straddle him.

Storzzi threw him off. He grabbed the knife and went for Groggins' throat.

Groggins grabbed Storzzi's wrist. And slowly forced it back.

Storzzi pushed closer.

The knife point was pressing against Groggins' neck. He could feel pain. But he pushed it back. Then with a burst of strength he twisted Storzzi's hand. The bones snapped. The knife dropped to the floor.

Storzzi groaned in agony and fell back.

Groggins was on him. He smashed his head against

the floor, knocking him senseless. Breathing hard, he
picked up his piece. He grabbed Storzzi by the collar
and dragged him out of the burning building.

Twenty minutes after the fighting began, Wolk's
men either killed or captured all of the UDAR men and
completely surrounded the mercenaries.

Using a bullhorn, Wolk ordered "Lay down your
arms. Put your hands in the air and take ten steps
backward." Then he sent in a dozen men to cover them.

"Now I want Groggins to come forward," Wolk
said.

Groggins dropped his weapon. Pulling Storzzi along
the ground he stepped toward Wolk.

"I'll go with him," Salito said.

"He's yours," Wolk answered. He began to issue
orders to destroy what was left of the camp, the overhead cover and the dam.

"Storzzi—I mean Colonel Grachev," Groggins
said. Stopping in front of Salito.

"Wolk," Salito called out, "send a couple of your
men here to take charge of a prisoner."

Groggins let Grachev drop to the ground. Then he
turned. And walked back to where Boyce lay.

Salito followed him. Groggins held Boyce's body in
his arms. He said to Salito, "He was a Shin Beth
agent."

"I know," Salito answered.

"A damn good man," Groggins said.

Salito nodded.

Groggins carried the body to where other KIAs were
being placed. "How man men did we lose?" he asked.

"Twenty, counting four mercs," Salito answered.

"It could have been much worse," Groggins said.
"What about the UDAR's casualties?"

"We're not staying around to count."

There were several large explosions, as the dam, power house, and control mechanism for the overhead cover were blown up.

The central area was suddenly illuminated by red flares. The first choppers began to arrive.

As Groggins and Salito watched the dead and wounded being loaded on to the choppers, Salito briefed him on the expected UDAR attack against the Dan Hotel in Elat. "That was supposed to precede the attack on the Aswan," he explained.

"Krudi will be told about what happened here. . . . Maybe he already has been told."

"You think it will stop him?"

"Hard to tell," Groggins said. "But the Israelis can handle it."

"What are you going to do when you get back to—"

"London," Groggins said. "I'm going to finish my book. I'm finished with the Company. I don't want any more adventures like this one or Angola, and I don't want to kill anymore."

"The Company Director thinks the President will ask you to the White House," Salito said, after several moments of silence.

Groggins nodded. He wasn't impressed. "If I'm in Washington, maybe I'll meet with him."

"Luise asked me to—"

"She's one hell of a woman!" Groggins exclaimed.

"She said that you were one hell of a man," Salito responded.

Groggins looked at him questioningly.

"She told me to give you her phone number," Salito said. "Are you interested?"

"Sure I'm interested," Groggins said. "She's about the only one I am interested in."

Salito grinned.

A moment later Wolk ordered him aboard a chopper.

"Listen," Groggins said, "there's a merc by the name of Woods. He's with the guys you rounded up. He was one of the captains. I owe him. I don't want him bothered by the Justice Department, or anyone else."

"You know I can't do that," Salito said.

"I know you can," Groggins answered flatly. "So you do it. Because you owe me a couple."

Salito thought for a few moments. "If I do this for you, we're even. I don't owe you anything more?"

"We're even," Groggins answered.

An hour after they left the UDAR camp they arrived at the airfield in Egypt, and two hours after that, the American Embassy in Cairo. Groggins was on the phone, arranging a date for the following day with Luise.

The attack on the Dan Hotel never materialized. But on the morning of the fifteenth of September Gershom received a phone call from a woman. "There is a body in the water, just off the beach of the Dan Hotel," she said and hung up.

By the time Gershom arrived at the beach, the police had already recovered the body. And Richter, the Chief of Police, was there. He motioned to Gershom and said, "It's someone you know."

Gershom walked over to where the body lay covered by a tarpaulin. He bent down, pulling back a portion of the canvas cover, exposing the face. It was Krudi! With a bullet hole in his forehead.

Gershom let the cover fall over Krudi's face. "I'm sorry I wasn't the one who did it," he said.

Richter shrugged. "Maybe it's better this way."

"Maybe," Gershom agreed. He turned and walked away.